JM

B.W

D1426602

AD 03060209

NO HIDING PLACE

Janet Tanner titles available from Severn House Large Print

All That Glisters
Forgotten Destiny
Hostage to Love
Morwennan House
Shadows of the Past
Tucker's Inn
The House by the Sea

NO HIDING PLACE

Janet Tanner

Severn House Large Print
London & New York

This first large print edition published in Great Britain 2006 by
SEVERN HOUSE LARGE PRINT BOOKS LTD of
9-15 High Street, Sutton, Surrey, SM1 1DF.
First world regular print edition published 2004 by
Severn House Publishers, London and New York.
This first large print edition published in the USA 2006 by
SEVERN HOUSE PUBLISHERS INC., of
595 Madison Avenue, New York, NY 10022.

Copyright © 2004 by Janet Tanner.

All rights reserved.
The moral right of the author has been asserted.

LINCOLNSHIRE
COUNTY COUNCIL

British Library Cataloguing in Publication Data

Tanner, Janet
  No hiding place - Large print ed.
  1. Women lawyers - Great Britain - Fiction
  2. Suspense fiction
  3. Large type books
  I. Title
  823.9'14 [F]

  ISBN-10: 0-7278-7510-8

Except where actual historical events and characters are being described
for the storyline of this novel, all situations in this publication are
fictitious and any resemblance to living persons is purely coincidental.

Printed and bound in Great Britain by
MPG Books Ltd, Bodmin, Cornwall.

Prologue

If you were to ask me to pinpoint the moment when the nightmare began, I could describe it exactly, though at the time I didn't realize its significance. At the time I was simply surprised and intrigued and, yes, perhaps a little concerned. I looked at the catalyst for catastrophe, wondered briefly, and forgot about it – almost. It was nothing – just one of those strange coincidental quirks of fate that happen from time to time. Or so I thought. But of course I was wrong.

If I had but known it, I was looking at the key to many nightmares and the beginning of my own. But I was blind to the danger lurking in everyday ordinariness, deaf to the whispering voice which might have warned me if I had cared to listen.

Such an unspectacular beginning, so commonplace that it made scarcely a ripple in my busy, fulfilled life. So that now, looking back with a shudder, I cannot help but wonder – how can I ever bring myself to trust normality again?

One

It began on a Friday afternoon in late February, 1996, an afternoon when the storm clouds which had rolled in from the east, threatening snow, cast an eerie yellow light over London and brought an early dusk. From my desk, which looked out on to the open-plan outer office through a frosted-glass screen, I could see that quite a few of our secretaries had packed up and left. Mostly they're on flexitime. I don't have set hours either, I work as long as the job demands. I love my work – Paul, my husband, says I'm obsessed by it, and perhaps he's right. But I just think I'm extremely lucky to be doing something I enjoy so much.

I'm a lawyer by profession, specializing in company law. I joined my firm, Havers and Havers, straight from university, and knew at once that I'd found my niche. That was ten years ago now. I'd worked my way up the ladder with a speed that had surprised even me, ambitious as I am. When I stop to think what I've achieved I feel a sense of pride, but mostly I'm too busy to think of anything but the job in hand.

Today was no exception. I'd been at my desk since eight and I still had a great deal I needed to get through before I could go home.

A tap on the glass screen. I looked up – Marian, my secretary, with a sheaf of papers and a slightly harassed expression. I really don't know why Marian needs to look harassed – she's unbelievably efficient.

'Your letters.'

I glanced at my watch. 'Heavens! Is that the time already?'

'I'm afraid so. If there's nothing else, I really would like to get away promptly tonight. I'm going home to Kent, and if the weather closes in, the branch line may close down.'

'Sure. Did you manage to run the checks I wanted for Poyson Associates?'

Her face fell. 'Oh gosh, I'm sorry, no. I thought the post was the most important thing. I'll do it now...'

She looked more fraught than ever, and I took pity on her.

'It's all right. I'll do it myself. Just wait for me to sign these and then you can get off.'

She hovered whilst I skimmed through the urgent letters and scribbled my signature on the bottom. Then she scurried away to take them down to the post room, calling: 'Have a good weekend!' and I was left in the rapidly emptying office.

I sighed and reached for the Poyson Associates file. This was an extra job I could have done without, but it was something that really needed to be cleared so that I could study the papers over the weekend.

Poyson Associates was one of my best clients – a small but thrusting conglomerate with their fingers in a great many pies. The company was forever involved in mergers and takeovers as they gobbled up failing businesses with good prospects for the future, and it was my job to sort out the legalities. A few months ago the managing director had made me an offer – he wanted me to join their payroll, even hinted at a non-executive directorship if I did, and I must admit I'd been tempted. I had a feeling Poyson Associates could end up huge – not to mention the fact that their offices were on the right side of London to give me easy access to the M4 and my home in Wiltshire. But I like my independence, and I like the variety my present position affords me. I thought about it for a day or two and decided I'd prefer to stay where I was.

The fact that they'd offered the job to me, however, meant they must be seriously considering having an in-house lawyer. I knew that if I wanted to keep their business I had to make their assignments top priority. And just yesterday they'd landed a new one in my lap, and rather an important one at that. A potentially lucrative and powerful deal was on the cards with an old established Hong Kong company. It was my job to check out that company and ensure there was nothing to its detriment that Poyson should know about before they involved themselves too deeply.

Sutherland Dewar had its origins in the days of the Empire. It had been founded by an expatriate Scot, and at one time it had probably built its foundations on the opium trade. Nowadays it has a Hong Kong Chinese at the helm – one Sun Li Yu, son of a New Territories peasant who made his fortune in property and land development – and lists construction and manufacturing, money-broking and hotels among its interests, as well as trade of all kinds.

Perhaps with one wary eye on the return of Hong Kong to the Chinese in 1997, Sutherland Dewar were looking to get a toe-hold in a British base, and they had made overtures to Poyson Associates, who were themselves looking to get into the expanding telecommunications market. One of their subsidiaries had the expertise, Sutherland Dewar had the wherewithal, and a suitable site had already been earmarked. But first, Poyson wanted to be sure of what they were getting into. And with Sutherland Dewar pressing them for a decision, Poyson were pressing me.

I opened the file, switched on my computer and began searching the Internet for the information I wanted. I'm not the world's greatest when it comes to computers, and I knew it would take me a good deal longer than it would have taken Marian. But after a few false starts I was into the information dealing with Hong Kong affairs.

I had been working steadily for the best part of an hour when my telephone rang. I cursed silently at the interruption, but since the switchboard in the foyer would be closed by now, I knew this must be someone who knew the number of my direct line. I reached for the receiver, my eyes still on the computer screen.

It was Paul.

'You're still there then! I thought you might already be on the way home.'

'No, I've still got a bit to do here, and the weather was really grotty the last time I looked. I'm not sure if I shouldn't just crash out at the flat tonight, and come home in the morning.'

Home, for Paul and me, is a lovely old rectory in Wiltshire within easy reach of the industrial estate where Paul and his partner, Josh, have their electrical components firm. But there's no way I'd want to commute daily, and I have a flat in Canary Wharf that

I use during the week. I'm lucky enough to have the best of both worlds, I always maintain – the buzz of the city from Monday to Friday, the peace of the countryside for weekends. I'm usually too busy to feel lonely in the evenings, and in any case I value my independence. But sometimes, when it's almost time to go home, I am consumed with longing to be there, as if all the hours before, when I've been my own person, have suddenly mounted up and transmuted into something which is not quite so desirable after all. Homesickness for Wiltshire. Homesickness for Paul. I felt it now, a reluctance to spend another night in London, however sensible that might be.

'What's it like down there?' I asked.

'OK, I think. It was quite sunny this afternoon. Hang on, I'll take a look.' There was a pause. I could hear his footsteps and the clink of the Venetian blind at the window of his office, and the longing to be with him sharpened as I imagined him, in his white cotton business shirt with the cuffs rolled back and his tie loosened a little at the neck, peering out into the floodlit yard which separated the office block from the warehouse. I tapped another reference into the computer as I waited, then he was back. 'Looks like a nice night. The stars are shining.'

'In that case I think I'll chance it. I should

12

think another half an hour should see me through here. I expect I can be home by eight or so, as long as I don't hit any problems.'

I was glancing at the computer screen as I spoke, idly scrolling down a list of companies which had, at some time, been prosecuted for irregularities by the Hong Kong authorities, when a name I recognized caught my eye.

'Weird!' I said.

'What?'

'That is really weird!'

'What is? Jules – are you listening to me or doing something else?'

'Sorry. Both really. It's just that I'm doing some checks on companies in Hong Kong for a client, and your principal supplier's name came up on the screen.'

'What are you talking about?'

'Kowloon and Victoria Enterprises. The ones you get your electrical thingummys from. I thought I was checking a list of dodgy businesses. I must have pulled up the wrong file.'

'It sounds to me,' Paul said, 'as if you've been at that computer too long. Don't you know you're supposed to have a break of at least ten minutes every hour? I suggest it's time you closed down and came home – now.'

'Yes, Paul.'

'If I was there I'd switch it off myself.'

'Yes, Paul.'

'I mean it, Julia. You'll damage your eyesight. Promise me you'll pack up and leave whatever it is you're doing until Monday.'

'OK, OK, I promise.' He was probably right; my eyes were aching and I could feel the stiffness in my shoulders. 'I'll see you later, right?'

'Sure. I'm going home myself now. I'll have a bottle of claret opened and waiting for you.'

'Great. And what can I look forward to to eat?'

'One of Ruth's casseroles, I think. I could smell it when I popped home at lunchtime.'

'Better and better.' Ruth was our daily housekeeper; her casseroles were legendary. 'I'm on my way.'

'Drive carefully, won't you? Love you.'

I melted inside. After three years of marriage Paul could still do this to me.

'Love you too. I'll see you.'

I put the phone down, smiling. Glanced back at the screen. Yes, I had pulled up the wrong file. This wasn't the one detailing prosecutions against Hong Kong companies, merely those investigated by the authorities. A list as long as your arm – not surprisingly, since corruption was so rife in Hong Kong and the authorities were so zealous in trying to stamp it out. Small wonder Kowloon and Victoria rated a mention. Given the number of investigations every year, it would almost have been more surprising if they had not.

Making a decision, I switched off the computer and began packing up my desk. A stack of files – including the Poyson Associates one – to go home with me, another stack that could wait until Monday. I leaned over, reaching for my briefcase, and the room suddenly swam. Paul was right, I had been working too long. I sat for a moment with my fingers pressed against my temples, then I drew a deep breath and finished gathering my things together. Definitely time to go home. I couldn't wait to be there.

Two

Paul had been right about the weather. Though the heavy cloud still hung threateningly over London, as I headed west I left it behind. By the time I crossed the border into Wiltshire the sky was clear and studded with stars.

I turned into our lane just before eight and slowed to squeeze between the imposing stone pillars which sit one each side of our drive. Paul had turned on the porch lantern and the helium security light on the eaves had come on when I broke the beam with the car; between them they illuminated the garden – the old trees bare and sharp for winter, the bushes soft smudges against the silvery lawn. From the church across the fields behind the house, the peal of bells clamoured in the frosty air – Friday night is ringing practice night.

Some city folk complain about the noise of church bells in the villages where they choose to live. Not me. I love the bells. To me, they are an essential part of the rural scene, though sometimes on a Sunday morning when I'm enjoying a lie-in, I'm quite glad the Old Rectory isn't actually bang next door to the church. Rumour has it that the village was razed to the ground after an outbreak of plague in the Middle Ages and rebuilt a mile or so further east, and the two or three fields between the houses and the church means the sound of the bells is muted and evocative. Bells Across The Meadow, as the old piece of music had it.

As I walked along the path to the back door, Oscar, the cat belonging to our nearest neighbours, came streaking out of the bushes and attached himself to me like a shadow. He's a nice cat, with thick black fur that makes him look like an enormous puffball, though underneath it all he's quite dainty. But he is a great deal too fond of our house. His owners are quite sniffy about it – I think they suspect us of encouraging him, and it has occurred to me to wonder if Ruth feeds him titbits when we're not there. Whatever the reason, he takes every opportunity to slip inside.

'Oh Oscar!' I chided him. 'Haven't you got a home to go to?'

For reply, he merely rubbed himself around my ankles.

I juggled my files and opened the back door. I'd known it wouldn't be locked. It never was until we went to bed – another thing I loved about living in the country. Yes, burglaries happen with increasing frequency, but even now, in 1996, no one thinks to lock a door unless they are actually going out.

'I'm home!' I called, kicking the door shut before Oscar could slip in.

After the sharp cold outside, the kitchen was glowingly warm and full of the aroma of Ruth's casserole. I was just dumping my files on to a chair, because the pine table was already set with a check cloth, cutlery and glasses, when Paul appeared in the doorway, bottle in one hand, corkscrew in the other.

'You've made good time! I didn't expect you for another half-hour or so.'

'You mean the wine's not ready?'

' 'Fraid not. Have a gin and tonic while it's breathing.'

'Sounds good to me. I'll have a kiss as well.'

He put the bottle down, hugging me. I snuggled into him, glad I'd decided to come home tonight, but also glad of all the nights we spent apart. They made our times together special, not just a habit. And we always had something to talk about, all the things that couldn't be said over the telephone, however regularly we called one another.

His sweater felt rough and comfortable beneath my cheek – Paul always changed into jumper and jeans as soon as he got home from work. It made me want to do the same. 'Pour me that G and T while I go up and change, will you?'

'At your service, ma'am!' He grinned, and I poked my tongue out at him.

By the time I came back downstairs wearing jogging pants, sweater and oversized aerobics socks, he had it ready for me. I leaned against the bar of the Rayburn sipping it, savouring the aroma of the casserole, enjoying the cosy warmth of the kitchen, anticipating the relaxed evening ahead. Work was good, but being here with Paul was good too.

'Oh, it's so nice to be home!' I said, and thought how very lucky I was. Really, my life could not have been more perfect.

Ruth's casserole was everything I'd anticipated – after simmering away all day, the meat and vegetables had absorbed all the flavour of the herbs and wine she'd obviously thrown in. It would have been awarded five rosettes in a good food guide, that casserole. When we'd finished eating, I made a pot of fresh coffee and we took it through to the living room.

I adore our living room. It's quite small really – what used to be called a parlour in the days when the house was the rectory, I imagine – a square room with an open fireplace, a bay window which looks out on to the lane, and window seats with fat cushions. The furniture is real curl-up-and-relax furniture, quite different to the sharp modern stuff I have in my London flat. The log fire was casting flickering shadows and making the brass fire irons gleam, and the little radiator, hidden away out of sight behind one of the chairs, ensured the room was always warm, even on a cold night such as this.

I set the coffee pot down on the low table in front of the sofa and poured two cups.

'Is there anything you want to watch on television?' Paul asked.

'I don't think so. Let's have some music.'

'Vivaldi?' He selected a CD, then sat down on the sofa beside me, jean-clad legs splay-ed, and I shifted so that my feet were curled up beneath me and my shoulder resting comfortably against his.

'So – what sort of a day have you had?' I asked.

'Oh, the usual, you know. Chasing late payments, trying to track down a consignment of components that has gone missing between our warehouse and the customer – pretty mundane, compared with what you do.'

'Rubbish. You love it.'

'It's a living.'

'It's more than that, and you know it.' Paul was very good at putting himself down sometimes. But Stattisford Electronics, the firm in which he and Josh Miller were partners, was doing well, and I knew its success was due in no small measure to Paul. Josh might be more flamboyant, the go-getter who did the deals and chatted up the customers, but he would have been lost without Paul's steady influence. When Paul had joined him nine years ago, Stattisford Electronics had been struggling. Now it had a healthy corner of the market sewn up.

'True. I just wish I could make a killing. Perhaps then you'd give up work and allow me to keep you in the manner to which you are accustomed.'

'Paul,' I said warningly, 'let's not get on to that now.'

Paul can be a bit old-fashioned in some ways. He'd like nothing better than for me to stay at home playing happy families while he does his stuff as the breadwinner. He knows it won't wash, knows I'd be wretched stuck in the house all day, and that having a large enough income to support our lifestyle has absolutely nothing to do with my intention to keep my career going. But still he mentions it from time to time, pretending that making his fortune would change everything.

'All right, all right!' He made a rueful face at me over the rim of his coffee cup. 'So – what were you going on about when we were on the phone this afternoon? You said something about Hong Kong.'

'It was one of those really odd things. I was making sure the company my client is interested in hasn't got a criminal record. I pulled up the wrong file by mistake – companies investigated. Practically everybody in Hong Kong has been investigated at some time, from the look of it. But Kowloon and Victoria was on the list. It gave me quite a start.'

'So when were they investigated?'

'Oh, ages ago – 1985, I think it said. But there couldn't have been anything in it. They weren't on the list of convictions, so you need not worry about it.'

'I'm not worried,' he said. 'Just curious.'

I laughed. 'Yes, you are worried! The slightest whiff of anything like that, and you're thinking the worst. Relax! On second thoughts, perhaps you'd better not. They might be after *you* next!' I ran my fingers teasingly across his chest, as if they were little scurrying policemen's legs. 'The yellow peril is coming to get you!'

He grabbed my hand, jerking it so that I half-fell across him.

'Think you can wind me up, do you? We'll see about that!'

The firelight was playing on his face, but I couldn't see it clearly. It was too close to mine, and he was kissing me.

'I think,' he said, 'that it is time we went to bed.'

'Already?'

'Why not? Have you got a better idea?'

I hadn't. So we did.

Three

When I woke next morning it was broad daylight, crisp clear sunshine creeping in between the half-drawn curtains. I opened my eyes gingerly, realizing I felt slightly queasy. Obviously I'd drunk too much claret on top of the gin and tonic last night.

Paul was still asleep. I raised myself on one elbow to look at him and felt a rush of tenderness. Sleeping, he looked impossibly young, nowhere near his thirty-two years, his face rosy and boyish, his hair falling in a thick fair lick over his forehead. One arm lay outside the duvet and the sunshine made the tiny fair hairs on his forearm gleam golden. His bare shoulder looked solid and inviting. I bent over to kiss it and suddenly the nausea was welling up, making me gulp. I sat up hurriedly, pressing a hand across my mouth, and the sudden movement disturbed Paul.

'Jules?' he said sleepily. 'Are you all right?'

'I feel a bit sick, that's all. You and your claret!'

'You did have quite a lot. But I wouldn't mind betting it's not just that. You've been overdoing things. It's a good thing it's the

23

weekend and I can spoil you. How would you like a cup of tea in bed?' He pushed back the duvet and got out of bed. His body looked as strong and inviting as his shoulder had done, and I thought I could very easily forget my hangover.

A few minutes later he was back, wearing his bathrobe and carrying the tea in one hand and the biscuit tin in the other.

'Aren't you having one?' I asked.

'I'll have mine downstairs. I want to go in to work for an hour or so.'

'On a Saturday?'

'There are a few things I want to go over with Josh. Anyway, you'll be going into town for your retail therapy, won't you?'

'Yes, I expect so. Have to have my weekly fix.'

'I don't know why you're so keen on the shops here when you've got all London to choose from all week.'

'When I'm in London I'm too busy working! In any case, it's much nicer here. Not so much trouble parking! There's always bags of room in the multi-storey if you go up high enough.'

Paul grinned, shaking his head. He hated shopping.

'I'm going to have my shower now.'

'OK, I'll stay in bed until you've finished,' I said. 'This is bliss.'

But whenever I'm inactive, I find myself

24

thinking about work. If I'm to get a day's break from it I have to be doing something, which is one of the reasons I make my weekly excursion into town. By the time I'd finished my tea, Paul was out of the shower and I joined him downstairs for a piece of toast. I'd have my own shower later, when he'd left. This was Saturday, my day for indulging myself. I intended to make the most of it.

I'd just got out of the shower and was rubbing cream into my legs when I heard what sounded like a car on the drive.

Not best pleased, I pulled on my bathrobe and padded along to the landing window. The car – a white Fiesta – had pulled into the space Paul had vacated, and I recognized it as Ruth's. I was relieved, but also a bit puzzled. Ruth didn't usually come in at weekends. I went back to the bathroom, wound a towel round my head, and went downstairs.

'Ruth – what are you doing here?'

'Oh hello, Julia. I just popped in with a couple of things I noticed you'd run short of – horseradish relish, in case you have beef on Sunday, and some more olive oil...'

Oscar had followed her in, I noticed. I scooped him up, carried him to the back door and deposited him outside.

'You shouldn't have bothered! I'm going

into town. I could have got some,' I said, coming back.

'No bother, honestly. It's my job, isn't it?'

I shook my head, marvelling at Ruth's commitment. She'd been with us for two and a half years now, and quite honestly I didn't know how I'd manage without her. When we were first married we had a daily three times a week, but she was worse than useless. She tended to vacuum round things where they lay and made scorch marks on my underwear by being too heavy-handed with the iron. Besides this, with me being in London all week, we really needed someone to cook as well. We got rid of the daily woman and advertised for a housekeeper. And along came Ruth.

My first impression was that she was far too young – she only looked about twenty. In fact, she was twenty-seven, and married to Jim Wood, the head storeman at Stattisford Electronics. At the time, she was working there herself as an office cleaner, and for want of a more suitable applicant, I decided to give her a try. I never regretted it.

Ruth took over all the mundane tasks associated with running the house, with the sort of enthusiasm that would have had our previous cleaning lady perspiring even more freely than she already did. Ruth did the laundry and organized the kitchen, she shopped, and she cooked like an angel.

When Ruth cleaned, everything sparkled –
no more gunk in the sink or dustings of
pepper escaped from the pepper mill on the
shelves of the dresser. By Tuesday of each
week, the fresh-scented sheets and towels
were stacked in the airing cupboard, Paul's
clean shirts were on hangers in his wardrobe,
and my undies back in the drawer with no
hint of a scorch mark. Old newspapers and
junk mail were disposed of, though I'd had
to ask her to take them to the recycling bank
rather than putting them in the dustbin,
because she was always keen to get rid of
them then and there. Ditto the empty
bottles. 'I can't stand muddle,' Ruth would
say. And I thought that was fine by me,
though I did spare a thought for her
husband. I could just imagine her chasing
him round their neat little semi (brand new,
of course – no picturesque cottage where
dust and spiders could gather in corners for
Ruth!) whipping off his grimy overalls to
wash the moment he got in from work and
binning his newspapers before he'd had the
chance to read them.

As far as we were concerned, Ruth was the
answer to a prayer. Now, still wearing her
coat, she was clearing away the breakfast
things I'd left on the table, putting the top
back on the marmalade, stacking the used
crockery on the draining board.

'There's no need for you to do that!' I

protested.

'It won't take me a minute.' She turned on the tap, running hot water into the sink. 'You go and dry your hair before you catch cold.'

I shook my head, smiling, and did as I was told.

That was the only trouble with Ruth – she did take over rather!

I was on my way into town when I suddenly realized I couldn't remember switching off the electric heater in the bathroom. The radiator there is always more full of air than hot water, and this morning had been no exception. I'd put on the heater to beat the chill in the air – but had I gone back into the bathroom after going downstairs to speak to Ruth? I didn't think I had.

I parked in my favourite multi-storey – as usual there was plenty of room on the top deck – and fished my mobile phone out of my bag to give Paul a call.

I tried the house first, but there was no reply. Next, I called Stattisford Electronics, and after a few moments, Josh, Paul's partner, answered.

'Is Paul about?' I asked.

'Paul? No, I don't think so.'

'Really? He left home ages ago saying he had some things to sort out with you.'

'Oh yes, he did pop in earlier. I don't know where he is now. Could be in the warehouse,

I suppose. Can I get him to call you? Where are you?'

'At this precise moment on the top deck of the multi-storey car park in Osbourne Street! No, don't get him to call me. I'm going into town now to do some shopping. But if you do see him, will you ask him to check that I switched off the electric fire in the bathroom?'

'Yes, sure. Are you in town all day then?'

'Probably. I'm going to have a good old browse.'

I put my mobile back into my bag, bought a pay-and-display ticket that would last me the whole day, and set out to enjoy what I thought of as my 'Saturday Treat'.

Four

It was five thirty and almost totally dark by the time I made my way back to the multi-storey. I'd had a marvellous day and picked up some bargains, too – a couple of tops that would go well with my business suits, a rugby shirt for Paul, and some bright Italian pottery bowls that would be great for al fresco meals on the patio when summer finally arrived.

The wind had turned to the east. It was bitingly cold and it had blown in the storm clouds which had been hanging over London yesterday. I shivered as I pushed open the heavy metal-clad door to the car park and found myself looking forward to the cosy evening ahead. Ruth had left a quiche in the fridge and some home-made onion soup on the Rayburn; we'd open another bottle of wine and perhaps watch a video.

I crossed to the lifts, and then I saw it. A placard draped across the doors – OUT OF ORDER – PLEASE USE STAIRS. Resigned, I started up.

It was dark and malodorous in the stair-well. The only light came from a dusty florescent lamp on the landing, and gallons of strong disinfectant failed to disguise the stench of urine and exhaust fumes and stale cigarette smoke.

For some reason, the seedy oppressiveness made me uncomfortable. I'm not normally the nervous sort – I have this belief, perhaps rather naive, that if you face up to things, they tend to go away. I knew that muggings and murders and rapes happen, but honestly, not that often.

Laden down with my purchases, it seemed to take forever to reach the top of the multi-storey. Then, at last, directly ahead of me was the door leading to the top floor, where I had parked – a solid-looking, metal-plated door like the one downstairs, which opened inward. It was fractionally ajar, showing a sliver of light in the gloom – no, not light, exactly, just *less dark*. I gave it a push, but it scraped open only a couple of inches and stuck again. I put my shoulder to the door as hard as I could, so hard it spun me round. The door gave with a suddenness that unbalanced me, and at that precise same second I experienced what felt like a hard push between my shoulder blades.

Shock and surprise flooded through me, liquid and scarlet. My legs, already like jelly from the climb, stumbled one pace forward, and then I was falling, tumbling, jolting. Each concrete step was a jar of shock, one after the other, one after the other, a momentum that seemed to go on forever, so that when I reached the bottom and there was nowhere else to go, that was a shock too.

For a long moment, a timeless, unreal, suspended moment, I lay there in a heap, too shaken to move, or even feel pain. And then, from the very edges of my mind, the blackness began to close in. I gasped, feeling a flash of utter panic. But the blackness was unrepentant. It washed over me, and I knew no more.

Five

It wouldn't be true to say I remember nothing of what happened afterwards. Very dimly, I was aware of someone standing over me, of voices which seemed to come from a long way off, of someone covering me with a coat, of the wail of an ambulance siren coming closer. I was on a stretcher, faces appeared above me, distorted, as if I were looking at them through a goldfish bowl, and I was trying to say something. But I knew I wasn't making any sense, and in any case the effort was too much. I closed my eyes and let the blackness come again, soft, comforting. Except that now I was hurting all over.

And then things get really fuzzy. The voices and the faces are all part of a dream – or a nightmare. I'm trying to say something again, but my voice won't come. It's all I can do to breathe. And I'm lapsing again, floating away...

But now there's someone holding my hand. And a voice I recognize. Paul's voice. Paul is here, I'm sure. How did he get here? I open my eyes and see him looking down at me, his face taut with anxiety.

'Julia? Oh, sweetheart...'

'Paul...?'

But I'm drifting again. All I want to do is go to sleep...

'Well,' the doctor said, 'you're back with us then.'

He was quite young and rather good-looking, with longish hair and a pair of round metal-framed glasses. I looked past him, to the room I had seen only fuzzily in the hours – days? – before: small and neat with primrose-yellow walls and green and yellow patterned curtains. A private room, I guessed. Beyond the green door I could hear the sounds of hospital life going on – the clank of what might have been metal food containers, the squeak of a trolley, a woman's voice, a little strident, footsteps on polished floors, but it all sounded vague and distant, as if I was removed from it, shut up in my little yellow and green cell.

'How are you feeling?' the doctor asked.

That took some thinking about. Mentally I explored myself. Stiff. Sore. With a thumping headache. And, when I tried to move it, a sharp jarring pain in my right wrist.

'Lousy, actually.'

'Not surprising. You took quite a fall.'

'I did?'

'Don't you remember?'

'I'm not sure...' I chased the elusive

34

memories round the cotton wool which seemed to be stuffing my brain. Bumping. Jolting. Yes, I could remember that. But bumping and jolting *where*? Concrete stairs. Of course – the car park. I'd climbed the stairs, tried to open the door, and then ... someone had pushed me. Someone had pushed me and I'd fallen down the stairs. But that couldn't be right. People didn't deliberately push other people downstairs.

The doctor must have seen the confusion in my face.

'Don't worry about it,' he said, smiling his best bedside-manner smile. 'You banged your head and you have mild concussion. There may be blanks at the moment – it's quite normal. It will all come back in time.'

I certainly hoped so. It was very unsettling, even a little frightening, not to be able to remember.

'What day is it?' I asked.

'Sunday. Lunchtime, actually.'

So I'd been right about the food containers.

'Does my husband know I'm here?' I asked in sudden panic, then remembered Paul's face fading in and out of the fog.

'He certainly does. He's scarcely left your bedside. I think he's gone home for a change of clothes and something to eat. He brought you those flowers,' he added.

I turned my head with difficulty, making

a sharp wave of pain wash over my entire skull. On the locker beside my bed was an enormous bouquet of yellow and bronze chrysanthemums, cream gladioli and some delicate spotted lilies. I wondered where he'd got them on a Sunday morning. The hospital flower shop, perhaps.

'How long...?' I stopped in mid-sentence.

'How long will you be here? Difficult to say at the moment. We shall want to keep an eye on you today, certainly. Tomorrow we'll give you a thorough check-over and it's possible we may allow you to go home then.'

Unbelievably, I was getting sleepy again. The good-looking face and the little round glasses were blurring into the yellow and green patterned curtains.

'Tell my husband I...' I never got around to finishing whatever it was I was going to say, because I'd totally lost the thread of it. My heavy eyes closed again and I slept.

Paul was there next time I woke, sitting in the chair beside the bed, flipping through the business section of the *Sunday Times*. When he realized I was awake, he put it down on the bedside locker, leant over and took my hand.

'Julia – you're awake. Thank God!'

'Oh Paul – I'm so sorry,' I said thickly.

'What on earth for?'

'Doing something so stupid! I just don't

know how it happened! One minute I was on the landing and the next...' I stopped, remembering again that sensation of being pushed. Strange how clear it was when everything else was so woozy and confused. I could almost feel that hand between my shoulder blades, even now. 'Paul, I know this sounds really off-the-wall, but I thought ... it felt just as if someone pushed me!'

'Pushed you?' Paul echoed. He sounded startled and disbelieving. 'What on earth are you talking about?'

'Oh, I know it's crazy. But I really thought...'

'No one would *push* you, Julia! You've banged your head. You're imagining things.'

'Yes, I suppose I must be. But all the same...'

'You didn't see anyone, did you?'

I tried to think about that. Had there been someone behind the door? I couldn't be sure. And though I could remember people bending over me as I lay on the landing, they must have been people looking after me – mustn't they?

'No, I didn't see anyone.'

'Well, there you are. No one would push you down the stairs. Unless it was a mugger. You know I don't like you using those multi-storey car parks.'

'Paul, I've been there hundreds of times. Nothing like this ever happened before.'

'Well, if it was a mugger, he didn't take anything,' Paul said. 'Your bag hasn't been stolen or anything. Somebody put it in the ambulance with you.'

My bag. My shopping.

'What happened to all the things I bought?' Suddenly – bizarrely – that seemed vastly more important than any other consideration. 'I'd got crockery! Oh, my God, it'll be smashed to smithereens!' I could hear my voice rising, feel idiotic hot tears filling my eyes.

'Your shopping is all safe too – apart from the crockery. Come on, now, don't cry. We can always get some more. The important thing is that you are all right. Well, almost. Oh Julia, don't...'

But I couldn't help it. The tears went on seeping out of the corners of my eyes and rolling down my cheeks.

'At least you didn't leave the bathroom fire on,' Paul said in the sort of tone intended to change the subject and jolly me along.

'The bathroom fire...? Oh yes, I tried to ring you, didn't I? Josh said you weren't there.'

'Well I was, all the time. He'd have found me in the warehouse checking stock if he'd taken the trouble to look. Anyway, as I say, you had nothing to worry about. The house didn't burn down. So, there is absolutely nothing to cry about. And it won't do you

38

any good at all.'

'I know. I do love you, Paul.'

'And I love you. Now, get some rest, huh? I'm going to leave you in peace for a bit.'

'Where are you going?'

'Things to do. Nothing you need worry about.'

'Oh, all right.' I felt too woozy to argue.

Paul kissed me and then he was gone. Gingerly I raised myself on one elbow, leaning over to the locker for a glass of water.

The *Sunday Times* business section lay across the corner, open to the article Paul had been reading. The headline said something about Hong Kong. It jolted a chord in my memory. Hong Kong. Work. I had a big job to do for Poyson Associates. I couldn't be here too long or I'd be letting them down. But just at the moment my brain ached too much to even think about it.

Six

I slept and slept. Once or twice I woke with a start, a replay of the horrible sensation of falling making me shake from head to foot. But by the next day I was feeling much more like myself, if a little queasy.

At around lunchtime the young doctor came to see me.

'You'll be glad to know we're on the point of giving you a clean bill of health,' he said cheerily. 'As you know, you managed to concuss yourself when you fell – hardly surprising. Concrete steps aren't really recommended for banging your head on. And you've got a badly sprained wrist and ankle and a variety of rather nasty bruises. But the chief thing is nothing is broken, and I know you'll be relieved to hear the baby is absolutely fine.'

I stared at him. 'I beg your pardon?'

'The baby. A nasty fall like that could have caused you to miscarry. Fortunately that hasn't happened.' He eased the metal frame of his glasses down on his nose and looked at me over the top of them. 'You did know about the baby?'

40

'No!'

'Well goodness me!' He laughed, slightly embarrassed. 'You are about two months pregnant, Mrs Wilson.'

My head was spinning, not from concussion this time, but in sheer confused shock. 'I had no idea!'

'In that case, I'm very pleased to be the bearer of good news. It is good news, I hope?'

'Well ... yes ... I suppose so. Bit of a shock, though. I'm on the pill...'

'Not always infallible. You haven't had antibiotics by any chance?'

'Oh yes! I did! I had tonsillitis over Christmas ... oh shit!'

'It's not good news then.'

'Oh ... yes ... no ... I don't know! I just can't believe it...'

'Well, I'll leave you to take in the news.'

Alone, I lay back against the pillows, my thoughts reeling. We'd always planned on having a family one day, of course. But not yet. At the moment my career was my first consideration and a baby would cause all kinds of unlooked-for complications. And how could I be two months pregnant and not know it? It certainly explained the nausea I'd been experiencing, though...

A tiny bubble of excitement twisted deep inside me. A baby. I was going to have a baby! The thought opened up whole new vistas of uncharted country and challenges totally outside my experience. A new life growing inside me – a small human being for whom I would be totally responsible. The next generation. The enormity of it was staggering, but also exhilarating. Suddenly I couldn't wait to tell Paul.

I rang the bell beside my bed and asked for a telephone. A few minutes later a nurse came in with a phone trolley. Because of my damaged wrist she offered to dial for me, but when I started dictating the number of the line to Paul's office, my mind went blank. I struggled to remember; failed. I had to ask her to look it up in my diary, which made me feel a complete fool, though I suppose she was used to patients with concussion having memory lapses – especially if they had also just been told they were pregnant!

'It's ringing.' She handed me the phone and bustled away. I waited expectantly to hear Paul's voice, and when Josh answered instead I could have wept with disappointment.

'Julia! Is something wrong?' he asked.

'No, no – I just wanted to speak to Paul about something. Is he there?'

'Not at the moment. Can I help?'

'Not really.' I had a sudden feeling of déjà-vu. This was practically a re-run of the conversation we'd had on Saturday. 'We must stop meeting like this,' I said in a weak attempt at humour.

'Oh, I don't know! Paul's loss is my gain.' His tone was light, but I heard the under-tones, and it made me uncomfortable. I'd always had the feeling that Josh fancied me. He'd never said a word out of place, certainly never made a move in my direction, yet somehow I could sense it – the unmistake-able certainty that if I were to let down my guard there could be something between us.

'I'm pretty sure I saw Paul drive out of the yard an hour or so ago,' Josh was saying. 'You could always try his mobile.'

'Yes, I suppose I could...' But I rather thought that number, too, was lost in the murky mists. I didn't want to bother the nurse again – she had quite enough to do without having to act as my secretary.

'Don't worry, I'll catch up with him later,' I said, but I suppose I must have sounded a little odd, because Josh said: 'Are you sure everything is all right, Julia?'

'Yes. Fine. Couldn't be better.'

I put the phone down and the twisting movement sent a jar of pain up my spine and into my neck and head.

Perhaps 'couldn't be better' was something of an exaggeration, I thought ruefully. But certainly I had a great deal to think about.

Later on, a nurse took me for the first bath I'd had since Saturday. It was something of a painful exercise, but the hot water was also soothing, and I'd been longing to feel really clean again. As I sat in the bath, letting her shampoo my hair, I looked down at my still-flat tummy and thought about the life that was growing inside. Overwhelming!

She had towel-dried both me and my hair when there was a knock at the bathroom door and another nurse popped her head round.

'Ah – nearly ready to go back to her room, is she? She's got a visitor – a very good-looking man. So it's as well she's got smartened up!'

'That will be my husband,' I said, pleased by the nurse's flattering description of Paul, and amused by the way she was talking as if I wasn't there at all.

The nurse winked at me. 'Well, *lucky you* is all I can say!'

The first nurse helped me into my dressing gown and passed me my comb. The small mirror was steamed up, but after she'd given it a wipe with a paper towel it was clear enough to show me just how pale I was – and how dreadful my eyes looked. I always think my eyes, tawny brown and almond shaped, are my best feature, but now they were horribly swollen and the dark circles beneath them spanned the colour spectrum from purple to bilious dark green.

I combed my towel-dried hair so that it

framed my face with spiky damp tendrils, and the nurse helped me back along the corridor.

The door of my private room was ajar. My visitor was standing at the window, looking out.

Not Paul at all.

Josh.

He turned round as we went in. He was holding a bouquet of long-stemmed yellow roses.

'Josh!' I said. 'What are you doing here?'

'Come to see you, of course. I brought these for you.' He held out the roses.

'You shouldn't have! But thanks, anyway.'

'Let's get you into bed,' my nurse said. 'Do you want to take your dressing gown off?'

'No – I'll keep it on.' I was very aware that beneath it I was wearing only my strappy nightdress. It made me feel very vulnerable with Josh standing there looking at me.

The nurse turned back the covers, helped me into bed, and took the roses from Josh.

'I'll put these in water.' She was a bit pink, a bit coy suddenly. Josh has that effect on women.

He's a very attractive man, no argument about that. Just over six feet tall, well-built – I think he works out two or three times a week at the gym – with very dark, very thick curly hair and the kind of swarthy com-

45

plexion that makes me think he has some Mediterranean blood. In his dark business suit and crisp white shirt, he managed to look like a cross between a film star and a rugby player, and though he is eight years older than Paul, he looks no more than early thirties. He's a confirmed bachelor, wedded, he jokes, to his powerful BMW motorcycle and the single-engine PA28 aircraft he owns a share in and flies whenever he can. But there's always one or another of a seemingly endless procession of beautiful women on his arm when it comes to social functions.

His commanding presence is a great asset in business – people don't easily ignore – or forget – Josh. But I do sometimes wonder if all that confidence is part of the reason why Paul is so self-effacing – because he feels somewhat in Josh's shadow.

Truth to tell, however, Paul was always self-effacing. Though we went to the same school – a grammar turned comprehensive which still sought to keep up its old standards – I remember very little about him, and at eighteen, when our paths divided, I went travelling in Australia and the Far East for a year before going to university without giving him a second thought, whilst he went straight into a job with an electronics company.

Seven years went by before we met up again – at a reunion of the class of '83. We got talking over a glass of wine and a sausage roll and I realized that the unremarkable boy I'd scarcely noticed in the old days had metamorphosed into a very attractive man whom I liked very much. There was a strength behind the rather reserved exterior, a twinkle of dry humour that shone through as he relaxed.

'You were always the golden girl,' he said when we got to know each other better. 'I always fancied you, but I didn't think I stood a chance.'

'Idiot!' But in a funny way, that remark sums Paul up. He's a successful businessman now, with all the trappings that go with it, and I hate it when he puts himself down, attributing his success to nothing more than 'a lucky break'. But to be perfectly honest, I have to admit to doubting whether he'd have had the drive to make it without Josh. In all likelihood he'd have stayed with the electronics company all his life, working his guts out, doing a marvellous job for them, for which he never received proper credit or remuneration. But he and Josh were a winning team. While Paul was superbly knowledgeable and a brilliant organizer, Josh was the one with the vision – and the charisma. Josh made things happen; Paul backed him up. If a lucky break was what he liked to attribute his success to, then that lucky break was undoubtedly called Josh Miller.

47

Now I lay back against my heaped-up pillows and smiled at Josh weakly.

'I didn't expect you to come and visit me.'

'Didn't you?' His eyes held mine a fraction too long. 'I was worried about you, Julia. When you telephoned, you sounded ... well, a little odd. I couldn't find the man himself, so I came instead.'

'That's very sweet of you, Josh,' I said, 'but really, I'm fine. Well, not *fine*, exactly. Feeling a bit the worse for wear, to tell the truth.'

'Hardly surprising! How on earth did it happen?'

'I don't know.' I wasn't about to tell Josh that I had this idiotic notion I'd been pushed. 'To be truthful, I can't remember much about it. I keep getting these stupid memory lapses. They say it's quite normal, but it's pretty frustrating, all the same.'

'Have they said how long it will be before you get back to normal?'

'Not really. I don't think they know. But I've got to get out of here soon. I've got several important jobs on...'

'Sounds interesting. Which companies are you working for at the moment?'

I sighed. 'Oh Josh, I don't want to talk about it. I don't even want to think about it. It makes my head hurt.'

'Poor old Julia.'

At that moment the door opened, and there was Paul. He didn't look very pleased to see Josh. In fact, he practically glared at him.

'What are you doing here?'

'Come to see your wife. I was concerned about her. She phoned for you sounding really anxious. I knew you were out. I saw you driving off a while before. Where were you going, anyway? I thought you were going to be in the office all afternoon.'

'Hello!' I said. 'Is anyone talking to me?'

'Darling!' Paul came over and kissed me. 'Are you all right? What did you want me for?'

'It's ... well, it's rather private, actually.'

'I'm going now,' Josh said, winking at me. 'Somebody has to mind the shop.'

Paul ignored him. I could sense the tension between them. They weren't going to start falling out, I hoped. That would be disastrous for the business.

Just to make matters worse, my nurse chose that very moment to come in with the long-stemmed roses in a vase. 'They look lovely, don't they?'

Paul's mouth tightened still more. I could see what he was thinking. He should have been the one to bring me roses. And yes, they did look lovely, managing to upstage his hospital flower shop chrysanthemums.

'I'll leave you two alone,' Josh said.

I thought it was probably the most tactful thing he'd said in a long while.

Seven

The minute we were alone, I told Paul my news. I simply could not wait any longer. There was no question of leading into it. I just came straight out with it and for a moment Paul stared at me in the same sort of blank disbelief I must have registered when the doctor told me.

'Well, this is a surprise!' he said. 'How do you feel about it?'

'Like you – shocked. But also happy.'

'It's going to mean a lot of changes. You're going to have to give up your job.'

'Not necessarily. Other women manage to juggle a career and motherhood. There's no reason why I can't do the same.'

'Other women don't live and work in two different places.'

'Some do. Anyway, I'll manage. Oh Paul, don't look so cross!'

'I'm not cross. Just a bit concerned. You're so committed to your career at the moment. In a few years' time, maybe you'd have got it out of your system.'

'Paul,' I said, 'my career isn't something to "get out of my system" like chicken pox. It's my life. It will still be just as important to me five years from now – and we'll both be five years older. Perhaps this is the best thing that could have happened. If we'd waited for the right time, it might never have come. We might have left it too late. That would be just awful. Oh please, don't make problems.'

'I'm not making problems. Just being realistic.'

'You don't want the baby,' I said flatly.

Paul sat down on the bed beside me, taking both my hands in his.

'Oh Julia, of course I do! I can't think of anything I'd like more.'

'That's all right then,' I said.

But I had this niggling little worry that there might yet be disagreements over just how we were going to organize our life.

By the time I was discharged from hospital two days later I'd become completely used to the idea that I was pregnant. I was still a little overawed and a little apprehensive, but mostly just very happy and excited.

I spent quite a lot of time daydreaming about it, and even started to make plans. There was nothing stopping me working right up until the baby was born. Then afterwards we'd have to find a nanny. That might be a problem – I'd heard horror stories from friends at work on that score.

And then I thought of Ruth. She would be

absolutely perfect if only she would agree to take on the extra responsibility. She'd already looked after Paul in my absence like a mother hen, and I couldn't think of anyone I'd rather entrust with the care of a baby.

There was only one snag as far as I could see – I knew that Ruth and Jim, her husband, had been trying for a baby themselves for ages. If she fell pregnant too, she might want to give up work altogether. And then again she might not. It hadn't happened yet, and if it did, she might well be prepared to look after two children instead of just one. Knowing her, she'd cope cheerfully and efficiently.

But aside from thinking about the baby, I was also beginning to feel very restless – a sure sign I was getting better! – and I was worried about all the unfinished work piling up at my office. Paul had flatly refused to bring my briefcase and files to the hospital, saying I should be resting, but that didn't stop me fretting about my clients, and Poyson Associates in particular. I'd telephoned to let them know what had happened, and they had been very understanding, but I knew they would be champing at the bit, waiting for my report, and I didn't want to risk them passing on the job to someone else. So it was an enormous relief when my doctor told me I could go home.

Paul came to collect me and insisted on

treating me like a piece of Dresden china. I only just managed to persuade him against putting me into a wheelchair, and on the staircase that led down from my private room he linked his arm very firmly through mine.

'We don't want you taking any more tumbles – especially now.'

'That was a one-off,' I said, biting my lip against the pain in my ankle. 'I definitely won't be trying that again!'

Neither of us mentioned my assertion that I thought I'd been pushed. Though I could still almost feel that hand in my back, I'd practically convinced myself it had been nothing more than a figment of my imagination. I'd fallen. End of story. Perhaps, given my condition, I'd had a dizzy spell after exerting myself on the stairs. That really was the most feasible explanation.

I went home.

I thought the nightmare was over. How wrong can you be?

In fact, it had only just begun.

Eight

Considering how much better I'd been feeling when I was in hospital, I'd thought, rather naively, that once I got home everything would be well on the way to being back to normal. I was wrong. Just making the short car journey left me exhausted, and the simplest task seemed like an obstacle course. With my wrist still strapped up, an ankle I couldn't put any weight on and a spine that jarred uncomfortably every time I moved, it took me forever to do the things I'd done before without even thinking, and I felt weak, useless, and horribly frustrated.

It wasn't only the physical, either. I was still a bit weepy, still suffering the annoying lapses of memory, and, worst of all, I'd be suddenly assailed by a terrifying sensation of vulnerability. For someone like me it was a new and disturbing experience.

For the first couple of days I did nothing but sit in one of the garden loungers, which Paul had brought in from the garage and aired with an electric blanket because the adjustable back, firm and at just the right angle, was the most comfortable for me.

Concentrating on anything more taxing than the stack of magazines Ruth had brought from the paper shop in the village was beyond me – I couldn't even be bothered with a book. No sooner did I try to start reading than my brain would be buzzing with all the pressing work I had to do. But I knew I wasn't up to concentrating on that either.

'Just relax and forget about everything but getting well,' Paul said, but I couldn't. I couldn't work, and I couldn't *not* work, and it was driving me crazy.

What on earth I would have done without Ruth, I don't know. If I'd thought she was a treasure before, now I was convinced of it. She made me appetizing little meals on a tray and endless cups of tea and coffee, and kept the house ticking comfortably around me.

I told her about the baby on my second day at home, because I felt I owed it to her to put her in the picture as soon as possible, and though she pretended to be pleased for me, there was no mistaking the fact that she was envious too.

'Well, that's life for you,' she said in a resigned tone. 'You just can't work it out, can you?'

But she plumped up the pillow behind my back with unusual vigour and a few minutes later I could hear her banging things around in the kitchen. I could guess what she was thinking. It wasn't fair that I should get pregnant without even trying, whilst she and Jim, who wanted a baby so desperately, were disappointed month after month. For a moment I felt quite guilty, as if I'd deliberately set out to hurt her. But I told myself that was pure silliness. Just another manifestation of all the very raw emotions which seemed to keep bubbling to the surface.

But I didn't mention my idea that perhaps Ruth could take on the role of nanny as well as housekeeper. That really would have been salt in the wound. And with seven months still to go, there was all the time in the world for making arrangements.

I had several visitors in those first days when I was a virtual prisoner in my own home. One of them was Josh.

He turned up unannounced in the middle of the afternoon. I was watching an Australian soap on TV when I heard the doorbell and a few minutes later he appeared in the doorway.

'Good afternoon, Mrs Wilson! I was just passing and I thought I'd look in and see how you are.'

I wished he'd let me know he was coming. I knew I looked a perfect fright in my comfortable old dressing gown, without a vestige of make-up.

I also knew he wasn't telling the truth when he said he'd been passing. No one 'passes' through our village, unless it's tourists doing the local beauty spots. From the industrial estate on the outskirts of town where Stattisford Electronics is situated, a dual carriageway leads directly on to the ring road, and just a few miles away is the junction with the M4. Business contacts don't hide away in sleepy villages miles off the beaten track. Josh had come especially to see me, and both he and I knew it.

'I thought these might cheer you up.' He handed me a box of extremely expensive Belgian chocolates tied with a red ribbon.

'Josh! You shouldn't have! I'll get as fat as a house!'

'You, Julia? Never!'

'Don't believe it! Sitting around all day doing nothing but eating chocolates is a recipe for disaster.'

'Well, I'll help you eat them if you insist.'

'Ah – do I scent an ulterior motive?' I untied the ribbon and opened the box. 'Choose!'

'You first. They are your chocolates.'

We were laughing, Josh bending over me to look at the chocolates, when Ruth came in.

'Oh, sorry...'

I looked up, puzzled. There was a very strange expression on Ruth's face, a mixture of disapproval and embarrassment, and something else, something I couldn't identify, but realized later was the same look she had worn when I told her about the baby. Envy.

'I ... just wondered if you'd like a cup of tea...' Her voice was odd too.

'That would be really nice, Ruth. Thanks.'

'It certainly would, Ruth.' Josh winked at her, and she turned faintly pink.

'I don't know what I'd have done without Ruth these last few days,' I said when she'd gone off to make the tea. 'She's been working far more hours than usual, looking after me.'

'A clock-watcher Ruth is not. We've never really found anyone to replace her at the office. Most cleaners do their job and go – some of them don't even do that! Ruth was never averse to a spot of overtime.'

It occurred to me to wonder just what Ruth's overtime had involved. There had been something in the way she'd looked at Josh. But I dismissed the idea almost instantly. Ruth might fancy Josh – most women did – but I couldn't imagine Josh fancying Ruth in a million years. His taste in women was far more sophisticated. And though Ruth was quite pretty, I couldn't imagine Josh would ever get involved with the wife of his storeman. No, if any candle-carrying was going on, it was almost certainly a one-sided affair.

'So, it's no work for you for a while then,' Josh said, sitting down in one of our comfortable chairs.

'Not for a day or two, no.'

'That must be a blow. Paul tells me you've got several big jobs on.'

'That's par for the course. But yes, it is a crashing nuisance.'

'A Hong Kong connection, he tells me.'

I frowned. 'He shouldn't have told you that. *I* shouldn't have told *him*.'

'It's no great secret, surely? Half the companies in Hong Kong are looking for European interests in case things go pear-shaped there after 1997. There was an article about it in the *Sunday Times* only this week.'

'I haven't read the papers,' I confessed. 'It's just that I like to feel my clients can trust they will get absolute confidentiality from me.'

'I'm sure they can. You are a very professional lady, Julia.'

'I don't feel very professional at the moment,' I said ruefully. 'I feel battered and bruised and rather sorry for myself.'

'How long will it be before you can be back at the grindstone?'

'As short a time as I can possibly make it! At least in this computer age I can do some work from home the moment I feel up to it.'

'Paul won't allow that, surely?'

'Let him try to stop me! There's a computer in his study that I can hijack, and if he makes it unusable somehow, I shall get my secretary to bring me a lap-top. She'll be coming down in a day or two in any case to bring me my post and take some dictation. I can't afford to let things slide, Josh.'

Ruth came back with the tea. She still looked slightly pink, slightly flustered, and as she handed Josh his cup, I could almost sense her eagerness. I smiled to myself. Irresistible Josh! What a way he had with the ladies!

I opened the box of Belgian chocolates again.

'Have a choccy, Ruth. They're rather special ones.'

'Oh, thanks...' She glanced at me. 'You don't know how lucky you are, Julia.'

'Oh yes I do,' I said.

But I had the distinct feeling that Ruth was referring to a great deal more than the chocolates.

Nine

That evening, after we'd eaten the meal Ruth had left for us, Paul and I sat down together to watch television. For the first time since my accident I was actually able to concentrate, but by ten o'clock I realized I was very tired again.

'I think I'm ready for bed,' I said.

'OK, sweetheart. We don't want you getting overtired, especially now.'

He helped me upstairs. The bed was already turned down – Ruth again, I guessed – and Paul had switched on the electric blanket during one of the commercial breaks in the film we'd been watching. With enormous relief I slid between the sheets and Paul pulled them up to my chin.

'Do you want a hot drink?'

'No, thanks.'

'Right. I'll be joining you soon. I'll just lock up and ... oh, damn it!'

'What's the matter?' I asked.

'It's the end of the month. I should have paid the bills today. I'll have to sort that out before I come to bed.'

'Do you have to?' I was sleepy, but some of

61

the insecurity that had resulted from my accident had returned. I longed to feel the comforting warmth of Paul lying beside me. 'I can do it tomorrow. I'm here kicking my heels. Just leave out the file and the cheque book.'

'No. You don't want to be bothered with that. You're supposed to be having a complete rest,' Paul said emphatically.

'I don't mind, honestly. I feel much better now, and tomorrow I'll feel better still. Anyway, it will give me something to do.'

'I said I will do it, Julia!' Paul's tone was quite sharp, taking me aback. 'Just go to sleep, please!'

He turned out the light and was gone, leaving me puzzled and rather stung by the way he had spoken to me. Anyone would think he hadn't wanted me seeing his accounts! Then, in a flash, it came to me, and I smiled to myself. It would be my birthday in a few weeks' time. Perhaps Paul had bought something for me on his credit card and didn't want me to see the bill for fear of spoiling the surprise. Perhaps he'd got tickets for a show, or even booked a weekend away somewhere. Once, he'd whisked me off to Paris for two glorious nights. Paris in the springtime, romantic and beautiful. The memory of it dispelled my resentment, making me feel warm and happy and loved.

The heat of the electric blanket was

making me drowsy. Full of blissful anticipation, I fell asleep.

When Ruth arrived next morning, she helped me to get dressed, and whilst I had breakfast she hoovered through, singing loudly and rather tunelessly.

'Would you like me to put your chair in the conservatory?' she asked, coming back as I was finishing my coffee. 'It's a lovely day. The sun's quite warm in there.'

It was a lovely day – a clear blue sky that promised spring just around the corner – but I had other things on my mind than more wasted hours.

'No, I'm going to try to do some work.'

She looked worried. 'Do you think you should?'

'Yes I do! I'm fed up with being an invalid. Have you seen my files lying about? They were here, but...'

'Aren't they in the study?'

'Oh yes, of course!'

I'd put them there myself, I remembered now. On Saturday morning before I'd gone out for my fateful shopping spree. These memory lapses were getting to be annoying!

'Actually, I think I'll work in the study,' I said. 'I can use Paul's desk and his computer, too, if I need to.'

I limped through to the study, leaving Ruth to clear away my breakfast things.

The study was almost as sunny as the conservatory would have been. It's cosy, panelled in oak and hung with some of the old cartoons Paul likes to collect, and I have to confess it's also rather cluttered, as we also use it to store things we haven't got room for anywhere else. Besides the box and lever-arch files with all our household documents, there are old photograph albums and a collection of records we don't play any more, and wallets of maps and brochures from our various jaunts. Paul and I both love travelling. I got a taste for it when I took my year out, backpacking in Australia and the Far East, and since we were married we have had at least one holiday a year in some exotic spot. There doesn't seem much point in keeping all that memorabilia, and I keep threatening to throw it all out, but somehow I never do. There are just too many precious memories amongst the yellowing plane tickets and the pictures of faraway places.

The desk, however, is almost always tidy. It belongs to Paul, and he is quite fastidious about working in a muddle. My files were on a corner of the desk, neatly stacked, and my briefcase was in the corner. I sat down in the big swivel chair overlooking the sunny garden and pulled the files towards me.

I realized straight away that working was not going to be easy. At least I was able to read through the papers and start getting myself back into a work-orientated frame of mind. But with my right wrist still strapped up, writing was well-nigh impossible.

As for the computer, managing it single-handed was awkward in the extreme, slow and laborious and frustrating. But I really did want to finish the Hong Kong checks I'd begun last Friday.

'Ruth!' I called. 'You couldn't come and help me, could you?'

She appeared in the doorway, duster in hand. 'Help you? How?'

'I'm really struggling here. Do you think you could be my hand?'

'I don't know anything about computers,' Ruth said doubtfully.

'You don't need to. I'll explain as we go along.'

'I'm in the middle of dusting...'

'I'm sure everything is spotless. This is far more important. Bring a chair, there's an angel.'

Ruth departed and returned with one of the pine kitchen chairs. She positioned it alongside mine and we moved the computer in her direction.

'Right, this is what you do...'

Under my instruction, Ruth pulled up the file of Hong Kong companies who had been prosecuted for fraudulent dealing. I wanted to be sure that I hadn't missed anything on Friday. But the result was the same. As far as

I could tell, Sutherland Dewar were clean. For good measure, I ran a few additional checks and then found myself remembering the other file I'd chanced upon – the one covering companies investigated.

It had been quite a shock, seeing the name of Stattisford Electronics' suppliers, Kowloon and Victoria Enterprises, appear on the screen, though, as I'd thought at the time, and Paul had confirmed, there was nothing very unusual about being under investigation in a place as corruption-conscious as Hong Kong. Sharp practice and crime were rife there, everything from counterfeiting and drug smuggling to fraud and vice, and the authorities were doing their very best to stamp it out. But I was curious, all the same. The date of the investigation I'd seen listed had been 1985, I remembered, but I'd take a quick peep to see if there had been anything since.

Because in the first place I'd come upon the file by mistake, it took me a while to tell Ruth how to find it again, but at last there it was, block upon block of names of companies with dates and brief notes explaining the reasons for the investigation.

I ran my eye down it; frowned. Strange. I'd thought Kowloon and Victoria were on the first page. But they weren't.

'Move on,' I said to Ruth.

She did as I told her; she was beginning to

get the hang of it now.

'What are we looking for?'

'Kowloon and Victoria Enterprises. The people who supply Stattisford with components.'

'Can't see them.'

'Neither can I. That is odd. Really odd. This was the file I pulled up on Friday. They were there then. But now they're not. Why on earth...?'

I was thinking aloud, but all the thinking in the world didn't change anything.

On Friday Kowloon and Victoria Enterprises had been on a list of companies under investigation. Now they weren't. Either I'd dreamed the whole thing – or somebody had removed the details from the file.

Ten

'I really ought to be getting the casserole in the oven if it's going to be done for your supper,' Ruth said.

I glanced at her, still deep in thought.

'Oh yes – all right. You go and do what you have to.'

'Can you manage here now?'

'Yes. But leave the chair. We'll close down the computer when you've finished your cooking.'

Ruth went off and I could hear pots and pans clanking in the kitchen. I sat for a few minutes, staring at the computer screen. I simply couldn't understand what had happened. I hadn't *imagined* seeing Kowloon and Victoria Enterprises listed, surely? I'd been talking to Paul at the time, but he hadn't mentioned them as far as I could remember, or said anything that would have caused my mind to play tricks. It had been before my accident, after all, before the bang to my head. If it had happened today, I'd have put it down to the after-effects of my concussion. But on Friday everything had been perfectly normal. I'd never have imagined something like that.

I gave my head a small shake. There was something very odd here, and before I was through, I was going to find out what it was. But just at the moment, the most important thing was making up lost time with the job in hand.

I pulled the Poyson Associates file towards me once more and tried to forget about Kowloon and Victoria Enterprises.

At one o'clock, Ruth appeared in the doorway. 'I've made a sandwich for lunch. Would you like it here, or are you coming back into the kitchen?'

'I'll come back to the kitchen. Just give me a hand here first. I'd like to look at that file just once more.'

We found it. But of course there was still no mention of Kowloon and Victoria. I'd known there wouldn't be – it was hardly likely to have reappeared as if by magic. But perhaps there was another file...

'Let's do a search,' I said to Ruth. 'We are looking for anything to do with Hong Kong businesses.'

Ruth sighed. It was a very quiet sigh, but I heard it. She was getting fed up with this, I realized.

'It won't take a minute, I promise.'

I was so engrossed, I didn't hear the car on the drive. Perhaps I wouldn't have heard it anyway – the study is, after all, on the other side of the house. The first indication I had that Paul was home was hearing the door slam and his voice calling: 'Hello! Where is everybody?'

'In the study,' I called back. 'What are you doing home at this time of day?'

'Just popped back for a couple of things...' He broke off in mid-sentence. He was in the study doorway now. 'What on earth do you think you're doing?'

'A bit of work, that's all...'

'You are supposed to be resting!'

'Oh Paul – I'm all right! I can't just sit around doing nothing when I've got so much work on.'

'You'll never get better unless you take things more easily!' He strode across the study, looking at the computer screen over Ruth's and my head. 'What are you doing, anyway?'

'Work! At least – I was. At this precise moment I'm searching for any mention of Kowloon and Victoria Enterprises. There's something very odd, Paul...'

'I don't want to hear it, Julia.' Paul leaned between us, switching off the computer.

'What do you think you're doing?' I demanded.

'Putting a stop to you endangering your health. If you haven't got the sense to look after yourself, I shall have to do it for you.'

70

'Paul, I am not a child...'

'Shall I...?' Ruth was looking from one to the other of us, clearly embarrassed at being caught in the middle of a fight.

'Yes, sure – go and put the kettle on,' I said.

She pushed back her chair and made a hasty exit.

'I really don't know what you are going on about, Paul,' I said when she had gone. 'A couple of hours at the computer hardly constitutes hard labour.'

'The trouble with you, Julia, is that you don't know when to stop. You worry me, do you know that?' He still sounded annoyed, but we'd both cooled down a bit, and the heat had gone out of the moment.

'I'm sorry. You know what I'm like.'

'Yes – a workaholic. And when you get your teeth into something, you just won't let go, either.'

'I know, I know.'

'You are going to have to slow down when the baby arrives.'

'We'll see about that.'

He let it go.

'I don't feel like going back to work and leaving you here if I can't trust you to take things easy.'

'Don't be so silly!'

'I mean it. I don't want you doing this, Julia. And I don't know that I like Ruth messing about with my computer, either.

71

She doesn't know the first thing about them. If she fouls anything up...'

'She won't. She was only doing as I told her.'

Paul sighed, shaking his head in exasperation.

'Are you going to have some lunch now that you're here?' I asked, trying to change the subject.

'What is there?'

'Ruth has made a sandwich for us. I'm sure it would only take her a minute to rustle up another.'

Paul glanced at his watch. 'I suppose I could. I'll just ring Josh, let him know I'm going to be longer than I said...'

He sounded mellower now, but I could guess what was going through his mind. The longer he stayed at home, the longer he could make sure I didn't do any more work.

A few moments later, when he had got through to Stattisford, my suspicions were confirmed.

'Hello, Josh ... yes, I'm at home, keeping an eye on Julia. When I came in I caught her working on my computer – that Hong Kong thing. And what do you think? She even had Ruth Wood helping her!'

When Paul had gone back to work I was tempted to return to the computer to make a point, if nothing else. I really resent being told what to do, by him or anyone else. I guess I've always been headstrong – or 'bloody-minded' as my father used to call me, because in my youth we disagreed violently about practically everything.

He was in the legal profession, too – a solicitor's clerk – and to my mind, very old-fashioned. Even when he'd been with the same firm for almost forty years he still called the partners 'Mister', while they called him 'Bob'. Since by the time he retired they were all considerably younger than he was, this struck me as being ridiculous and also rather offensive, a throwback to the days when forelocks had to be tugged to those who were considered 'our betters'. But to Dad it was a point of etiquette, and it epitomized the gulf between our ways of looking at the world.

I suppose I've modified my thinking a little from those days when – much to Dad's horror – I thought that demonstrations and marches and sit-ins were the way to bring about change – but I still care passionately about injustice and inequality. I'll still fight to the bitter end if I believe something to be right. Inside, I'm still the same person. 'Bloody-minded', and very, very persistent.

Sometimes I thought Paul was almost as bemused by me as Dad used to be. But determined as I was to show I would make my own decisions about what I would and wouldn't do, I realized that it would not be wise to overtax myself too much today. The morning's work had taken more out of me than I had realized; I was beginning to feel very tired again.

I settled down for a quiet afternoon with nothing more taxing than the day-time soaps and old films, and though I did have my files on the nesting table within easy reach, I didn't so much as glance at them. As for the computer, once Ruth left at four, there was no way I could have managed it.

Paul was a little late coming home that evening. I had no idea what hours he worked when I was in London, of course, but certainly since my accident he had been getting in around six. Tonight it was past seven when I heard the back door open.

'You're late,' I said when he came in.

'Not really.' He grinned, a little sheepishly. 'You've been behaving yourself, I hope. No more working the moment my back was turned.'

'Not a thing.'

'Let's eat, then. What have we got?'

'Spiced lamb, I think.'

Paul dished up and we ate sitting at the kitchen table.

'What were you going on about at lunch-time?' he asked, forking rice into the thick syrupy sauce. 'Kowloon and Victoria? You said there was something odd.'

'Yes, I can't understand it. You know I said I'd seen them listed amongst those Hong Kong companies who had been investigated? Well, I tried to look them up again today, and they weren't there. Someone has wiped them off, it's the only explanation. But why should they do that?'

'Haven't a clue! You must have been wrong, Julia. We were talking at the time, after all.'

'I wasn't wrong. I just don't understand it – that's why I was trying out other websites when you came in and let fly at me. If you hadn't, I might have found something out.'

'And given yourself another filthy head-ache into the bargain, staring at the screen too long.'

'Well, I am going to look into it,' I said. 'As soon as I have time. If there is something funny going on with Kowloon and Victoria, you need to know about it. I mean, suppose they were involved in something dishonest? Or still are? Counterfeiting, for example – you could be buying components in good faith, thinking they're genuine, when all the time they're fakes.'

'It would hardly matter really, would it?' Paul said reasonably. 'An electrical compo-nent is an electrical component. If it works, it doesn't make much difference who's sup-posed to have manufactured it.'

'True. Sweatshop labour, then. They may have women and even children cooped up in appalling conditions turning out the stuff you buy from them. I wouldn't like to think we were contributing in any way to keeping a company like that going. In fact, I'd fight it, tooth and nail.'

'Don't you think you're getting a bit carried away, Julia?' Paul said.

'Perhaps. But why has the name been wiped off?'

To that, Paul had no answer.

I went to bed about ten o'clock. Paul helped me to get undressed, then went back downstairs.

I lay for a while, my mind still too busy for sleep, but I must have begun to dose off because when I heard the telephone ringing, I came to with a sudden jolt, wondering who on earth could be calling in the middle of the night.

It wasn't the middle of the night, of course. The luminous dial of the clock on my bedside table showed it was only twenty to eleven. But it was still late for anyone to ring.

A few moments later I heard Paul's footsteps on the stairs.

'Julia – are you still awake?' he asked in a soft whisper from the other side of the door.

'Yes – what's wrong?'

Paul pushed open the door. 'What time did

Ruth leave this afternoon?'

'Oh, I don't know ... four, half-past. Why?'

Paul hesitated. 'I've got Jim Wood on the phone. He doesn't know where she is. She wasn't there when he got home from work, and from the look of things, he thinks she hasn't been back since she left to come here this morning.'

Eleven

I didn't sleep well. Several times in the night I woke, wondering about Ruth and feeling anxious. I simply couldn't understand what it was all about. Ruth wasn't the sort to disappear without telling anyone, especially her husband. In the end, I practically convinced myself that I had been asleep and dreamed Paul coming up to say Jim was on the telephone. And I must have fallen into a deep slumber, because it was daylight when I woke again.

I turned over to snuggle into Paul, but his side of the bed was empty – hardly surprising, since the clock on the bedside table said ten to nine. I sat up, and the nausea was there again. For a minute or two I sat quite still with the back of my hand pressed against my mouth, wondering how long morning sickness lasted, and remembering with a sinking heart that Beverley, my sister, had complained that hers had continued for the entire nine months. It didn't seem to have put her off, though. She had three children now, twins of five and a two-year-old, Alice, and it would never surprise me to hear she had another one on the way. All Bev had ever wanted was to get married and have a large family.

In that, as in practically every other way, we were just about as different as two sisters could be. Even when we were children, she had always been the one playing with dolls, dressing and undressing them and pushing them round the garden in her dolls' pram, while I had my head in a book. Later on, as soon as she was old enough, she'd taken up babysitting for the neighbours to earn some spending money, whereas I'd preferred to work part-time in the local bookshop. The very idea of being responsible for children who might wake up and cry had terrified me. As, to be honest, it terrified me now. But it would be different if the child was your own ... wouldn't it?

Bev was going to be delighted about the baby, I knew. Whenever I saw her – which wasn't that often, since she lived in Newquay – she dropped hints about how nice it would be for her three to have a cousin. But I suspected that, like Paul, she would nag me to give up work and be a full-time mother, and so I'd put off ringing to tell her my news.

In any case, I hadn't wanted to have to explain about my accident. I was reluctant to talk about it, and I knew she would tell my mother, who had moved to Cornwall to be near her. Mum always got herself into a dreadful state about things and I didn't want her worried. If she had known I was in hospital, she would probably have been on the first train up, well-meaning, but making complications I could do without.

Much as I loved my family, there were times when they stifled me. Paul couldn't understand the way I felt, I knew. His parents had been killed in a road accident when he was just twenty, and he had never really got over it. He still missed them dreadfully, I knew – as I missed my father, and as I would miss my mother and Bev if they weren't there. I loved them very much. I just didn't want them fussing round me.

When the nausea began to pass I got up and put on my dressing gown. I couldn't tie the belt by myself, and I had to hold the folds of material up with my left hand as I limped downstairs.

Paul was in the kitchen, refilling the coffee maker. 'You're awake at last, then? Do you want some breakfast? The toast I made earlier is cold now, but I can soon make some more.'

'I think I could eat it, yes. And please could you tie my dressing gown for me?'

He did, and I sat down on one of the pine chairs while he put bread in the toaster.

'You haven't heard anything from Jim this morning, have you?' I asked.

'From Jim?'

80

'Yes. I thought he might have phoned to let us know if Ruth got home all right in the end. He must know we'd be concerned about her.'

'I'm sure he'd have been in touch again by now if she *hadn't* got home,' Paul said. 'I expect it was all a storm in a teacup. They probably had a row, and she took off in her car to cool down.'

'I thought the whole point was that she hadn't been home.'

'That's what Jim said, yes, but maybe he just felt awkward about admitting the truth. He's got a pretty fiery temper, though he's always ashamed of it afterwards.'

'No, Paul, it doesn't add up. If she *had* been home, why should he phone here to ask what time she left?'

'Perhaps he thought she might have come to us. Or perhaps the row was in the morning before they left for work. How should I know?' Paul said, a little irritably. 'Stop worrying about it, Julia.'

When I'd had breakfast Paul helped me to get dressed, then left me to fiddle with my face and hair. Managing it one-handed took me quite some time. From the bedroom window, I saw the postman's bicycle propped up against our gatepost, and when I finally went downstairs I went into the hall to see what he had dropped through the letter box. There were no letters on the mat – Paul must have already collected them. I went into the kitchen, but there were no letters on the table either.

'What post did we have?' I asked.

'Post?' Paul was fiddling with his torch, fitting new batteries. 'None that I know of.'

'None?' I repeated, surprised. 'But I saw the postman's bicycle by the gate.'

'Oh, there was an invitation to play the pools. I binned it.' But he looked faintly sheepish. Ah! I thought. Perhaps he *did* send for something for my birthday that he doesn't want me to know about.

'Oh, right,' I said, pretending to be taken in.

'How do you fancy going to the Dog and Duck for lunch?' Paul suggested – changing the subject, I couldn't help feeling.

'We could, I suppose. Ruth left a quiche though...'

'We can have it for supper. It would do you good to get out of the house.'

'OK. I'll run with that.' But the mention of Ruth had set me thinking about her again. 'I'm going to phone,' I said. 'I can't get her off my mind.'

'Julia! Leave well alone! What goes on between Ruth and Jim is really none of our business. They won't appreciate you poking your nose in.'

'Don't worry, I'll think of some excuse,' I

said, reaching for the phone. 'I'll ask her to get some tomatoes on her way in on Monday or something.'

With some difficulty I managed to punch in Ruth's number, but the phone just rang and rang and no one answered.

'Seems like they're out,' I said.

'There you are. He's probably taken her out shopping as a way of making the peace. Now will you forget about it?'

'I suppose I'll have to.'

But I knew I wouldn't.

We had our lunch at the Dog and Duck. They do the most wonderful fish soup I've ever tasted, and serve it with little French bread croûtes and a mustard dip. I suppose there's every chance it's made from all the leftover bits from the exotic fish dishes they serve in their restaurant, but I think that it's the variety that makes it so good.

Being a Saturday, the bar trade was brisk and it was almost three by the time we got home again. There was a police car parked in the road outside our gate. I felt a stab of alarm.

'What now...?'

'Don't tell me I've forgotten to renew my car tax,' Paul said, rather flippantly.

'Oh, don't be silly!' I snapped. 'You know very well the police don't come for something like that. It's all dealt with at Swansea.'

Paul said nothing. I wondered if underneath that blasé exterior he was as worried as I was.

We turned into our drive. A uniformed policeman was outside our door, ringing the bell. Paul parked and helped me out. 'Hello, can I help you?' he said to the policeman.

'I'd like a word if possible, sir. If you could spare me a minute.'

'Well, I suppose so. Just let me find my keys.'

He led the way around to the back of the house – we always used the kitchen door – and unlocked it. The policeman followed us in.

'Would you like a coffee?' Paul said. Again, I had the feeling he might be putting off the moment when we learned the purpose of the policeman's visit.

The policeman put his cap down on the kitchen table. 'If you're making one, I wouldn't say no.'

'It will only be instant at this time of the day, I'm afraid.' Paul put the kettle on; turned back. 'Right. How can we help you?'

'I'm making enquiries about a Mrs Ruth Wood. She works for you, I believe?'

'That's right, she's our housekeeper,' Paul began.

'She's not still missing, is she?' I interrupted.

The policeman looked at me sharply. He

84

was young and fresh-faced. 'You knew?'

'Her husband phoned last night. We just assumed they'd had a tiff or something.'

'That's very likely what it is,' the policeman said. 'But he's reported her missing, so we have to check.'

'You mean she still hasn't come home?'

'She hadn't an hour ago. You haven't seen her today, I take it?'

'We wouldn't, on a Saturday,' Paul said. 'She doesn't usually come to us at weekends.'

'But she was here yesterday?'

'Yes, of course.'

'Did you notice anything unusual about her?'

'I didn't see her,' Paul said. 'I was at work myself. Julia?'

'You did see her,' I said. 'You came home at lunch time yesterday, don't you remember?'

'Well, all right, I *saw* her, but only for a few minutes. She seemed quite normal to me.'

'And to me.'

'What time did she leave?'

'Oh, four-ish. The same time she always leaves.'

'Did she say where she was going?'

'No. I assumed she was going straight home. Unless of course she had some shopping to do.'

'Which she would do ... where?'

'I really don't know. She'd get odds and ends from the Spar shop in the village, I imagine, but I think she goes to the Tesco in town to do her big shop. If she does any for us, it's usually a Tesco receipt.'

The kettle had boiled; Paul made three mugs of instant coffee. I sipped mine with my fingers spread out around the mug to warm them. I felt very cold suddenly.

'What on earth can have happened to her?' I said.

'That's what we're trying to establish,' the policeman said. 'It's possible she's with a friend, or a relative. Do you know anything about her family?'

'Her mother lives in the village and she's got a couple of brothers.'

'We've already checked with them. They haven't seen her. What about friends?'

'For heaven's sake, how should we know who her friends are?' Paul said. 'You'll have to ask her husband that.'

'He's given a list, of course,' the policeman said. 'I just wondered if there was anybody else you could think of. Someone he might not know about.'

'You mean a man?' I said. 'Oh, I don't think so. Not Ruth! She's not the type...'

My naivety must have amused the policeman. 'You'd be surprised, Mrs Wilson,' he said drily. 'You just never can tell.'

He was right, of course, I thought. And in

reality, I hardly knew Ruth at all. Most of the time I wasn't even here when she was, and even when I was, we weren't exactly on intimate terms. For all I knew she might have been having an affair. She'd certainly tried to flirt with Josh in a rather clumsy way. Yet still I felt honour bound to defend her.

'I'm sure she and Jim are very happy,' I said firmly.

The policeman had finished his coffee. He set his cup down and picked up his cap. 'Well, thank you. You've been very helpful.'

'I didn't think we'd been any help at all!' I said. 'I only wish we could have been.'

'It's all pieces of the jigsaw,' the policeman said. 'And one more place that we know she isn't, if you get my meaning. Don't worry.' He smiled at me reassuringly. 'I'm sure she'll turn up safe and sound.'

'I shouldn't like to be in her shoes when she does,' Paul said. 'Jim hates to be made to look a fool, and he has one hell of a temper when he's roused.'

I said nothing. All very well for the policeman to say Ruth was going to turn up safe and sound. I had the sickening feeling we were never going to see her again.

Twelve

It was a very odd weekend, as unreal in its own way as last weekend had been. I simply couldn't get Ruth out of my mind. Paul, on the other hand, seemed unconcerned.

'She's just gone off somewhere,' he said. 'She'll be back. Unless she really has run off with someone else, in which case she won't. Either way, I'm sure she's all right.'

I wished I could be so sure. Disappearing in this way was so totally out of character with the Ruth I knew. Every time the phone rang I wondered if it might be news of her, but it never was. As Paul quite reasonably said, why should it be? No one was likely to let us know what was going on. We were simply her employers.

On Monday morning, after Paul had left for work, I found myself watching the lane, hoping to see her car turning into the drive, yet knowing all the time it would not. Rain was lashing down and the trees were dripping miserably, turning last autumn's fallen leaves on the lawn into a sodden brown carpet. Even the patch of crocus which had come into flower looked faded instead of the bright battalion of harbingers of early spring which had lightened my heart in last week's sunshine.

I cleared away the remains of the breakfast without too much trouble. My wrist was definitely improving, and in any case I had begun to get used to doing things left-handed. Then I settled down with my files, determined to try to put everything else out of my mind and get on with some work. But it all seemed frustratingly distant.

At ten fifteen I rang my secretary in London. She sounded very relieved to hear from me.

'I've had Poyson Associates on the phone several times asking how things are progressing.'

'Right. I'll ring them and let them know I've more or less tied up their enquiries. Now – is there anything in the post I should know about?'

Marian mentioned one or two matters pending and the results of a legal search I'd instituted.

'OK. Now, do you think you could come down here to me? I know it's a bit of an imposition, but I can't drive at the moment, and there are some things I really do need to deal with. I'll make sure you're well compensated.'

'Come on the train, you mean?' Marian sounded doubtful.

'It would be better if you drove. Hire a car and charge it to the company. You shouldn't have any trouble finding me. It's simplicity itself. All you do is get on to the M4 and—'

'Don't try to tell me over the phone. You'll just muddle me,' Marian interrupted. 'I'll ask Richard. He can draw me a map.'

Richard was the junior Havers in Havers and Havers.

'Yes, do that. And listen – can you also bring me the Prentis file, which should be in my tray, and the book of telephone contact numbers and addresses from the top left-hand drawer of my desk? I'm lost without it.'

'Will do.'

'Good. I'll see you tomorrow.'

'I hope so!' Marian laughed, a little nervously. 'If I don't turn up, you'll have to phone the motorway police and ask them to look out for someone heading west and utterly confused.'

'Oh, don't even *go* there, Marian...'

'What?'

'Never mind. I'll explain tomorrow. Drive carefully, won't you?'

I put the phone down feeling that at last I was getting somewhere, and pulled my files towards me again. But I still felt oddly detached and unable to concentrate. The house was very quiet with no Ruth bustling about, singing tunelessly as she dusted and vacuumed, and her absence was somehow more distracting than her presence had been. I simply couldn't get her off my mind. There were practical considerations impinging on my concentration too, things I didn't usually have to worry about, such as what on earth were we going to have for supper?

Almost glad of the excuse to take a break, I went into the back lobby to investigate the contents of the deep freeze. I found a pack of chicken breasts, and got them out to thaw. I'd phone Paul at work and ask him to get some bean sprouts, peppers and mushrooms on his way home, and we could have a stir-fry.

It was as I dialled his number on the phone in the study that I noticed an airmail envelope in the waste-paper basket. Curious, I fished it out, and as I waited for the line to connect, I uncrumpled it. I don't know what I was expecting – nothing at all really – but as the postmark and stamp leaped out at me, I experienced a sense of shock.

Hong Kong! The wretched place seemed to be haunting me!

'Hello? Paul Wilson.'

'Paul – it's me. I just wondered if you could pick up a few things on your way home...' I was speaking automatically, but my mind was on that crumpled empty envelope.

It hadn't been there on Friday, I was sure. Ruth was meticulous in emptying all the bins daily. So, could it be that this was the letter the postman had delivered on Saturday, the letter Paul had tried to pretend hadn't come at all? But why should he do that? And why, come to that, should anyone in Hong Kong be writing to Paul here, at home? The only connection he had with the colony that I was aware of was with Kowloon and Victoria, and business letters normally went straight to the office. This, on top of the fact that I had discovered that Kowloon and Victoria had been investigated for some irregularity by the authorities, only to find their name had mysteriously disappeared from the Net. Something was going on – something highly peculiar. And one way or another, I was going to find out what it was.

The idea came to me in the middle of the afternoon. I'd speak to Tony Bowman.

Tony was a financial consultant in the City; he had an office in the same street as my firm. We called on his services from time to time and found him to be straightforward and utterly professional. But it wasn't because of his knowledge of finance that I thought of Tony now.

He was, I knew, an expert on the Far East. He'd worked there for some years and if anyone could tell me how I could find out what, if anything, was going on with Kowloon and Victoria, it was him.

My hand hovered over the telephone as I

debated whether to get the number of Bowman Associates from directory enquiries. But the number they would give me would be that of the general office. I'd have to get past his receptionist, who would probably tell me that he was 'in a meeting'. But in my book of telephone contact numbers was the one that would connect me direct to Tony's office. Marian would be bringing that book down for me tomorrow; my call to Tony could wait until then.

Thirteen

Paul got home just before six.

'Good day?' I asked.

'Oh, the usual.' But I thought he looked tired. 'How about you?'

'Weird. I kept expecting Ruth to turn up. I'm really worried about her, Paul.'

'It is odd,' he conceded, 'but to be honest I'm more worried as to how you are going to cope here on your own without her.'

'I'm managing. I'm much better now. And I've got Marian coming down tomorrow. Organizing meals is the biggest headache. Did you remember to get the mushrooms and beansprouts?'

Paul swore.

'Oh Paul! You forgot!'

'No – I got the shopping.' He fished into the deep pocket of his Barbour and dumped the beansprouts and a paper bag containing far too many mushrooms on the work top. 'But why is Marian coming down here?'

'She's bringing me things I need to work, and to sort out some correspondence. What's wrong with that?'

Paul looked absolutely furious. 'Julia, I just

don't know how to stop you from overdoing things. It's too late now to stop her from coming, I suppose.'

'Of course it is. She'll have gone home by now – and she'll have arranged for the hire car, and everything. In any case, I have absolutely no intention of changing the arrangements.'

'I see. Well, in that case the only thing is for me to be here to make sure you don't overdo things.'

'What on earth are you talking about?'

'God knows how hard you'll drive yourself to get through as much work as possible if I'm not here to stop you. Plus the fact you'll be running round after her, trying to make lunch or something. I haven't had a day off in ages – I shall take one tomorrow and work from home so that I can keep an eye on you.'

'Paul – you can't take time off just because of me!' I protested, irritated.

'Why not? You're my wife – and a great deal more important to me than work – though I wish I could say I thought you felt the same way. It's pretty obvious what the first priority in your life is.'

'Oh please, don't start that again!' I could not understand what he was getting so worked up about. 'I've got commitments. It's not just that I'm missing my work, but if I don't deliver, I'll lose clients. I can't afford to do that.'

'Just stop and think for a moment, Julia. You've had a nasty accident and you're still groggy. Added to which, you're pregnant. You have to take care of yourself.'

'Oh for goodness' sake!' I snapped, exasperated. 'I'm beginning to wish I *wasn't* pregnant!'

The moment the words were out I regretted them. I certainly didn't mean it – it was just that everything was getting on top of me.

'I'm sorry,' I said. 'I am glad I'm having our baby, of course I am. I just wish you wouldn't treat me as if I were different all of a sudden. I mean – this business of staying home tomorrow to keep an eye on me! It's ludicrous. I resent you trying to nanny me as if I were three years old.'

He glanced at me. 'I worry about you, Julia. I worry about *us...*'

I went to him, linking my arm through his. 'There's no need, honestly.'

'There's every need. I don't want to lose you.'

'You're not going to lose me, Paul, I assure you. I intend to be around for a very long time.'

'Oh Julia, come here!' He pulled me close and I buried my head in his chest, wanting only for things to be right between us. He kissed me fiercely and I kissed him back, but I could still feel the tension in his body, in his arms, in his shoulders, and after a moment he said: 'I was going to stay home tomorrow anyway. I don't like leaving you on your own, with Ruth not here.' He paused. 'They found her car today. In Hawley Woods.'

'Oh my God!'

'I know. It is a bit worrying, I must admit.' He said it lightly enough, but I understood now why he was being so overprotective.

'How is Jim taking it?' I asked.

'I don't know. He hasn't been in to work today.'

We were silent for a few minutes, reluctant to put into words what must have been in both our minds. Then Paul glanced at his watch.

'I ought to get on. I've got a Round Table meeting this evening. I'd give it a miss, but we have to finalize arrangements for the consignment of aid we're sending to Romania. As chairman, I really have to be there.'

I nodded. Paul took his Round Table commitments very seriously, especially this year, now that he was in the chair.

'In that case we'd better get on, hadn't we? What time is your meeting?'

'Eight. I'll go and get changed.'

'And I'll start the supper.'

But I couldn't. There was no way I could prepare food. I might be a good deal better, but I had some way to go yet before I was back to normal.

Little as I might like it, I realized Paul was probably right when he insisted I still needed a little tender loving care.

By about nine I was feeling tired again and I decided to have a bath and go to bed. Paul wouldn't be home for a couple of hours yet – the Round Table met at the local country club and when their meeting was over they usually adjourned to the bar for a nightcap. Perhaps Paul wouldn't stay any longer than he had to tonight, seeing that I was on my own, but the meeting was likely to be a long one anyway.

I went upstairs, taking my transistor radio with me, poured some perfumed oil into the bath, and set the hot tap running on to it. Ten minutes later I was relaxing in the sweet-smelling bubbles, my head resting against the bath pillow, luxuriating in the way the warm water was floating the tension out of my still-achy body. I was tuned in to the local radio station; at nine thirty the programme broke for the news headlines, and suddenly I wasn't relaxed any more.

'Concern is growing for a local woman, missing since Friday. Ruth Wood, twenty-seven, has not been seen since she left her place of employment at four in the afternoon. Her car, a white Ford Fiesta, has been found abandoned in Hawley Woods, a local beauty spot. Tonight her husband, James, appealed for Ruth to get in touch, or for anyone who knows anything of her whereabouts to come forward.'

Although the news bulletin had not told me anything I didn't already know, hearing it read out in those impersonal, professional tones somehow made it more real. Abruptly I turned off the radio and got out of the bath, reaching into the airing cupboard for a clean towel, then changing my mind and slipping on my towelling robe instead. My wrist still wasn't up to the rigours of drying myself properly.

I was standing there, my feet making damp footprints on the bath mat, when I heard what sounded like the creak of a door downstairs. The bathroom is directly over the kitchen, and sounds funnel straight up the channel that carries the water pipes.

Paul home? Surely not! It was only just after half past nine. I cocked my head, listening, half-expecting his voice to call up the stairs even though I was sure it was far too early for him.

Silence. I must have imagined that creak. And yet some instinct, prickling on my skin like the drying bath water, was telling me I had not. I went out on to the landing, holding the bathrobe tightly around me, and padded to the head of the stairs. I'd left the hall light on; its warm glow showed total emptiness.

'Paul?' I called 'Are you there?'

No answer.

'Paul?'

And then I heard a crash – something that sounded like smashing china.

I froze. There's no other way to describe the icy wash that totally immobilized me for a moment, I swear I even stopped breathing.

Someone was in the house, and it wasn't Paul.

Fourteen

For a moment or two my mind was a total blank. Like my limbs, it was totally incapable of functioning. Then I realized I was listening, straining my ears for some other sound of movement downstairs. There was none. Just the rain lashing against the landing window and the wind creaking in the branches of the trees outside.

A creak! That was definitely a creak! My skin prickled again, and then I remembered the way the timbers settled, as they do in all old houses. Was that all it had been? Timbers settling – air in the central-heating pipes – a branch tapping against the window? Or was there somebody down there – a burglar, perhaps? I should have locked the back door. It was madness to leave it open. I just hadn't thought. Locking doors when we were in the house just wasn't something we did.

The silence stretched on. I hugged my bathrobe around me, shivering, my mind chasing in all directions. What the hell should I do? Lock myself in a bedroom? Investigate – and risk confronting an intruder? I was in no fit state for that. And the nearest telephone was in the hall, thirteen stairs away. If there was someone downstairs they could reach me before I could reach the telephone.

But I couldn't just stay here and do nothing, and everything seemed quiet now. Perhaps, unnerved as I was, I'd imagined the whole thing.

I took a step, stopped. I could feel my heart beating against my ribs and my legs were like jelly. *Oh, for heaven's sake, DO something, woman!*

I crept down the first stair. The second one creaked loudly. I froze again. Then, growing bolder, I went halfway down the stairs, holding tightly to the banister, listening, listening. Nothing. Three-quarters of the way down I had a view into the sitting room. The standard lamp was on, casting a soft glow, and as far as I could see, the room was empty.

I took the last two or three steps in a rush, thinking that at least I could reach the phone now if I needed to. But whether I'd have time to dial 999 was another matter. *You won't need to*, I told myself. *There's no one there.*

I forced myself to walk along the hall to the kitchen. It was as empty as the sitting room, and I could see no sign that anything had been disturbed or stolen. The portable TV was still on its shelf, the antique carriage clock in its place on the dresser, my handbag on the table where I'd left it. It really didn't look as if we'd been burgled, but I was still too much on edge to be able to feel any sort of confidence.

Again I looked around, checking, and that was when I saw it. On the floor, directly in front of the sink, were two halves of a plate. That explained the crash I'd heard, then. I'd washed up a few things in the sink instead of using the dishwasher and clearly I couldn't have stood that plate in the drainer properly. It had toppled over on to the floor and smashed. I almost sobbed with relief. *Julia Wilson, you are turning into a bag of nerves...*

But I certainly wasn't going to leave the back door unlocked again when I was alone in the house, especially after dark! I turned the key, took it out and hung it on the hook nearby so that Paul would be able to get his own key into the lock when he got home.

Relief and release of tension were making me shiver convulsively now, and my knees felt weak. Stupid! What was happening to me? Was it my fall that was turning me into a frightened rabbit – or was it because I was pregnant, and suddenly so protective of the baby I was carrying that I felt in need of protection myself? Whichever, I didn't much like it. I'd never had much patience with clingy little women and I hated the thought that I might be turning into one. Added to which, if Paul came home and found me like this he'd be even more insistent that he should wrap me in cotton wool.

I picked up the two halves of the broken plate and dumped them in the bin. Beneath my bare feet the kitchen floor felt damp – splashes from when we'd washed up? I tore a piece of kitchen paper off the roll and wiped the floor. It looked grimy as well as wet. The house was fast turning into a tip without Ruth's attention!

Thinking of Ruth made me uncomfortable all over again. Deliberately I squashed the thoughts. *Calm down, calm down!*

I made myself a cup of hot chocolate and took it into the living room. What I really wanted was a good stiff drink. I fought the temptation to pour myself a glass of Paul's cognac and lost. I shouldn't be drinking alcohol when I was pregnant, I knew, but surely a few sips couldn't do any harm, just this once. My jangling nerves must be just as bad for the baby. But the spirit burned my throat and made me feel guilty all over again. I set it down, almost untouched, on the dresser out of reach, turned on the television, and settled myself on the sofa. I didn't know what programme I was tuned to and I didn't much care. Just as long as there was something to fill the silence.

The touch of fur on the back of my neck made me jump. I twisted too quickly, jarring a nerve, and next door's cat leaped down silently and agilely from the back of the sofa and stepped delicately on to my lap.

I relaxed momentarily. It must have been Oscar who had knocked over the plate. He really was getting to be something of a menace, not to mention the friction he was going to cause between ourselves and our neighbours if they thought we were encouraging him. We'd really have to make sure we kept the door shut...

A sudden shiver prickled over my skin. The door! The only way for Oscar to get in was through the back door! I hadn't opened it since Paul left, and Oscar certainly hadn't been in the house then. That he was here now could mean only one thing.

Someone else had opened it. Someone *had* been in the house.

Fifteen

I don't remember very much about what happened next. Just the terror. Sheer, stultifying, debilitating terror. For a long time I was afraid even to move, afraid the intruder might still be in the house, that when I'd locked the door and taken out the key I might have locked him in with me. I sat there, literally frozen by fear, with Oscar a warm alien lump on my lap, and felt that the very stillness of the room was breathing.

And then suddenly I was pushing Oscar away, because the feel of him was making my skin crawl, and standing up, jerkily, like a marionette when somebody is pulling the strings all wrong. I was creeping to the door, a step at a time, and then I was running along the hall, running though my bad ankle almost gave way each time the weight went on to it, grabbing the phone, starting to dial 999 and then stopping, realizing I didn't want an unknown policeman here, wanting only Paul. The phone clattered down on to the table as I fumbled for the phone book.

My fingers were like wads of cotton wool, clumsy and unresponsive, and even when I turned up the number of the country club, I couldn't read it properly. The light in the hall was dim and my eyes weren't focusing properly.

I forced myself into the kitchen, where the light was better – and something on the carpet caught my eye. Something I hadn't noticed before because it wasn't near the sink, but on the far side of the table. A leaf – a muddy wet leaf! How had *that* got there? Had it been trodden in on the intruder's shoe? I was shaking again, almost sobbing.

Back into the hall. Dial the number. The bell ringing endlessly and then the receptionist's voice, cool and a little superior.

'Sycamore Grove Country Club.'

'Can I speak to Paul Wilson? He's at a meeting of the Round Table. In your conference room.'

'Oh, I don't think they're there now. The meeting is over.'

'The bar. They're probably in the bar. Will you go and look for me, please?'

An endless wait. Heels clacking on tiled floors, people talking in the background. Someone calling 'goodnight'. More heels clacking.

'I'm sorry. Mr Wilson's not here.'

'Are you sure?'

'I've spoken to one of his friends. He left some time ago.'

If Paul had left he must be on his way

home now. *Please, God, let him be on his way home! Please let him get here soon!*

I went to the window, peering out anxiously to catch the first sight of the lights of his car turning into the lane. But the darkness was complete. No moon. No stars. No shaft of headlights. I leaned my forehead against the glass, chewing my lip.

And then I saw something move in the shadows and heard what sounded like the crunch of footsteps on the gravel path that ran around the front of the house. Someone was out there – and I knew that someone wasn't Paul.

The terror closed in again, yet at the same time my mind was racing furiously. The bolts. I must shoot all the bolts on the doors. Make quite certain that whoever was prowling about out there couldn't get in. I tried to move, even managed a step or two, but my knees were buckling. I grabbed at the doorpost, but my fingers, useless as my legs, simply slid down it. I could feel myself going limp like a rag doll, and everything was going away from me. I was falling, falling, into the darkness. I had never felt more helpless in my life.

There was a loud knocking impinging on my semi-consciousness. For a moment I could not identify it. Then I realized – someone was banging on the back door. Weak, sick, trembling, I crawled towards it.

'Who is it?' My voice was nothing but a croaking whisper. I tried again. 'Who's there? What do you want?'

'Julia?' A voice I recognized, calling my name. 'It's me – Josh!'

Josh!

'Josh – is it really you?'

'Of course it is! What's the matter? Julia – are you all right?'

Somehow I got the key from the hook. Managed to fit it into the lock. Opened the door. Felt the blast of cold air. And his hands on my arms, steadying me.

'Julia – what on earth is wrong?'

'I thought ... oh Josh, I've been so frightened! I thought someone was trying to break into the house ... I thought...' *I was going to be raped or murdered* ... I couldn't say it. It sounded so melodramatic, so feeble.

'Julia, you're shivering.' Josh was looking at me, puzzled, very concerned. 'Can I come in?'

I nodded wordlessly, backing into the kitchen, hugging my bathrobe round me.

'Let me get you a drink.'

'I already poured one ... it's in the living room...'

'Come and have it then.' He led me through and sat me down on the sofa. Then he found the brandy, dropped to his haunches beside me, and pressed the glass

109

into my shaking hand.

'Drink this now and you'll feel better.'

I took a sip and felt a little warmth return to my body.

'Now, what's been going on?' He was still crouching beside me, looking at me anxiously.

'I was in the bath and I thought I heard someone down here. But there wasn't anyone. And then Oscar...' I gesticulated towards the cat, curled comfortably now in the fireside chair. 'I realized that someone must have opened the door, or Oscar couldn't have got in.'

'The door was locked, Julia.'

'No – not before. I've only just locked it. A few minutes ago. And then I thought I saw something moving in the garden and there were footsteps on the path...' I knew I was babbling, almost incoherent.

'Oh Julia, that was *me*. I'm really sorry to have given you such a scare.'

'I didn't hear your car. I didn't see any lights...'

'I didn't bring my car. Well, at least, I left it on the pub forecourt in the village. Your lane is so narrow it's difficult turning in the dark. I thought it would be easier to walk down. I never meant to frighten you.'

'Well you certainly managed it!' A thought occurred to me. 'You didn't see anyone else in the lane, did you?'

'Only a man walking a Dalmatian.'

'Brian Roper from the house on the corner. No, he's all right. I know him. Though his dog does chase Oscar. Perhaps that's why the cat came in, to get out of his way. But no, that doesn't explain *how* he got in...'

'Through a window? The downstairs cloakroom, perhaps?'

'Is it open? I don't think so. And he's never come in that way before.'

'I'll go and see. I'll also have a good look round – see if there's any sign of an intruder.' Josh got up purposefully.

'Josh – be careful!' I begged him.

He didn't answer. I waited nervously, listening to him moving about the house, opening doors, switching on lights. After a few minutes he was back.

'I can't find anything. There's certainly nobody here now, and nothing appears to have been touched. And the cloakroom window *is* open, by the way – only a couple of notches, but enough for a determined cat to slip through.'

'Oh.' I didn't know what to say. I was relieved, of course, but also concerned. Had I really got myself into such a state over nothing at all? What on earth was happening to me?

'Josh – I feel a complete fool,' I said shakily. 'I haven't even asked you why you're here.'

'Oh, I just came to pick up a file I need. Paul's not coming in to work tomorrow, is he, and as he had a meeting, I said I'd call round for it. I thought he'd be home by now.'

'He should be actually. I don't know what's keeping him...' As if on cue, I heard a car on the drive. 'There he is now!' A great wash of relief made me go weak again. 'Oh, thank goodness! I'm beginning to get to the stage where I'm wondering what on earth is going to happen next!'

'Nothing else is going to happen.' Josh's hand covered mine briefly, and at that precise moment Paul appeared in the doorway.

'Oh Paul, I'm so glad you're home!' I burst out.

Paul was looking from one of us to the other, surprised and not very pleased. 'Julia? Josh? What's going on?'

Josh laughed shortly. 'It's not the way it looks, I can assure you.'

'I hope not!' Paul snapped.

I was shocked. It had not even occurred to me that Paul might misinterpret the scene, or that Josh should think he might. Now I was suddenly acutely aware of my dishevelled state and the fact that I was alone with Josh, wearing nothing but my bathrobe.

'I think Julia's had something of a fright,' Josh went on. He was his usual suave self, quite unfazed by Paul's virtually accusing him of adultery. 'She thought she heard someone in the house, and then I made things worse by walking down the lane rather than driving. She thought I was a prowler.'

'I was just being stupid,' I said quickly. I was calming down now, and beginning to feel very ashamed of myself. Besides which, I knew that if I allowed Josh to tell Paul just what a state he'd found me in, Paul would become more over-protective than ever.

'I'm really sorry,' Josh said. 'The last thing I'd want is to scare Julia like that. I really thought you'd be home from your meeting before now. I only came to pick up the tender for the haulage contract if you've finished with it. I want to have a look at it tomorrow.'

'I'll get it for you.' Paul disappeared into the office and returned with an envelope file which he handed to Josh. 'Here we are. You'll see I've made some notes on the costings...'

But I could sense the tension still there between them, and knew it was all my fault.

'What am I going to do with you, Julia?' Paul asked tenderly after Josh had gone.

'Let me get back to work as soon as possible?' I suggested. 'I'm usually far too busy to let my imagination run away with me. This is the result when I've got nothing else to think about!'

Paul's mouth tightened a shade, but he didn't argue. He went into the sitting room to turn off the lights – and came out carrying Oscar unceremoniously under his arm.

'What's this cat doing in here? We're going to have Molly and Jeff accusing us of kidnapping it.'

'I think he must have come in through the cloakroom window.' But even as I said it, I still found it difficult to believe, though it seemed there was no other explanation. 'We shall have to keep it shut, I suppose.'

Paul went to dump Oscar outside the back door.

'Just in time,' he said when he came back. 'I can hear Molly out on her doorstep calling him. Now – you look decidedly ropey, Mrs Wilson, and I think it's time you were in bed.'

'Are you coming up now?'

'In a few minutes.'

'Then I'll wait for you.' Weak and shaky as I still felt, good as it would be to lie down and pull the covers up to my chin, I really didn't feel like being left alone for a single second.

Sixteen

Next morning I woke to the sound of the shower running, and a few minutes later Paul came into the bedroom wearing his dark business suit and a tie.

'Hi, sweetheart. How are you feeling?'

'All right.' Actually I felt nauseous again but I wasn't going to admit it. 'You're dressed. I thought you weren't going in to work today.'

'Changed my mind. I suppose if Marian is coming down, you'll insist on working whether I'm here or not, and I thought if I took tomorrow off instead, we could go somewhere nice. In fact, I could take the rest of the week off and we could get right away. Exmoor maybe – or we could go to Cornwall and see your folks.'

'It's a nice thought.'

'We'll talk about it tonight. Now – I want you to promise you won't overdo things today.'

'I won't.'

'I could cheerfully murder Josh for frightening you like that last night.'

'It wasn't his fault. He wasn't to know I'd

overreact like that.' I didn't want Paul blaming Josh – if there were tensions between them it would only make things worse. 'It's just that everything is getting on top of me. First my accident, then Ruth going missing, then all that ... it's like living in a nightmare. I keep wondering what's going to happen next.' I thought, but didn't add, my uncomfortable suspicion that there was something odd going on at Kowloon and Victoria Enterprises.

Paul squeezed my hand. 'I suppose life's like that sometimes. You know the old saying – it never rains but it pours.'

'Well, I must say I shall be glad when the storm passes and the sun comes out again.'

He grinned mischievously. 'The forecast is good. Lovely weather for Cornwall.'

'You've had the radio on this morning, have you?' I asked.

'While I was having breakfast.'

'Nothing about Ruth, I suppose?'

'No mention. I think she's done a runner.' Clearly he'd decided to put the least sinister interpretation on her disappearance, and I knew I should try to do the same. After all, what could possibly have happened to her on a March afternoon in a sleepy village where everyone knew everyone else?

'I have to go, sweetheart,' Paul said. 'I'll see you this afternoon.'

'I must get up now anyway if I don't want

Marian to find me still in bed.'

He kissed me. 'Remember what I said – no overdoing things.'

'Stop nagging me!'

He laid a hand on the duvet in the region of my stomach. 'You have to take care of this little one, remember.'

I nodded. 'I know, I know.'

I listened to his footsteps on the stairs, the sound of his car starting up. Then I pushed back the duvet and got out of bed. As I'd said, I really needed to get on – Marian had probably left London at the crack of dawn. But that wasn't my only reason for getting up. Now that Paul had gone and I was alone, I didn't want to be upstairs and vulnerable. Not with the back door unlocked. My fright last night was still too fresh in my mind. Perhaps it had been all over nothing, but it had been very real to me. It would be a long time, I suspected, before I felt totally safe again.

Marian arrived soon after ten. She was dressed as if for the office in a neat grey suit and she was wearing her slightly flustered expression.

'You found us then,' I said, opening the door to her.

'Yes, no trouble at all really. Oh Julia, you do look pale! What an awful thing to happen!'

'I'm much better now.' Marian's concern had the effect of making me determined to behave as normally as possible. 'Shall we have a cup of coffee before we start work? I'm sure you're ready for one after driving all this way.'

'Oh yes! I didn't dare have one before I left, in case I needed the loo on the motorway.'

I smiled to myself. With all the service stations between here and London, finding a loo was hardly enough of a problem to warrant foregoing an early-morning coffee, but Marian had to have something to worry about!

'You must be dying of thirst,' I said. 'I'll get the filter going.'

'And I'll get the rest of the stuff from the car.'

Marian had already dumped a pile of files on the corner of the table.

'Did you bring my telephone book?' I asked.

'I'm sure I did. Yes, there it is – under the post.'

'Good. Get the other stuff, then, and we can get weaving.' My enthusiasm for work, always simmering away just waiting to be ignited, had been excited by the stack of post and the files awaiting my attention.

The hours to lunch flew by. Marian filled me in on what had been happening in my absence, I dictated a report for Poyson Associates, and together we dealt with the mail she'd brought with her.

Lunchtime brought a problem. As Ruth hadn't been in since Friday, stocks of food were getting low, but I couldn't send Marian all the way back to London without feeding her. I found some rather soft tomatoes and the remains of the mushrooms in the fridge, and a stick of garlic bread, foil-wrapped, in the freezer. We defrosted the garlic bread in the oven and grilled the tomatoes and mushrooms. Not exactly a feast, but it would have to do.

After we'd eaten I told Marian I thought she should be setting out for home. Since she was driving a car she was unfamiliar with, on a route she didn't know, I was concerned that she should get back to London in daylight. I didn't want to be worrying about Marian too!

We packed up and I went outside to see her off. It seemed the weather forecast had been right for once: it was quite a pleasant afternoon with the promise of spring in the air. After Marian had driven off, I spent a few moments pottering a little painfully round the garden. The crocus had taken on a new lease of life, perking up in the sunshine to make a patch of bright yellow, and clumps of daffodils were opening their trumpets. I thought of Ruth, remembering how she had filled vases with them last year to cheer up every room in the house, and felt a dull ache of anxiety for her stir again.

Yesterday I'd still been half-expecting her to walk into the kitchen as if nothing had happened; now I couldn't imagine her ever walking in again. I shivered, cold suddenly in spite of the warmth in the afternoon sunshine, and went back into the house.

We'd got through quite a bit of work, I realized, as I flicked again through the pile of papers Marian had left me, but it had only served to remind me of all the jobs waiting for me at the office that couldn't be dealt with from home, and the clients depending on me. The sooner I could get back the better. Not this week, perhaps, but certainly next. Paul would try to talk me out of it, of course – and there would be another disagreement.

I sighed. Since my accident we'd had too many of those. Disagreements about me doing too much, about how we saw the future now that I was pregnant, even about this peculiar Kowloon and Victoria thing. Though it had been marginalized a little by everything else that had happened, it was still bothering me. I didn't like the thought that Paul's company had connections with a company who might be up to something illegal or immoral, yet he'd dismissed it almost out of hand. It was as if he simply didn't want to know anything that might suggest Kowloon and Victoria were not all they should be. Of course, that was Paul all over, burying his head in the sand, and taking the view that as long as Stattisford Electronics was in the clear, that was all that mattered. But I couldn't help feeling that there could be repercussions. It was very short-sighted to ignore potential trouble.

Or *was* he ignoring it? Suddenly I remembered the airmail envelope with the Hong Kong postmark which I'd thought might have arrived on Saturday, and I went into the study, intending to check the date of the postmark. But the envelope was no longer in the waste-paper basket.

I frowned. Paul never emptied the waste-paper basket himself – Ruth always did that. But Ruth hadn't been in. I couldn't understand it. Either I was going totally mad, or Paul had removed the envelope. But why? It had been scrapped as rubbish.

Only one explanation occurred to me – and I didn't like it. Paul had got rid of the envelope because he didn't want me to see it. Not the contents, since the envelope had been empty, but the evidence that he had received a letter from Hong Kong at all.

I chewed my lip, puzzled and anxious, wondering whether to ring Tony Bowman and pick his brains as I'd planned or wait and talk to Paul – insist he told me what was going on. It might cause unpleasantness – given the chip he had on his shoulder, Paul might think I was trying to interfere in his business again – the hot-shot city lawyer thinking she knew better than the small-town businessman. And it may well be that I was making something out of nothing. But my gut instinct was worrying away at me and I knew I couldn't just let it go.

Best to be sure of my facts first, though. Then I could work out the best strategy for dealing with it and finding a way to put it to Paul without making him feel he was some-how at fault, or at best, lacking in judgement.

I flipped through my telephone book and turned up Tony Bowman's number. But when I rang it, the phone was answered by a female voice.

'I'm sorry, Mr Bowman is not in the office this week,' she said when I asked for him. 'He'll be back on Monday.'

'Right. Thanks. I'll call him then.'

So for the moment there was nothing more I could do. Or was there? What was to stop me contacting Hong Kong myself and asking them direct if they had any reason to suspect Kowloon and Victoria Enterprises of some illegal activity? I switched the computer back on and searched for details of whom I should contact, then typed up a letter and faxed it off on Paul's machine. I'd have to wait a few days for a reply, of course, but a few more days would make no difference one way or the other.

Or so I thought. In this, as in so many things that were happening in my life, I couldn't have been more wrong.

Seventeen

About ten minutes later the doorbell rang. It was Peter Dawson, our GP, who is also a friend and a neighbour.

He checked me over and, much to my relief, removed the strapping from my wrist, though my ankle, he said, needed supporting for a while longer. I told him about our proposed break in Cornwall and he gave his approval.

'Do you good, Julia. Just what you need.'

'That's what Paul said.'

'And he's right. Knowing you, he's probably having problems keeping you quiet!'

I laughed ruefully. 'He'd agree with you there.'

'You took a nasty bang to the head. And with a baby on the way you must take care of yourself. So – rest and recuperation is the best thing. Just take things steadily and don't try to do too much too soon.'

Peter had barely left when Paul got home – unusually early for him.

'Marian gone?' he asked. 'Or didn't she come in the end?'

'She left soon after lunch. I've had Peter

124

Dawson here since then. He took the strapping off my wrist – look!' I waved my hand at him. It felt really weird and floppy, as if heavy strapping was its natural state and I was missing it.

'Good.' Paul put a supermarket carrier bag on the kitchen table. 'Here's some food. For tonight. I got some of those ready-prepared meals they do – some sort of seafood pasta thing. And some salad.'

'Oh, well done!'

'Well, it will have to do. We can't go on like this, though. If Ruth's done a runner, we'll have to find a replacement for her.'

'I suppose so. There's no news of her then?'

'No, not a thing.'

'Is Jim at work?'

'No. He came in, but we sent him home. He was in no fit state. We can manage without him for a day or two. As they can manage without me. I've told Josh I'm taking the rest of the week off.'

'Oh Paul, you shouldn't have! Not on my account!'

'Why not? I haven't had any time off since I don't know when. Did you think any more about my suggestion?'

'Going away, you mean? Yes, I mentioned it to Peter, and he thought it was a good idea.'

'Exactly. A break will do us both good. If we pack up tonight we could get off first thing in the morning. We'll have no trouble

125

getting into a hotel at this time of year. Agreed?'

'Agreed.'

Paul grinned a little sheepishly. 'That's just as well. I've already booked. A hotel on the Roseland Peninsula that Josh recommended. Close enough to your folks for us to be able to visit, far enough away so they won't expect us to spend all our time with them.'

'Paul, you are a schemer!'

'Well, sometimes one has to be a little devious.' He took the supermarket dinners out of the carrier bag, looking at them critically. 'I don't know what these are going to be like, but I think I can put up with them if I know that tomorrow night we'll be eating in style.'

'Very true.'

Already I was looking forward to it. Now the decision had been made, I couldn't wait to get away and leave all the problems and traumas behind.

As the forecast had promised, the weather held. We set off next morning in spring-like sunshine that was making fresh green leaf speckle the sad brown hedges, and drifts of yellow daffodils brightened the verges. We left the motorway in Devon and stopped for a lunchtime drink at a country pub, and Paul, hungry no doubt after the delicious but rather small portions of seafood pasta we'd had for supper last night, devoured a pasty and chips. He seemed not to have a care in the world.

The hotel, when we found it, was everything Josh had said it was. It stood on a promontory on the beautiful Roseland Peninsula, looking out over the thrift-studded cliffs to the dancing sea beyond. A log fire burned in an open grate and afternoon tea had been set out – Indian or China, milk or lemon, tiny squares of shortbread, slices of seed cake and fruit loaf, and a Madeira cake so light it melted in the mouth. Again, Paul piled his plate high.

'You'll spoil your appetite for dinner!' I chided him.

'Don't you believe it! I shall go for a walk and the sea air will make me hungry again. Do you want to come? Oh no, I suppose you can't really, with that ankle of yours.'

'I think I might cramp your style,' I said regretfully. 'You go, though, if you want to. I'll ring Bev, tell her we're here, and fix up to go and see them – tomorrow, perhaps.'

'Whatever.'

'This is bliss. I'm really glad you suggested it.'

'Well, there you are! Sometimes your husband does know what he's talking about.'

That chip on his shoulder again. 'Have I ever said different?' I asked.

He pulled a face. 'No. But you have to

admit you always think you know best.'

'Oh Paul, that's not fair!' But even as I said it I felt a twinge of guilt. I supposed that sometimes it might seem that way. Perhaps it was the nature of my job that made me trust my own judgement rather than anyone else's; perhaps it was just *me*. And I did think that Paul could be a bit naive and trusting, accepting what he was told at face value, believing everyone else to be as straight-forward and honest as he was. This business with Kowloon and Victoria was a case in point. I was suspicious, he dismissed it. I was determined to get to the bottom of it, he thought I was making complications where none need exist.

But this was our much-needed break, and I wasn't going to allow anything to spoil it. I gave him a playful little push.

'Go on, you go for your walk. I'm just going to sit here and enjoy the view!'

Those few stolen days were some of the most special I can remember. We took the car and explored the wild Cornish country-side, we played Scrabble in the sea-view room with the log fire crackling, we ate and drank far more than was good for us, and at night, in the big comfortable bed, we made wonderful, leisurely love. The shadow of the problems which had seemed so darkly over-whelming at home blew away on the stiff sea breeze as we relaxed into leisure mode.

On the second day, we visited my mother and Bev and took them, and the three children, out for the afternoon.

The little beach Bev directed us to was deserted but for a couple of people walking dogs. Mum, Bev and I perched on big flat rocks at the foot of the towering cliffs while Paul took the children down to the water's edge. As we watched them go, William and Haydn, the five-year-old twins, running ahead in great swooping circles, two-year-old Alice riding piggy-back on Paul's shoulders, my heart filled with love. He enjoyed the children, and though we saw them so seldom, he was marvellous with them. Now, soon, he was going to enjoy having a child of his own.

'I've got something to tell you,' I said, not wanting to keep my news a secret from my family for a moment longer, wanting to share the burst of joy that was lightening my heart.

Mum looked at me expectantly; Bev was still preoccupied with keeping an eye on the children. Even though they were safe with Paul, she couldn't break the habit of watching over them; they were too precious to her for her to be able to completely entrust their welfare to anyone else. I wondered if I would feel the same powerful emotion, and if I did, how I would feel about leaving my baby in the care of a nanny.

'I suppose it's a bit soon to say anything really, but...' I began, and Mum smiled suddenly.

'You're pregnant, aren't you?'

'Well ... yes.'

'I knew it!' Her smile widened, smoothing out the deep lines that time – and Dad's death – had etched into her face, making her look years younger.

'Is it so obvious?' I asked, returning her smile.

'Yes, it is really. You look ... well, softer somehow, Julia. Rounder.'

'That's all the food we've been eating!' I said ruefully.

'No – no, it's not. I don't mean you're any fatter, though it wouldn't be a bad thing if you were. You've always been too thin for my liking. No, it's your face. You just look more ... womanly.'

'What a thing to say!' Bev turned, grinning at me. The wind had whipped her no-nonsense, collar-length hair around her face – her round, rosy, unmade-up face – and suddenly I knew exactly what Mum meant.

Bev had that look too – a glow which transcended physical attributes or the lack of them, a sort of contentment that came from fulfilling a biological role for which nature had intended her. In that moment I knew I wasn't the only one who was pregnant, and I wondered why I'd never noticed that look before, either in others, or, more importantly, in myself.

'Not you too!' I said.

'Yep, 'fraid so! No stopping me, is there? But I must say I'm surprised you've found time to join the club, Ju. I thought your career was all that mattered to you.'

'There's no reason why I can't have both, is there?' I asked, though I knew her opinion would coincide exactly with Paul's – that a child needed its mother's full attention in the early formative years.

'I'm sure Julia will manage it all perfectly,' my mother said hastily. She knew Bev and I could spar all too easily.

'I'm sure she will.' But the edge was there, that same edge, and I thought: *Is that what everyone thinks of me? Career-obsessed, over-confident, opinionated?* And why did I suddenly mind if they did? Because impending motherhood was already changing me, making me – what had my mother said? – more womanly? Surely not! But it was certainly true that I was a good deal more emotional, a good deal more vulnerable, in more ways than one.

'I'm really pleased, Julia.' Mum reached across, squeezing my hand where it lay on the sun-warmed rock. 'I was always afraid you might leave it too late and then regret it.' She glanced at Paul, who was now skimming

131

pebbles into the breakers to the delight of the children. 'I expect Paul is pleased, too.'

'Yes, he is.'

'He'll be a wonderful father.'

'I know.'

And he would, he would. Not a doubt of it. In a few years, we could be bringing *our* children here, and how they would love it, more even than Bev's three, whose whole lives were spent within easy reach of the sea. I could picture it now – exploring the rock pools with them, building sandcastles, teaching them to swim ... it was an idyll where the sun shone from morning to night and the shadows of the last days could not reach, a future all wrapped up in the cocoon of a secure family unit, tight-knit protection against the pressures and anxieties of the outside world.

Even as I basked in the warmth of the vision, I knew it was rose-tinted and unrealistic, but for the moment it was enough to make me totally, utterly happy. More than enough. And I wanted, less than ever, to return to the real world of unexplained falls and missing housekeepers and intruders in the night and business dealings which might or might not be suspect. I wanted to stay forever on that sunny Cornish beach with the seagulls crying as they rode the wind and Paul playing with the children at the water's edge.

Eighteen

We were a little later that night going down to dinner. We'd made our way back early evening when it was time for Bev to start getting the children ready for bed, we'd bathed, made love, bathed again and got dressed, all in the lovely leisurely fashion that a couple of days of pleasant inactivity had engendered. We stopped in the bar for an aperitif (though mine was just an orange juice!) and by the time we reached our table, the dining room was quite busy.

It was as I chose an hors d'oeuvre from the trolley, laden with seafood and interesting salads, that I first had the feeling that someone was watching me. I looked round and saw a young woman of about my own age, who was sitting at a neighbouring table, staring at me. As our eyes met, she half-smiled, then looked away as if embarrassed. But a few minutes later I felt her eyes on me again.

I was puzzled and a little disconcerted. I couldn't imagine why I should be the subject of her attention. It was usually Paul who attracted glances from the women! I

133

watched her covertly. She had almost finished her meal – the waiter was offering her coffee. She shook her head, stood up to go – then came directly over to our table.

'Julia? It is Julia, isn't it?' She sounded slightly hesitant.

'I'm Julia, yes. I'm sorry ... do I know you?'

'It's Helen. Helen Gibbs. You've forgotten me, haven't you?'

I searched her face and my memory. Tall, fair, with shoulder-length hair tied back with a black velvet squidgee, and china-blue eyes – disconcertingly blue almost, as if the shade was not natural but came from tinted contact lenses. Not eyes one would easily forget, I would have thought. But they stirred no chord of recognition. I met a lot of people through my job, of course, but I had no recollection of how or when I had met her, and her name was equally unfamiliar.

'I'm sorry. I really don't...'

'Magnetic Island? 1984?' She laughed, a small brittle giggle of embarrassment. 'Oh, it's a long time ago, I know. I'm not surprised you don't remember.'

'Magnetic Island.' I remembered Magnetic Island, all right. A little piece of paradise off the coast of Queensland. I'd visited it during the year out I'd spent backpacking in Australia, spent a few idyllic days there, soaking up the sun on the white sand beaches, snorkelling in the warm azure water, jolting around the island in a four-wheel-drive buggy known as a 'moke' with a handful of other young people, mostly students like myself, all laid-back yet bursting inwardly with the enthusiasm of youth, the determination to make the most of this stolen time before succumbing to the responsibilities of the real world. 'No worries,' the Australians say, and we'd made that our slogan. 'No worries.' And there hadn't been. Lack of money, mosquitoes, hostels where we slept eight or ten to a room and privacy was an unheard-of luxury, cold-water showers and canteen-style food – none of these things had mattered in the slightest. Magic moments out of time, that was my overriding memory of a year in Australia. And apart from the mystique of Ayers Rock, Magnetic Island had perhaps been the most magical of all.

'You were there when I was?' I said.

'Yes. We went over on the boat together. And we were at the same backpackers' hostel. I was quite a little mouse at the time. And you were ... well, you always seemed to be at the centre of whatever was going on. Surrounded by boys, mostly...' She broke off, glancing at Paul. 'I'm sorry, I'm talking too much. I was just so surprised to see you!'

'Well, yes, it is...' I was still searching my memory. I still couldn't remember her, but then I'd met so many people during that

year, some fleetingly, some who had popped up time and again at the network of
backpackers' hostels and places of interest,
acquaintances who always greeted one
another as old friends because we were
sharing the same unreal existence.

'I'm interrupting your meal.' She glanced
at Paul again. 'I just had to say hello, though.
They were such happy days!'

'You're not interrupting at all!' Paul said.
He was becoming a little garrulous –
probably as a result of all the wine he'd been
getting through. 'I'm sure Julia would love to
have a chat about – what's it called? – Magnetic Island. Why don't you join us for a
drink when we've had dinner?'

'Oh, I couldn't intrude...'

'Don't be silly,' I said, more because I felt
guilty about not remembering her than for
any other reason. 'Paul's right – it would be
lovely to talk over old times. Unless you have
other plans, of course.'

'No, I'm on my own. Just having a break...'

'We'll see you in the bar, then. In about –
half an hour, say?'

'That will be really nice.'

'What a coincidence!' Paul said when she
had gone.

'Yes. It's weird, though. I don't remember
her at all.'

Paul was looking at me narrowly. The
shadow of concern was back in his eyes. 'You

don't think you're having another memory lapse, do you?'

'Oh God, I hope not! I thought I was getting better! Oh, I'm sure it's not that. I met so many people in those days, and it's such a long time ago...'

'When you start reminiscing, I expect it will all come back,' he said, the glow of the wine overriding his momentary concern once more.

'Perhaps so,' I said.

But I had caught a flickering shadow of the same darkness I'd experienced in the first days after my fall, and felt uncomfortably certain that for one reason or another, Helen Gibbs was lost somewhere in that murky pool, and totally beyond my recollection.

She was sitting in the lounge when we emerged from the dining room, leafing through a copy of *Country Life*. She glanced up, smiling a little uncertainly, as though she thought we might have changed our minds about her joining us. I returned her smile, feeling guilty again, this time because I had rather hoped she wouldn't be there, and sat down beside her on the chintz-covered Chesterfield.

'What would you like to drink?' Paul asked her.

'Oh, nothing alcoholic, thank you. I don't drink. I never have. Don't you remember,

Julia? I used to get teased terribly about it. Everyone else getting pie-eyed on Castlemaine XXXX and me on the fruit juice.'

'I certainly remember the Castlemaine XXXX.'

'Would you like fruit juice now then?' Paul asked.

'No, I'll have another coffee. They're still serving it, aren't they?'

'I certainly hope so. Julia – what about you?'

'I suppose I'd better just have coffee too,' I said regretfully, thinking how much I would have liked a Cointreau.

'Well, I'm going to have a cognac,' Paul said, causing me a stab of misgiving. I rather thought he'd had quite enough to drink already. 'It's all right,' he went on quickly, as if to pre-empt any possible objection on my part, 'you two girls stay here and renew your acquaintance. I'll get the coffee.'

'Your husband, I presume,' Helen said as he walked away across the lounge.

'Yes. I'm sorry, I should have introduced you.'

'Don't worry about it. You were taken by surprise. I have to say, I was pretty bowled over myself when I saw you sitting there. It was like going back in time.'

'Yes.'

'How long have you been married?'

'Oh, three years now.'

'You're lucky.'

'You're not married?'

'I was. Unfortunately it didn't work out.'

'I'm sorry.'

'Oh well, these things happen. I just didn't imagine it would happen to me. I loved Jeremy so much, I suppose I closed my eyes to the warning signals. By the time I woke up to what was happening it was too late. We'd passed the point of no return.'

I didn't know what to say. It was so bizarre, hearing what sounded very like confidences from someone who purported to be a friend, but whom I really didn't know from Adam.

'It's really odd, seeing you like this,' she went on. 'I was only thinking about you the other day. I was doing some turning out and I came across some photographs I took when I was in Australia. Some of them were on Magnetic Island, of course – and you were in them. You were wearing a yellow bikini. Do you remember it?'

I remembered the yellow bikini, all right. It had had a halter neck and three gold rings on the front of the pants. I'd felt like a million dollars in it and I'd been very upset when it became faded by too much sun and sea water. I hadn't been able to afford to replace it either, existing as I was on the meagre wages I could earn waitressing and fruit picking.

'It was really sassy, that bikini,' Helen went

on. 'You were wearing it the day you got bitten by something, remember? We thought it was a jellyfish and panicked that you'd be dead in minutes. And then that gorgeous Aussie lifeguard carried you to the first-aid centre, and we'd all have willingly swapped places with you.'

'Yes, I certainly remember that.' I'd often recounted the tale to the amusement of dinner-party guests, but for no reason that I could explain, it made me uncomfortable now to hear Helen refer to it. 'Anyway, it's all a long time ago now.'

'You're right, it is.' She sounded regretful.

'So what are you doing now?' I asked.

'Oh, this and that – you know me. Jill of all trades, master of none. Jeremy was prepared to be very generous when we split up – he felt guilty, I expect. He moved out and allowed me to stay on in the house, and he made sure I was never short of money, so I didn't have any immediate worries. But now...' She broke off. Paul was back with the coffees – three of them – and an assortment of petits fours. She smiled up at him, rather winsomely, I thought – as he put them on the low table in front of us. 'They look delicious! The food here is first-class, isn't it?'

'Not bad, I must admit.' Paul turned to take a balloon of brandy from the barman, who had followed him over, put it down on the table beside his coffee cup and settled himself into a brocaded chair.

'When I saw the brochure, I decided it was just what I needed,' Helen was saying. 'Log fires – afternoon tea – a deserted beach with only the gulls for company ... it seemed the ideal place to try to sort out my life. Trouble is, however lovely the spot, it doesn't really change anything, does it? The real world is still there waiting, just as it was when we came back from Australia. But I suppose you don't have those sorts of problems, do you, Julia? You always seemed to know exactly where you were going. And it's obviously happened for you. I can't imagine you not having every detail of your life perfectly worked out.'

There was something slightly sycophantic about the tone she was taking, which grated on me. 'Oh, I don't know, we all have our problems,' I said.

'You were going to study law, weren't you?' she went on, unabashed. 'I bet you did really well. You're probably a famous barrister now.'

'A solicitor, actually.'

'I knew it! You always had that aura of success. Oh, you don't know how I envied you! A career in law – it sounded so glamorous! I'd have loved to do something like that, but I knew I didn't have the brains for it.'

'I'm sure that's not true,' I protested politely.

'Oh, believe me, it is! Never mind, we can't all be high-fliers, can we?'

'What do you do?' Paul asked. Not, I thought, the most tactful question in the circumstances.

Helen smiled almost apologetically. 'Oh, I've done all sorts of things. I trained as a nurse when I got back from my globe-trotting, but that went by the board when I hurt my back lifting a patient. I helped out in a nursery school for a bit, and then I met Jeremy. I'd have liked to go back to nursing when my back was better, but he didn't like the idea of me working shifts. Didn't like the idea of me working at all, truth to tell. He was in a pretty high-powered position, and what he really wanted was a trophy wife. But I couldn't just stay at home all day, and I'm not the sort to shop and lunch with the crowd he thought I should be friendly with. So I managed to persuade him to let me do a course at the Pru Leith and set up a catering service. Buffets for weddings, little dinner parties, some corporate catering, you know the sort of thing. The kind of work that fitted in with the image he wanted me to portray.' She laughed a little bitterly. 'I have to say, I did enjoy it, though it was pretty hard work.'

'Was? Past tense? You don't do it any

more?' Paul asked.

'I'm afraid the recession put paid to it,' Helen said ruefully. 'I've tried my best to struggle on, but not many people seem to be able to do much entertaining any more. Most of my clients were Thatcher's children – whizz-kids with money to burn. Now they've got families and school fees and enormous mortgages and the City isn't buzzing any more. They have to count their pennies like the rest of us.'

'I thought you said your husband had a good job,' Paul said garrulously. I wanted to die of embarrassment, but Helen didn't take any offence.

'I was explaining to Julia – we're not together any more.'

'Oh, right.' For the first time, Paul looked slightly uncomfortable. 'Oh well, not to worry. Your business will pick up again, I'm sure. All the signs are we're beginning to come out of the recession at last.'

'A bit late for me, I'm afraid. I don't think I shall have a kitchen to cook in for much longer...' She broke off, flushing slightly. 'I'm sorry, you shouldn't have let me get on to this subject. You don't want to hear about my problems.'

No, we don't, I thought, not very charitably perhaps. Helen Gibbs was really beginning to get on my nerves. But Paul's brandy, on top of the other alcohol he'd got through this

143

evening, seemed to be having the effect of making him warm to all humankind.

'Surely that's what friends are for?' he said expansively.

Helen sipped her coffee. 'I must say, it's nice to be able to talk about it. As I said, I came away for this break to give myself the chance to think things out. But all I've succeeded in doing is going round and round in circles. Sometimes saying things out loud helps you to get them clear in your own mind, doesn't it?'

'Ab-so-lute-ly!' Paul said heartily, emphasizing each syllable with careful deliberation. 'Always helps.'

'I'm not sure that it does,' I said, giving him a straight look. 'Very often it's possible to say something and then later wish you hadn't, especially when you've had a drink.'

Helen laughed, a little nervously, but Paul missed the point of my comment entirely. 'Just consider yourself among friends,' he said heartily.

'Oh I do, I do! It's just that it's so depressing, and depression is like measles, isn't it – dreadfully catching...'

'Julia and I won't get depressed, I promise.'

Speak for yourself! I thought as Helen began to drone on again.

'Well, the thing is, not only is my business on its last legs, it looks now as if I'm going to lose my home too. As I was telling Julia,

144

when we first split up, Jeremy was very generous. He let me stay on in the house, but we never put the arrangement on a formal footing. Now he's met someone else and wants to set up home with her. It's all a bit of a mess, and it looks as though the house will have to be sold so we can divide things up between us. That means I shall be without a roof over my head. There's no way I can afford to buy anything else out of my share when I've got no regular income.'

'Oh dear, oh dear!' Paul was shaking his head and making rather silly clucking noises with his tongue and teeth.

'I shall have to rent, I suppose,' she went on. 'Find a flat – maybe even share. It's a pretty bleak prospect at my age. I mean – living ten to a room was all very well in Australia when we were youngsters. Now, after having been used to my own home ... well, I must say I'm dreading it.'

'You shouldn't have to! It's all wrong!' Paul said vehemently. 'Where *do* you live, by the way? London?'

'Oxford. But to be honest, I don't think I shall stay there. Too many memories. No, I really don't know what to do for the best. I have been doing a bit of child-minding as a sideline since the catering business hit the buffers, but of course that will be out of the question too when I don't have a home of my own. I can hardly look after four or five little ones in a rented shared flat with no proper facilities and probably no garden for them to play in.' She glanced at me. Her face was flushed now, and she looked on the point of tears. 'You haven't any magic legal remedy, I suppose, Julia? As a solicitor? Where do you think I stand?'

'I'm afraid family affairs aren't my forte,' I said, not wanting to get involved in this any more than I had to. 'Company law is my speciality.'

'We might be able to do something for you, though,' Paul said.

I looked at him in surprise. He tossed back his brandy and signalled to the barman for another.

'Well, it's only a thought, of course, but...' He grinned, managing to look pleased with himself and also a little bashful both at the same time, and suddenly I realized just what it was he was on the point of suggesting.

'Paul ... hang on! Don't you think we should...'

But Paul burbled on, seemingly totally unaware of my cautionary interruption.

'Well ... Helen, isn't it? ... we've just lost our housekeeper, and we shall have to find a replacement. Julia is in London all week and we need someone to keep things ticking over at home. It seems to me as if you have all the right qualifications, and since you two are old friends...'

146

'I'm sure Helen wouldn't want to bury herself in the country!' I said swiftly. 'I'm sorry, Helen, Paul's had rather a lot to drink, and when he's like that, he speaks without thinking.'

'No I don't!' Paul said indignantly. 'I think it's a brilliant idea! Pru-Leith-trained cook, nurse, childminder ... what more could we want?'

I was furious now. How dare Paul suggest Helen came to us as a housekeeper without even consulting me! Worse, he seemed on the point of appointing her as a nanny too!

'This needs thought. On all our parts,' I said firmly.

'Yes, yes...' Paul waved his brandy balloon airily so that he was in danger of slopping it down his jacket. 'But it is brilliant, you've got to agree!' He put down his glass, fished in his wallet for one of his business cards, and passed it to Helen. 'Why don't you give us a call when we get home? Come down and see what you think.'

'Thank you – I will.' Helen looked as if she might be about to burst into tears of gratitude, which made me feel guilty as well as angry. 'I'll give you my number too.' She tore a page out of her diary, scribbling on it and passing it to Paul. 'You know, this is almost beyond belief! To bump into Julia again after all these years and then ... well, it's seren-dipity, isn't it? One minute I don't know which way to turn for the best, the next ... well, it seems as though we've both found the answer to our problems!'

'I think it's a little early to assume that,' I said icily, but Paul seemed not to notice.

'I'm going to have another brandy on the strength of it!' he declared heartily.

I glared at him. 'Don't you think you've had enough already?'

'No! Hotel measures can't exactly be called generous! And it's not as if I have to drive.' He looked at Helen. 'Are you sure you won't have one too, to celebrate?'

'She's already said she doesn't drink, Paul,' I snapped, wishing the floor would open and swallow me – or him – or both of us.

'I must be making a move in any case.' Helen slid out of her chair. 'I like to go for a walk before bed. I find it helps me sleep – especially when it's sea air.'

'Will we see you tomorrow?' Paul asked.

'Possibly not. I'm leaving in the morning. This was a mid-week break only. They're cheaper. And I have to be out of my room by ten. So unless we happen to be having breakfast at the same time...'

'Well, don't forget, then – give us a call, won't you?' Paul rose, a little unsteadily, to shake her hand. 'We shall be home at the weekend.'

'I don't believe you, Paul!' I said furiously when Helen had gone.

'What do you mean?' He looked genuinely puzzled and a little hurt. His face was flushed and his tie slightly askew.

'You are drunk, do you know that?' I flared. 'How dare you offer that woman a job without discussing it with me first?'

'I am not drunk!' Paul retorted indignantly. 'And anyway, what are you getting so steamed up about? I should think it's a heaven-sent opportunity! She seems to be just what we need, and it would be helping her out of a hole too. And if the two of you are old friends, I thought...'

'I wish you wouldn't keep saying that!' I snapped. 'We are not old friends! We just happened to be in the same place at the same time more than ten years ago. I don't even remember her.'

'Well, I'm sorry! I didn't realize you felt like that...' Paul sounded really hurt.

'You never stopped to ask me! I can't believe you did it, I really can't! We don't even know for certain that Ruth won't be coming back.'

'But it is beginning to look that way, you must agree. She's done a runner, not much doubt of it.' He sighed heavily. 'Still, if you feel so strongly about it, we'll forget the whole idea. It was only a suggestion.'

He looked utterly crestfallen, and I thought guiltily that so soon after making up my mind not to do it, here I was treading once more on his fragile ego, once again taking the stand that I knew best. And it was always possible that I was over-reacting. Certainly, Helen seemed very well qualified for the position of housekeeper.

'Oh, I don't know,' I said helplessly. 'I suppose it's a bit late to back down now. Just let's think about it for a day or two and see what happens when we get home. She may not even get in touch.' But the feeling of being trapped by circumstances was too strong and I was unable to resist adding: 'Though I have a nasty feeling that she will.'

'Look, Jules, the last thing I want is for you to feel I've foisted someone on you.' My obvious annoyance seemed to have sobered Paul abruptly. 'Perhaps I was a bit hasty. It's just that she seemed so perfect, and I do worry about you, especially now, with the baby coming and everything...'

I tried my hardest to put my irritation aside. Paul was only trying to do what he thought was best, I told myself. And his judgement had been rather impaired by having had too much to drink.

'Let's forget about it for now,' I said. 'We are supposed to be relaxing and enjoying ourselves, not worrying about something that may never happen. Do you want to go to bed, or shall we have a game of Scrabble?'

Paul looked visibly relieved. 'Scrabble, if

you like,' he said.

I found myself smiling again. I had a feeling this was one game I was going to win hands down!

Nineteen

'I think I should go into the office on Monday,' I said.

We were driving home, speeding up the motorway. I hate motorway driving. Odd, really, when you consider how many hours I spend travelling between home and London. But I find motorways a weird mix of the tedious and the stressful, the monotony of an endless carriageway coupled with the need for constant sharp concentration, and I dislike the feeling that my safety is as much in the hands of all the other drivers racing along that same stretch of tarmac as it is in my own. Today, for some reason, I felt more tense and apprehensive than usual. All the knots in my nerves which had unravelled during our brief break were snarling up again and the only remedy I could think of was work, and more work.

I felt Paul glance in my direction.

'I know, you think it's too soon,' I said defensively. 'But I am much better. I can't just let things slide, Paul. I have clients who depend on me. And inactivity is driving me mad.'

'Sure.' Paul said lightly. 'Well, it's not really up to me, is it? If you feel well enough to go back to work, then it has to be your decision.'

I was totally taken by surprise. I'd expected another argument since Paul had consistently tried to talk me out of doing anything at all since my accident. The holiday had certainly mellowed him!

Or was there something else behind his change of attitude?

I didn't like the sneaky suspicion that suddenly crossed my mind. It was ridiculous, of course, too ridiculous to mention – but I couldn't entirely dismiss it either.

'You're not trying to get me out of the way by any chance, are you?' I said before I could stop myself.

Paul pulled into the outside lane to overtake a large delivery lorry. 'What on earth do you mean?'

'So that you can take on Helen Gibbs as housekeeper while my back's turned?'

'What a thing to say!' Paul sounded outraged.

'Well, you were very pro-her, weren't you?' I said defensively. 'And I was throwing spanners in the works.'

'I didn't realize how you felt at the time,' Paul said. 'You were probably right – I had had too much to drink, though I hate to admit it. It made me see her in a rosy light.

But of course the decision about who should keep house for us has to be a joint one. I'd never dream of appointing anyone unless you were in agreement.'

The edge of friction was there between us again and this time it was entirely my fault.

'I know,' I said quickly. 'I was only joking, really...'

'I hope so.' Paul reached over, fiddling with the car radio. 'I wonder if the reception is any better now?'

'I'll do it,' I said hastily. 'You keep your eyes on the road.'

The radio crackled into life, but crackled was the operative word. We'd already tried it several times since getting on to the motorway, but there was a lot of interference and we'd given up and switched off.

'Still pretty hopeless,' I said.

'Try the local radio station,' Paul suggested. 'That might be better.'

I depressed the tuner and caught a few snatches of a man's voice before the crackles began again.

'I'll have to get the aerial sorted out,' Paul was saying. 'I think it must have come loose...'

'Paul!' I said sharply. 'Shut up a minute!'

'What's the matter?'

'I thought I heard them say something about Ruth...'

But we were sandwiched now between

another lorry and a clapped-out-looking old Ford that was trying to overtake us in the fast lane, and the reception was worse than ever, making comprehension totally impossible.

'Oh, that racket is terrible!' Paul said, ignoring my comment, probably because he thought I'd imagined hearing Ruth's name. 'Put some music on instead. The cassettes are all in the glove pocket.'

Reluctantly I turned off the radio and opened the glove pocket. The moment I did, a pile of cassettes shot out into my lap.

'For goodness' sake, Paul!' I groaned. The cassettes had obviously been catapulted out because of a wad of papers shoved into the glove pocket behind them. 'What on earth have you got in here?'

'Nothing. Just leave it alone.' Paul reached across me, slamming the pocket shut before I could investigate, and grabbing one of the cassettes from my lap. 'This one will do. Bette Midler.'

'You really should have a clear-out,' I said, but I was still thinking about the fact that I'd thought I'd heard Ruth's name mentioned in the news bulletin. If I was right, what had they been saying about her? Was it just another 'concern is growing' report to fill a few seconds of air time? Or was there fresh news? Had she turned up? Or...

A chill whispered across my skin, a feeling

of dread made me feel slightly sick. Suddenly I was impatient to be home, with a television and a radio that worked perfectly. Though I wasn't at all sure I wanted to hear what it might say.

In the event, I didn't have to wait until we got home. We had turned off the motorway, driven along a stretch of road that cut a swathe through open countryside, and slowed to thirty as we approached a village. We passed a row of houses, identical boxes built, probably, in the fifties, a garage, and a pub, then came upon a set of temporary traffic lights set up around a trench where men were working.

'Blasted roadworks!' Paul said, pulling up at the designated spot, which happened to be alongside a row of small shops.

I scarcely heard him. One of the shops was a newsagent's; outside was a billboard advertising the evening paper. And scrawled across it in uneven black capitals were the words: LOCAL WOMAN FOUND MURDERED.

For a moment I was totally stunned. I've heard the expression 'blood turning to ice', but I don't think I've ever experienced it before. It happened to me then, though. Happened with such a rush that I felt as if not just my blood but my whole body had turned into a frozen block. And then I was trembling violently.

'Paul! Paul – stop!'

'I am stopped. The lights are red.'

'No – I mean stop properly! Pull in somewhere! I have to get a paper!'

'What...?'

And then he saw it too.

'Oh my God!' he said.

The lights were changing.

'Quick – jump out!' he said. 'I'll wait down the road.'

I fumbled with the door catch, my fingers shaking so much I could hardly manage it, then half-fell out on to the pavement. I glanced back and the last thing I saw before he pulled away was Paul's shocked face.

It seemed to reflect everything I was feeling.

The newspaper report was every bit as bad as I had feared it would be.

Paul had pulled into a bus lay-by just past the traffic lights, and we spread the paper out between us, both craning to read it at the same time. Though the print had seemed to be burning my fingers as I hobbled back to the car, I hadn't dared look at it until I was sitting in the passenger seat once more. Part of me didn't want to look at it ever. But of course I did.

It didn't say a great deal. Most of the front

page was given over to the headline which echoed the hook on the hoarding: LOCAL WOMAN FOUND MURDERED, and a three-inch-square photograph of Ruth. It was a bit grainy, as if it were a snapshot enlarged more times than the camera had ever intended it to be, and she looked very young, with her hair longer than I'd ever seen her wearing it. She had on a big brimmed hat, too far back on her head, so that it resembled a halo, and I guessed it had been taken at a family wedding. But it was unmistakeably Ruth.

I read the first, bold-print paragraph. *A body, discovered yesterday in Hawley Quarry by two schoolboys, has been identified as that of missing local woman Ruth Wood*, but the smaller print that followed was blurring before my eyes, and I realized it was because I was crying.

'What else does it say?' I asked, my voice unsteady.

Paul reread the first paragraph aloud, and then went on:

'Mrs Wood, twenty-seven, has been missing for a week since she failed to return home from her job as housekeeper to a professional couple. Her car had been found abandoned in nearby Hawley Woods, a local beauty spot. All efforts to trace her had proved unsuc-

158

cessful. But last evening two school-boys, Richard Trent and Nathan Johnson, spotted what looked like the body of a woman partially submerged in water at the disused quarry. They raised the alarm, and police divers recovered the body...'

'Hang on, the rest is inside...'

Newspaper crackled as Paul turned the pages, searching for the continuation of the story, folding the paper open against the steering wheel. Then he went on:

'Initial reports suggest that Mrs Wood, wife of storeman James Wood, thirty, had been strangled. A police spokesman told a press conference that although some items of clothing were missing, Mrs Wood did not appear to have been the victim of a sex attack. The death was, however, being treated as murder. Mrs Wood was undoubtedly dead when her body entered the water, where it is believed to have lain undetected for some days, possibly from the time when she went missing. Recent rains had swollen the water in the quarry above its usual level, but in the last few days this had subsided.

"'We saw what looked like an old

blue jacket in the water," Nathan Johnson told the *Evening Echo*. "When we got closer we saw a hand. It was a bit of a shock. We got out of there as fast as we could."

'A full-scale murder hunt will now be launched into Mrs Wood's death, and anyone with any information which might aid the police in their enquiries is asked to contact the incident room which has been set up, or their own local police station.'

He broke off, running a hand across his mouth. 'My God, Jules, I never thought for a minute...'

'I did,' I said. 'I knew it, Paul. Didn't I say? It just wouldn't be Ruth to simply disappear like that. But what on earth happened to her? Who would do such a terrible thing? And in broad daylight, too?'

'Obviously she must have had a secret life we didn't know anything about,' Paul said.

'What makes you say that?'

'Well, what was she doing in Hawley Woods? It's a bit off the beaten track, isn't it? You'd hardly expect her to go there after a day's work at our house – unless she was meeting someone.'

'Ruth? No, I don't believe it!'

'Then how else do you explain her being there?'

160

'Perhaps she picked up a hitchhiker and they forced her to drive there at knife-point ... I don't know. I just don't know! It's too awful to think about!' I pressed my hand over my mouth. I was shaking convulsively now, and the tears were threatening again.

A honking sound. I jumped, turned my head, and saw a bus directly behind us, the driver gesticulating angrily. Paul swore. 'I'm going to have to move. We're in the way.'

He dumped the paper on my knees, started the engine and pulled away with a screech of tyres.

We drove the rest of the way home in shocked silence.

'Do you think she did pick up a hitchhiker or something after she left here last Friday?' I said.

We were in the kitchen, our cases, un-opened, dumped in the centre of the floor. The kettle was singing – I'd put it on the moment we got in the door – but there was no comfort in the usually homely sound. It was simply an irrelevant background accompaniment to my churning thoughts.

'I don't know,' Paul said. 'I should have thought she'd have had more sense.'

'So would I, really. I'd certainly never stop for anyone if I was on my own. But what else could it be? Unless...' Suddenly I was re-membering my own bizarre experience.

'Maybe she went into town – parked in the multi-storey car park, and someone hid in her car, took her hostage when she got back to it ... I've heard of something like that happening, I'm sure.'

'An urban myth, I think,' Paul said flatly.

'Oh, I don't know...' All too clearly I could remember my own unease in that car park. The dark stairwell. The nauseating smell of disinfectant and petrol fumes and stale smoke and urine. And then the moment I'd relived so many times in nightmares – the moment when I'd fallen. When, however unlikely it seemed, I felt sure someone had actually pushed me. 'Perhaps there's some lunatic who hangs around that car park, just for the kicks he gets out of attacking lone women. Perhaps...'

'Julia, you are letting your imagination run away with you. There's not a single shred of evidence for such a theory. It's sheer fantasy.'

'I'm beginning to think anything is possible!' I said. 'It's like a nightmare, all of it. And I just can't seem to wake up...' My voice was rising hysterically, and Paul put his arms round me, pulling me close.

'Come on, now. Calm down, sweetheart.'

'But it could have happened that way!' I insisted. 'Suppose the same man who push-ed me forced Ruth to drive out to Hawley Woods! It could have been *me*, Paul! He could have abducted *me* instead of just pushing me down the stairs.'

'Julia!' Paul sighed helplessly. 'Nobody pushed you. I thought you'd put that idea out of your head.'

'Well, I haven't,' I said doggedly. 'I felt a push, Paul, I'm sure I did, and nobody can tell me any different.'

'You *imagined* it.'

'Oh, I know you don't believe me. But now someone has murdered poor Ruth. That's not just in my imagination. She's dead, Paul. Ruth is dead!'

'I know, and it's terrible. But there's no connection, Julia, between that and what happened to you. If you'll only think logically for a moment, how could there be?'

'I don't know...' I was weeping now, burying my face in Paul's shoulder, the tears hot on my cheeks, my body convulsing with the violence of my emotion.

'Sweetheart, don't, please! You mustn't! You'll make yourself ill. And what about the baby?' Paul sounded distressed, and I tried to control myself.

He was right, of course. I wasn't doing myself any good crying like this. There was a nasty crampy pain in my stomach where the sobs were coming from and I felt weak and sick. I had to calm down. I had to stop this. Think of my baby, as he said.

But I couldn't. I couldn't think of anything but that Ruth, who had cooked and cleaned and shopped for us, was dead – strangled – and for the last week her body had lain undetected in a flooded quarry less than five miles away. All the time we'd been speculating about what had happened to her. All the time we'd been enjoying ourselves in Cornwall. All that time. It was so mind-bogglingly appalling I couldn't believe I'd ever be able to get it out of my head.

Twenty

The police came to see us around six thirty. Not the uniformed constable who had called before, but two plain-clothes detectives – a man in his forties in a striped shirt and leather bomber jacket, whose purplish, bulbous nose and red-veined cheeks suggested he had spent too many hours on a bar stool cultivating contacts or unwinding after a long tour of duty, and a girl with bobbed brown hair and a snub nose wearing a blazer and knee-length skirt.

Paul had answered the front door, and the voices carried along the hall and into the kitchen, where I was half-heartedly trying to cobble together something for supper.

'Sorry to bother you, sir, but we're making enquiries into the death of Ruth Wood. We'd like to talk to you and your wife if it's convenient.'

'Yes, of course.' I heard the front door close, and the sounds of Paul taking them into the sitting room. Then he appeared in the kitchen doorway. 'Julia, could you come? The police...'

'Yes, I heard.'

165

I put the lid back on the pan, turned off the ring. The risotto wouldn't come to any harm, and what did it matter if it did? I couldn't imagine either Paul or I would have much appetite.

The two police officers had sat down in our comfortable chairs, but Paul was standing in front of the fireplace. Today, instead of the welcoming glow of the log fire, there was nothing in the grate but a heap of dead ashes left over from before our Cornish break.

'This is DS Wright and DC Smedley,' Paul said. 'They want to ask us some questions about Ruth. They particularly want to talk to you.'

'Yes, of course.' I tried to keep my voice level.

'As far as we can make out, you were one of the last people to see Mrs Wood alive,' the sergeant said. There was a brusque quality to his voice, probably unintentional, simply his natural manner, acquired from years of questioning witnesses – and suspects. But, upset as I was, I found it vaguely threatening. Instinctively I went to stand beside Paul, and he put his arm round me.

Where was the self-sufficient, high-flying lawyer now? I wondered wryly. Fast submerging beneath a sea of frightening circumstances!

'So – what can you tell us about her?'

'Not a great deal, really,' I said. 'In fact, I

don't think I can be of any real help at all. As we told the officer who called the day after she went missing, she left here on the Friday afternoon at the usual time and didn't say anything about where she was going. But then, she wouldn't. She wasn't in the habit of discussing her domestic arrangements or private life with me. She just ... well ... did her job ... and went. I can't really tell you any more than that.'

'She didn't seem to have anything on her mind? Appear worried about anything?'

'No. Not that I noticed.'

'And nothing unusual happened that day?'

'No. I've racked my brains since we heard she was missing, but I can't think of anything.'

'She didn't see anyone? Speak to anyone?'

'No...' I hesitated. 'I think she might have made a telephone call. During the afternoon – when I was watching the soaps on TV. I did think I heard the phone ping, the way it does sometimes when someone puts down the receiver on another extension. But it hadn't rung, so if there was a call, she must have made it herself.'

Paul looked at me sharply. 'You haven't mentioned that before.'

'I've only just thought of it. I didn't attach any importance to it at the time or since – I assumed she was just ringing the butcher to order the meat. Or maybe making herself an appointment at the hairdresser's or the dentist's.'

'You don't mind her using your phone then?' DS Wright asked.

'Within reason, no. She's never taken advantage. If the bills went sky-high we'd have to put a stop to it, of course. But just the odd call here and there ... no, of course we don't mind that.'

'And you're quite sure you didn't hear anything of what was said? Anything that might give us some indication as to who it was she was ringing?'

I shook my head. 'No. As I said, I had the television on.'

'So it might not have been the butcher or her dentist or whatever. It could have been a friend.'

'It could have been.'

'Do you have an itemized phone bill?' the young woman DC asked, speaking for the first time.

'We do, yes.'

'Then it's just possible it might tell us the number Mrs Wood called.'

'Calls have to be a certain length of time before they show up,' Paul said. 'But if Ruth had been making lengthy calls to strange numbers, I'd certainly have picked up on it.' He sounded defensive, as if his grip on the household accounts was being challenged.

'Point taken – but it's something worth

checking,' the detective sergeant said. 'You won't have had a bill yet covering last Friday, will you? We'll get on to BT, get a list of numbers, and you can run your eye over it to see if any of them are calls you don't recognize as having been made by yourselves.'

'We're virtually at the end of the quarter,' Paul said. 'The bill is due any day now, so there's really no need for you to go to all that trouble.'

The detective sergeant gave him a straight look. 'This is a murder enquiry, sir. We need to follow up any lead, however slight, without delay.' His tone was somehow patronizing in the extreme, and it stung me. Of course we'd do anything we possibly could to help catch Ruth's killer, but there was no need for him to treat us as if we were under suspicion.

'It's a pity you didn't treat Ruth's disappearance more seriously a good deal earlier,' I retorted. 'If you had, her body might not have lain undetected for so long. And though it would have been too late to help her, at least it would have saved her husband a week of wondering what on earth had happened to her. He must have been going through hell.'

'And still is, of course,' Paul added.

The sergeant shifted his position, slumping deeper into the chair and crossing his legs. Something in his expression, however, told me that the apparent relaxation was a tactic calculated to lull us into a false sense of security.

'Talking of the husband. He works for you too, I believe.'

'That's right,' Paul said. 'He's our storeman.'

'What sort of a man is he?'

'Jim? Quiet, reliable, typical countryman born and bred ... why? What are you getting at?'

'Were they happily married, would you say?'

'As far as I know ... Hang on a minute, what's this all about?'

I levered myself away from Paul, crossing to the sofa. My ankle was beginning to ache badly and besides, I really felt I needed to sit down.

'I think it's fairly obvious,' I said. 'DS...?'

'Wright.'

'DS Wright is asking whether we think it's possible that *Jim* killed Ruth.'

'That's ridiculous!' Paul said sharply. 'Jim wouldn't hurt a fly! Besides, he worshipped the ground Ruth walked on.'

'Hmm.' The sergeant's mouth twisted wryly. *I've heard it all before*, I could imagine him thinking.

'Jim is devastated!' Paul went on. 'You can't for one moment think that *Jim—*'

'It's a fact that most murders are committed within the family,' I said. 'Of course that's what he thinks.'

'No one is accusing Mr Wood of anything at the moment,' the sergeant said smoothly. 'Your wife is right, of course. The majority of murders *are* committed by the spouse, or at any rate by someone well known to the victim. But for the moment we are keeping an open mind. Looking at every possibility.'

Paul shook his head. 'Well, I hope so, because I'm sorry, but I just don't see Jim Wood as a wife-killer. He's just not the type.'

'And what type is that, sir?'

Paul gave him a withering look.

'They were happy, I'm sure of it,' I said. 'From the little Ruth said to me, they had a perfectly normal life. Probably more normal than ours.' The sergeant threw me a questioning glance and I went on: 'As a rule I live and work in London during the week. The only reason I've been at home for the last couple of weeks is because I'm recovering from an accident. But Ruth and Jim ... well, Ruth was very domesticated. And I know they had been trying for ages to start a family.'

'Ah! So she did talk to you then!' He said it triumphantly; I was beginning to dislike the man.

'Occasionally, when I was here. But only in the most casual, general way. As we have already explained, all Ruth did was to look

171

after the house for us. I really don't know anything about the intimate details of her life.'

'Nor you, sir?' Detective Sergeant Wright looked directly at Paul. 'If your wife is away all the week, I imagine you had more contact with Mrs Wood than she did.'

Once again, his tone was vaguely offensive, and Paul reacted angrily.

'If you are suggesting there was something between me and Mrs Wood, you have got it quite wrong. I employed her, sergeant, because she was an excellent cook and very good at keeping this house running smoothly, not for any other reason. And before you suggest that too, it was not me who met her at Hawley Woods and murdered her, for whatever reason. But I can tell you this – I'd like to get my hands on the bastard who did!'

The policeman smiled grimly. 'In that case, sir, I take it we can rely on you to give us every assistance with our enquiries.' He got up and the silent girl who was his shadow got up too. 'I don't think there's anything more at the moment, but we'll be in touch. And if anything else occurs to you that might be of use, perhaps you'll contact us.'

'Naturally,' Paul said stiffly. 'That goes without saying.'

'What an insufferable man!' I exploded when they had left. 'Poor Jim – having to deal with someone like that on top of everything else!'

'I don't suppose he's the one questioning Jim,' Paul said grimly. 'I expect Jim has got someone more senior – and probably infinitely worse!'

'Probably. I know they're only doing their job, and nobody wants Ruth's killer caught more than I do, but all the same...'

'They shouldn't approach it from the standpoint of assuming people to be guilty, I agree. He even made *me* feel guilty, for heaven's sake, as if *I* had something to hide, and it's nothing whatever to do with me.'

'It's their way, I suppose,' I said, trying to be reasonable.

'When they're in uniform it's even worse,' Paul went on. 'If I'm driving and see a police car behind me with its light flashing, I immediately wonder what the hell I've done wrong, even though they're probably just on their way to an accident or something. Stupid really, but it reduces me to a naughty schoolboy again, with the headmaster on my tail. I dread to think what poor Jim Wood must be going through. Just as if he'd take his wife out to Hawley Quarry and strangle her!'

'Nobody said she was strangled at Hawley Quarry,' I pointed out.

Paul frowned. 'But her car was found in the woods.'

'Yes, but somebody else could have driven

it there – *after* she'd been killed. To make it look as if that was where the attack took place. Rather than somewhere else ... somewhere that might have been awkward or incriminating for the killer.'

'You're suggesting *Jim* drove the car there? With her in it – dead?'

'No, of course not. I'm saying we don't know where she was killed. Not that Jim was responsible.'

'I'll bet that's what the police are saying, though – or insinuating, at least. And to him. Poor bloke – as if he didn't have enough to bear, without that too.'

'Paul,' I said. 'If Jim is grieving as I'd expect him to, I'm sure he won't even notice.'

Twenty-One

We were so preoccupied by the shock of learning Ruth had been murdered that it was halfway through the evening before we even thought of checking the answering machine to see if anyone had called us whilst we were away.

The little digital dial showed seven calls. Paul hit the replay button, and we listened rather abstractedly as the voices came on one after the other.

One from Josh, passing on a message from a client, two from Marian, confirming, amongst other things, that she had sent my report off to Poyson Associates, one from Tony Bowman.

'Julia. My secretary tells me you were trying to get hold of me. I'm not in the office this week, but if it's urgent call me on...'

'Who the hell is Tony Bowman?' Paul asked, stopping the machine whilst I jotted down the number.

'Oh, he's a financial consultant.'

'Why were you ringing a financial consultant?'

'Nothing to do with finance. I wanted to

175

pick his brains. He used to be based in Hong Kong and there's nothing he doesn't know about the colony. Well, perhaps that's a bit of an exaggeration. But he is pretty knowledgeable.'

'Hong Kong.' There was a slight edge to Paul's voice – or was I imagining it? 'The project you were working on, I presume.'

'Not exactly.' I hesitated, reluctant to tell Paul the real reason for my call to Tony Bowman. 'I'll explain later. Let's finish the messages.'

He gave me a look, and restarted the machine.

Josh again. 'Paul – can you give me a ring when you get back? I need to talk to you in case you haven't heard the news.' He sounded shocked and stressed, not at all the usual breezy Josh. I guessed he must have phoned as soon as he had heard that Ruth's body had been found.

We looked at one another without speaking, and Paul reached over to squeeze my hand.

The sixth message was my mother: 'Just to say how lovely it was to see you. Lots of love.'

The seventh made my heart sink as I recognized the voice.

'Oh hello, Julia ... Paul. This is Helen Gibbs. You're obviously not back yet, so I'll call again at the weekend to arrange a suitable time to come down and see you about

... well, the job. I hope you didn't have second thoughts. I'm really looking forward to it. Bye!'

'Oh shit!' I said. 'Now see what you've done!'

'Oh Julia, I am sorry. It seemed such a good idea at the time.'

'Because you were three sheets in the wind,' I said bluntly. 'Honestly, Paul, I could cheerfully strangle you...' I broke off, feeling sick as I realized what I'd said.

'I suppose I did get a bit carried away,' Paul said ruefully. 'And I know you seem to be set against the idea. But to be honest, I can't see what's so wrong with it. She sounded really well qualified. It's not as if I offered the job to someone totally unsuitable just because I felt sorry for them. And we are going to need someone fairly urgently if you intend going back to London next week. It could take ages to find the right person through the usual channels.'

'Mm, I know. We were so lucky with Ruth.'

'I think we should at least let her come down and have a look at the place – see how we all feel then,' Paul suggested.

I grimaced. 'I know how I feel now! I feel that I've been backed into a corner. And I also feel as if I'm betraying Ruth by even thinking of replacing her so soon after...' I broke off, unable to say the words.

'I know.' Paul squeezed my hand again.

'But we have to be practical, Jules. And Helen did seem heaven-sent. If you still hate the idea after we've talked to her, we'll think again. But she could be the answer to all our problems.'

'Perhaps you're right,' I said doubtfully. The thinking part of my mind was telling me that he was. Helen did seem ideal – added to which we'd be helping her out of a hole at a difficult time of her life. But none of that made any difference to my instinctive resentment of her. Had something happened on Magnetic Island which had made me dislike her, even though I'd forgotten all about it – and her? Or was I just taking it out on her because I *couldn't* remember her, whilst she seemed to remember me so well? I simply didn't know.

It was much later, as I lay tossing and turning in bed, unable to sleep, that something rather odd occurred to me.

'Paul – are you awake?' I whispered.

No reply. Just Paul's even breathing. How on earth could he go to sleep after such a terrible day I wondered. But that was Paul all over. Perhaps it was men in general. Able to switch off, whatever. After a blazing row, probably even if the house was falling down around us. I only wished I could be the same. But I couldn't. I lay turning over in my mind the thought that had occurred to me, trying to find an explanation for it.

When Paul had told Helen to call us, he'd given her one of his business cards – and they were printed with the address and telephone number of Stattisford Electronics. Yet Helen had rung here – our home – and we were ex-directory. How had she known the number?

She must have rung Stattisford first and somebody had given it to her, I supposed. Or maybe Paul had scribbled it on the back of the card. He did that sometimes. I hadn't seen him do it, but maybe it was one he'd inscribed for someone else and never given it to them, so it was still in his wallet, the one that had come to hand most easily. But for some reason I found the explanation un-satisfactory, and it made me uneasy.

'You are getting paranoid, Julia,' I told myself.

But still it nagged at me.

It was a very long time before I fell asleep.

Twenty-Two

Paul had been right about the phone bill being due any day. It dropped through the letter box next morning, along with the monthly bank statement, and a sheaf of junk mail.

Paul had gone into the village to buy bread and milk and a morning paper and to fill his car up with petrol. By the time we had got home last night, the tank had been almost empty, but after seeing the report about Ruth's murder, getting petrol had been the last thing on our minds.

I put the bank statement on one side for him, and tore open the envelope containing the telephone bill. There was so much of it in these days of itemized accounts – several sheets covering the breakdown of calls as well as the bill itself, which was, I noted with a sense of shock, a good deal larger than I would have dreamed it would be. Perhaps that was normal, though. As I've mentioned before, Paul deals with the bills and I don't usually get to see them.

I flicked down the list of calls, looking for last Friday's date. There were just three calls listed – and all the numbers were familiar and instantly recognizable – two that I'd made to London whilst I'd been working, and one to Stattisford – when Paul had rung Josh, presumably. So – nothing there. The police were going to be disappointed.

I let my eye run idly back up the list. There were several numbers that meant nothing at all to me – *Leatherhead?* Who did we know in *Leatherhead?* Fascinating! I wondered if Paul bothered to check them, which was, after all, the whole point of having an itemized bill. He probably did, knowing him.

I skimmed on, simply out of interest, then stopped, frowning. In the last quarter, three calls had been made to a Hong Kong number – expensive calls, too! Why on earth had Paul made them from home instead of from the office? I hoped he'd remembered to claim the cost of them back on expenses.

The sound of his car on the drive; the slam of the back door. Paul was back. He came into the kitchen juggling a loaf of bread in a paper bag and a carton of milk. The morning paper was tucked underneath his arm.

'You've been a long time,' I said as he went to put the milk in the fridge.

'I popped over to the office after I'd filled the car up, just to see if anything important had come in.' He returned to the table for the bread and noticed the pile of envelopes. 'Post?'

'The bank statement.' I pushed it towards him. 'And the phone bill has arrived. I can't see anything on it that might have been the call Ruth made. The only ones with last Friday's date are those two of mine, and one which must have been you ringing Josh.'

Paul came to look over my shoulder. 'Of course, if it was a local call it wouldn't necessarily show up,' he said thoughtfully. 'They don't if they're less than forty pence, and you can get quite a lot of time for that.'

'I suppose so...' I frowned suddenly. 'How long, exactly?'

'Oh, I don't know ... about three minutes for thirty pence? Something like that.'

'So why is your call to Josh showing up?' I asked. 'You were on the phone hardly any time at all.'

'It must have been longer than you realized. It's very difficult to judge these things.'

'Well, I wouldn't have thought it would have taken anything like ... what? six or seven minutes ... to say what you did. Unless you rang them some other time, of course, and we're talking about two different calls. Did you?'

'I don't think so. I don't remember. What are you getting at?'

'Just wondering if it was Ruth – calling Jim. For all we know they might have had daily conversations every hour on the hour at our expense. You'd never have thought twice about it, would you, since it's your own firm's number.'

'True. But it hardly matters now.'

'No.' I felt a stab of guilt, as if I were begrudging poor Ruth her last conversations with her husband, and also for the thought which had fleetingly crossed my mind – had Ruth phoned to arrange to meet Jim somewhere after she left work? But, of course, it simply didn't add up. If, as the police suspected, a husband had killed his wife, he wouldn't need to arrange to meet her in an out-of-the-way place to do it. And in any case, I really couldn't believe it of Jim.

'You know, I've never really looked at an itemized phone bill before,' I said. 'You always deal with ours, and at the office they're checked out by accounts. But it's fascinating! Take this – there's a call here to Leatherhead. Who on earth is that?'

'Haven't a clue. Unless it's the mail-order company I got those handmade shirts from.'

'And Hong Kong. You've been making business calls from home, Paul. I hope you're charging them.'

I glanced up and caught the most peculiar expression on his face, something that might almost have been guilt, a quick red flush staining his fair skin.

'You haven't been charging them?' I said.

'Yes – yes, of course I have!'

The doorbell, loud and piercing, made me

183

jump almost out of my skin. I can't stand melodic chimes, but our bell, the old-fashioned sort, screwed on to one of the beams in the kitchen, can be pretty ear-splitting when someone leans heavily on the button.

'Who on earth is that?' I exclaimed. 'The police again, do you think?'

'I'll go.' Paul disappeared into the hall and I waited apprehensively. Then, as I recognized the voice of the caller, I relaxed. It wasn't the police. It was Peter Dawson, our GP.

'Just popped in on my way home from Saturday-morning surgery to check you out, Julia,' he said, following Paul into the kitchen.

'Peter! That's nice of you. I'm much better, thank you – as regards my accident, anyway. I'm pretty shocked though, I must admit, about what's happened to Ruth.'

'Yes – dreadful business, isn't it? I've had the police at the house asking questions, and also at the surgery. She was a patient of mine. But let's not get sidetracked. It's you I came to see. How's the wrist?'

'Still a bit achy, but otherwise improving. I'm hoping to go back to work next week.'

'Mm ... well, we'll see about that...'

'Look, if you'd like to check Julia out in the sitting room, I'll put the coffee pot on,' Paul said. 'I'm sure you could do with a cup after

184

wrestling with the village hypochondriacs.'

'The heart-sink patients, you mean. The ones who think they'll be dead before Monday if they don't get an urgent appointment. Why is it my surgery is full of them, while people like Julia, who actually need my attention, make it a point of honour to stay away?'

I shrugged and tried to smile. 'Sorry, Peter, it's nothing personal.'

'I hope not!'

We went into the sitting room. Peter had a look at my wrist and my ankle and asked me a good many searching questions.

'Well, Julia, if you feel up to it, I see no reason why you shouldn't go back to work next week, though I do think you should be looking at a shorter than usual working day. And certainly nothing to aggravate that wrist. But then, you've got someone to type your letters for you, I presume.'

'Of course.'

'OK. What about headaches?'

'Better. Not completely, but better. Until this business with Ruth.'

'And the memory? No more lapses?'

I hesitated, thinking of the annoying blanks that persisted. Helen Gibbs, for instance. But I didn't want to go into that now.

'Better too.'

'Well,' Peter said, giving me a direct look, 'I think you're on the mend. But I wouldn't

185

advise you to drive, for another week or so at least. And you also have to bear in mind that you are pregnant and try to discipline yourself accordingly.'

I thought, but didn't say, that I had no intention of letting a little thing like pregnancy interfere with my working life until I absolutely had to. Once I was a hundred per cent fit, there was no reason why I couldn't go on working right up until the baby was born.

'Make an appointment at the surgery,' Peter went on. 'We need to sort out your antenatal care, dates for scans, and so on. And keep an eye out to make sure everything is progressing as it should be.'

In spite of myself I felt a moment's sharp apprehension. 'And is it?' I asked, keeping my tone light. 'Progressing as it should be, I mean?'

'At the moment – fine, as far as I can tell. And your blood pressure is normal, which is more than I can say for some of my patients – or myself, come to that.'

I smiled. Peter looked the sort who might well suffer from blood pressure. He was thickset, with a bullet-shaped head and the beginnings of a formidable paunch.

'So – you think it would be all right for me to go back to London?' I asked.

'Given the provisos I've already mentioned, I think it might actually be a good

186

idea,' Peter said. 'It's not exactly what you might call the best environment for recuperation here at the moment, is it? I think a change of scene and a little dose of normal office life might help to take your mind off things.'

'Good. I hope you'll tell Paul that. He does tend to try to wrap me in cotton wool, and though he didn't object when I suggested going back next week, I wouldn't be at all surprised if he doesn't have a change of heart and try to persuade me against it.'

'I expect he's pleased to have you here for a change – and that's quite understandable,' Peter said easily. 'And he did tell me how much he was looking forward to the baby and you being at home when it arrives.'

'Really?' I looked at him closely. 'When did he tell you that?'

'Oh, we had a beer together down at the local whilst you were in hospital. Now, how about that coffee he promised me? I have to call in on Doris Franklin in a minute and I could do with some fortification first. She's a dear old soul, but she does tend to bend my ear! Comes from living alone, I expect. And today she'll have a field day. She'll want to chew over every bit of news about poor Ruth.'

A thought struck me. Peter was a police surgeon, I knew. Once, when he and his wife had been having supper with us, he'd been called out to a sudden death – a fatal road accident, if I remembered rightly.

'Was it you who got called out when they found Ruth?' I asked now.

'No, thank God. They brought in a chap from town.' His eyes levelled with mine, as if he had read my mind. 'I'm afraid I know no more about it than the rest of you.'

We went back into the kitchen, which was now full of the delicious aroma of fresh coffee.

'The real stuff – lovely!' Peter said, sniffing appreciatively. 'I've had nothing but stewed tea since breakfast. Though I dare say Doris Franklin might spoil me with a glass of sweet sherry...'

We sat around the big pine table, chatting over the coffee.

'How's business?' Peter asked Paul.

'Oh – ticking over, you know.'

'Not hit too hard by the recession?'

'No more than anyone else,' Paul said. 'We've seen a few of our best customers go under, of course, but then, who hasn't?'

His tone was nonchalant, but I detected a slight note of strain, and I wondered if perhaps there was something Paul was not telling me. I thought again of the itemized telephone bill and the calls to Hong Kong which he'd made from home. What had they been about, and had he had a reason for not making them from the office? Might it be that he hadn't wanted the staff overhearing his conversation?

Peter stayed for another half-hour or so. He seemed not at all anxious to go, and I couldn't say I blamed him. I was glad I wasn't the one who had to call on Doris Franklin, with her ulcerated legs and her sweet sherry and her incessant chatter which never bore any real resemblance to a proper conversation. Doris was very deaf, but steadfastly refused to wear the hearing aid her long-suffering son had forked out good money for. As a GP, looking after Doris and all the others like her was just part of Peter's job, and it was the life he'd chosen. But all the same, I had a deep admiration for anyone who worked in the caring professions. I certainly couldn't have faced it day after day!

'Better go, I suppose,' he said at last, getting up reluctantly and reaching for the tweed jacket he'd draped across the back of one of the kitchen chairs. With it he was wearing cords, rather shiny and bagged at the knees, and a violently checked shirt. His socks, I'd noticed with some amusement, were odd, one brown, and one navy blue. Peter might be an excellent doctor and a good friend, but a fashion plate he was not.

'We really must get together again sometime soon,' he said, picking up his battered brown leather medical bag. 'I rather think it's our turn to do the honours. I'll have a word with my social secretary and get her to give you a call.'

Peter always referred to Lucy, his wife, as his social secretary when it came to making arrangements for supper parties, summer barbeques or New Year celebrations.

'We'll look forward to it,' I said, and thought with a pang that it was a good thing it was Peter and Lucy's turn to play host. When they, or any of our other friends, came to us, I usually relied on Ruth for the preparation of the food. Not any more!

'Well, at least he's given me a clean bill of health,' I said when Paul came back from seeing Peter out. 'He says I can go back to work on Monday provided I don't overdo it.'

Although Paul had seemed fairly resigned to my plans when I'd mentioned going back to London yesterday, I was still half-expecting him to object now that the moment had come, especially after Peter's comments. To my surprise, he didn't.

'Yes, sure. It might be the best thing.'

Though objections were the last thing I wanted, somehow this complete change in attitude niggled at me oddly.

'You *are* trying to get rid of me, aren't you?' I said teasingly, but not entirely jokingly.

Paul's face was serious. 'In a way, yes. I think you might be better off in London with things as they are.'

A chill whispered over my skin, a feeling of

apprehension I couldn't quite put a name to.

'Peter said much the same. That this isn't exactly the ideal atmosphere for rest and recuperation at the moment.' Yet somehow I felt it was more than that. It was no more than the truth, yet it didn't quite explain the sombre expression on Paul's face.

'It's not the atmosphere I'm worried about,' he said, confirming my suspicion. 'It's the thought that there might be a psychopath on the loose round here. I'd be worried to death going off to work and leaving you here on your own. Ruth has been murdered, for God's sake. For all we know whoever killed her might do it again, and we are very isolated out here.'

I can look after myself ... On the point of saying it, automatically, without thinking, because it was my usual confident response, I stopped, the unspoken words sounding banal and trite even to me. The truth of the matter was I was no longer sure I could look after myself any more – the events of the last couple of weeks had seriously undermined my normal brimming self-confidence.

The shadow of the things that had happened to me was bad enough. The stench of the car park was still all too real to me, along with the horrible feeling of apprehension and the shock of falling – being pushed – down the stairs. Then there was the terror I'd felt when I'd believed there was an intruder

191

in the house. I couldn't forget that either. And now it was even worse. As Paul had pointed out, someone had strangled Ruth and dumped her body in the brackish water at Hawley Quarry. Sometimes the things that seemed like figments of an overworked imagination weren't just silly insubstantial fears at all. Sometimes they were real. And realizing that was a shock in itself, as debilitating as the fear, because one never really expected such things to happen in the course of one's mundane, ordered life.

'You really think it was just a random killing?' I asked. 'Some crazy madman? And poor Ruth was just in the wrong place at the wrong time?'

Paul shook his head. 'I don't know what to think. I only know that I simply can't believe that Jim had anything to do with it.'

'I know,' I agreed. 'Neither can I. Oh Paul, it's like a nightmare.'

'One which I'll be glad to see you out of. You know I'd like nothing better than for you to be here all the time, Julia, and I never thought I'd say it, but to be honest, until we know what the hell is going on round here, I really think you'd be safer in London.'

'Oh Paul!' I went to him, burying my face in his shoulder, ashamed that I should have thought for a single moment that he had his own reasons for wanting me out of the way. He held me for a moment, very tightly, then raised the very subject I'd wanted to avoid.

'There's just one thing. Before you go, we've got to decide what we're going to do about Helen Gibbs.'

I sighed. I didn't want to think about Helen Gibbs.

'Oh, I suppose we have. She said she was going to ring again, didn't she?'

'Yes, and I'm sure she will. She seems very keen. Personally, Jules, I think we should give her a chance. But I don't want to put my foot in it again. We really need to talk to her together, if you'll agree to see her, and come to a joint decision. I know you have your reservations, but...'

'Well, yes, I have...' I hesitated. I was finding it more and more difficult to justify, even to myself, my aversion to the idea of employing Helen. There was absolutely nothing to back up the unease I felt about it, and I was beginning to think it was an overreaction on my part born of my recent feelings of vulnerability. 'Oh, maybe I'm just being silly. I mean, you're quite right really. She does seem to have quite a lot going for her.'

'Including being available to start more or less immediately, I imagine. Goodness knows how long it would be before someone as well qualified as she seems to be comes along. This isn't exactly the metropolis when it comes to finding staff. A cleaning woman, maybe, but...'

193

'Even that wasn't as simple as you'd think,' I interrupted. 'Don't you remember what a disaster that first woman we had turned out to be? She drove me mad, not to mention ruining all my best underwear...'

'So you agree we should at least talk to Helen again?' Paul persisted.

I found myself nodding reluctantly. 'Yes, I suppose so.'

'Then in that case, I suggest I give her a call and see if she can come down tomorrow, while you're still here. Otherwise it will be another week before we can talk to her together.'

Again I encountered a nugget of resistance; again I tried to overcome it. The thought of our last day before I returned to London being disrupted by having to interview Helen Gibbs made my heart sink – though I supposed 'interview' was scarcely the right word to describe what would be more of a social call, since Helen was supposed to be a long-lost friend. What was more, if we took her on, I was going to have to get used to her being around on other precious Sundays, since she'd be living under our roof, and that was not an appealing prospect either. But Paul was right; we had to do something about finding a replacement for Ruth fairly urgently, and it was foolish to dismiss Helen as a possibility without even talking to her again. As for my resentment, that probably came from the way I felt she'd foisted herself on us. I really should give her a chance.

'I'll phone her now then, shall I? Strike while the iron's hot?' Paul was saying.

'All right,' I agreed, then heard myself adding hopefully: 'Though she might have changed her mind, of course, if she's heard about Ruth...'

Paul smiled slightly and I wondered if he was thinking the same as me – that given Helen's eagerness to find herself a niche, it was probably just wishful thinking on my part that something like that would put her off. If it had occurred to him too though, he didn't say so. He went off to telephone, and I sat down at the kitchen table. The itemized phone bill still lay there – unusual for Paul not to have put it away. Perhaps he had left it out in case the police called again and wanted to see it. I pulled it towards me, running my eye down the list of calls again.

Times! My eyes narrowed suddenly as I noticed that the times of the calls were printed in a column next to the dates. Why hadn't I spotted that before? Because I'd been too preoccupied with who had been on the receiving end, presumably. I turned back to the sheet covering the Friday when Ruth had disappeared, and skimmed down the list until I found the call that had been made to the Stattisford number.

Fifteen forty-three. Somehow, deep down, I think I'd already known it, but seeing it in black and white still jarred me with a sense of heightened awareness. So, I'd been right to query the fact that Paul's short call to Josh was the one that had shown up. There *had* been another call – at about the time when I'd thought I'd heard the ping of the receiver going down. And only Ruth could have made it.

'I've spoken to Helen. She's coming down to see us tomorrow afternoon,' Paul said, coming back into the kitchen.

'Oh, right...' My mind was only half on what he was saying. 'Paul – look at this. It *was* Ruth who phoned Stattisford. The call is timed at a quarter to four – just before she left. It was lunchtime when you rang Josh.'

Paul stared at the bill over my shoulder. 'Well, I'll be blowed! I never realized before that they gave the times as well as the dates.'

'Nor me. I've only just noticed it. Do you think we should call the police and tell them?'

'Oh I don't think so,' Paul said, rather hastily, I thought. 'She must have been ringing Jim and they'll only start hassling him again to know what it was about. They might even think it's more evidence to build a case against him.'

'But suppose it *wasn't* Jim she called,' I persisted.

Paul frowned. 'Who else could it have been?'

'I don't know. But she used to work at Stattisford before she came to us. Maybe there's someone she's still friendly with.'

'She was an office cleaner, Julia.' Paul's tone was dismissive. 'She worked in the evenings and early mornings. The only people who would have been in the office at the same time as she was would be the other cleaners. And in any case, that was two and a half years ago.'

I chewed on my lip. 'Yes, I suppose that's true.'

'In any case, the police said they were going to get a copy of the printout. They'll probably pick this up without any help from us, and follow it up if they think there's any mileage in it.' Paul leaned across and took the bill from me. 'I'll file this away with my bills to be paid. I don't want it going missing so we forget all about it and get cut off.'

He went off into his study but I remained where I was, deep in thought. Paul felt quite protective towards Jim, I knew, but all the same he had been very quick to stamp on the suggestion that we should mention Ruth's call to the police. And there had been a look in his eyes I hadn't been able to read. A look that was almost ... shifty. Was it possible he had some suspicion as to who it was Ruth had spoken to on that last afternoon just

197

before she met her death? And if so, why was he keeping quiet about it?

With slow dawning horror, I realized what it was that had been niggling away at my subconscious.

I'd assumed there was no connection between all the disturbing and downright terrible things that had been happening recently. But there was.

The connection was Stattisford Electronics.

Twenty-Three

For a moment I sat totally still, so shocked by the realization, I might have been carved out of stone. Even my mind seemed to go blank for a few seconds. Only my nerves twanging and prickling seemed to have any sort of life in them.

My first instinct was to tell Paul, ask him if he could think of any possible connection. But with almost total certainty I knew he'd pooh-pooh it. And certainly it did seem almost too far-fetched for words. I chewed on a fingernail, my mind racing.

My accident – Ruth's murder – something highly suspicious about Stattisford's components suppliers, Kowloon and Victoria ... was there a link? Or was I letting my imagination run away with me? Just because awful things kept happening didn't necessarily mean they were connected in any way. *When sorrows come, they come not as single spies but in battalions.* Wasn't that one of the unwritten laws of the universe? Perhaps I was trying to make sense of something that had no rhyme or reason in it at all. And yet...

Paul came back into the kitchen, startling

me almost, since I was so lost in my thoughts.

'I think we ought to go to the supermarket, you know. There's hardly any food in the house. The milk and bread I got in the village isn't enough to keep us going all weekend.'

It took me a moment to drag myself back to the mundane world. Food had been the last thing on my mind. But he was right, of course. Whatever else was going on in our lives, and however preoccupied I was with it, we had to eat!

'I suppose we'd better,' I said with a sigh.

Paul gave me a narrow look. 'Do you feel up to it?'

'Considering I'm going back to work on Monday, I don't suppose a jaunt round the supermarket should be beyond me,' I said, trying to sound light-hearted. 'I'll make a list.'

I found a pencil and began scribbling on the back of one of the envelopes that had contained junk mail, whilst Paul opened cupboards and the fridge, checking the contents and calling out to me the items we needed.

When we were ready, I threw on a fleece over my sweatshirt and jeans and put on my trainers. It was lovely to be able to wear them again. The strapping on my ankle had been too bulky to fit under the high cuff of the trainer; now that Peter had removed it I felt like a kid on holiday as I laced my trainer and wriggled my toes appreciatively.

We drove to the out-of-town Tesco where Ruth had always done our weekly shop, and pushed the trolley round the aisles. It seemed to take forever – the store was crowded, with long queues at the delicatessen counter and the checkouts, and we kept missing things and having to retrace our steps, partly because we weren't very familiar with the layout, and partly because we weren't really concentrating on what we were doing.

'We could stop off for a pub lunch,' Paul suggested hopefully as we emerged from the store into the bright but chilly sunshine.

'We could – if we hadn't bought so much frozen stuff. If we don't get home soon it will all defrost,' I pointed out.

'So we'll take it home and then go out. I think I'm just about ready to do justice to a bowl of fish soup at the Dog and Duck. God, how I hate shopping!'

'Has to be done!'

'The sooner we get someone to take care of it again the better as far as I'm concerned,' Paul said with feeling.

'I'm not sure that I want to go out,' I said when he'd loaded the overflowing bags into the boot of the car. 'We've only just come back from holiday, and we did go to the Dog and Duck last Saturday. I think I'd rather have something at home.'

'That doesn't sound like you, Julia.' Paul sounded vaguely surprised.

I settled myself into the passenger seat and fastened my seat belt. 'I quite fancy making an omelette,' I said thoughtfully. 'I picked up some fresh herbs with the vegetables, and the tomatoes looked really quite good for the time of year.'

'Just as you like.' But he still sounded almost disbelieving, and I must admit I could hardly believe it myself that I was turning down the offer to be waited on in favour of cooking myself. But somehow the thought of the Dog and Duck, much as I liked the place, was not nearly as appealing as being in my own kitchen, just the two of us, and I actually had this peculiar and very unusual urge to wield a frying pan.

As I unlocked the back door, Oscar came streaking out of the bushes, rubbing himself against my legs and watching hopefully for the door to be opened.

'What is it about our house that attracts that cat so?' Paul asked, shooing him away.

'He's all right,' I said. 'If it wasn't for Molly and Jeff thinking we're trying to entice him away from them, I'd be only too pleased for him to come in. I rather like having him around.'

As we went into the lobby, I noticed through the half-open cloakroom door that the window was also ajar, and I was struck by the thought that Oscar hadn't made any attempt to get in that way this morning. All my misgivings about that night when I'd found him in the sitting room resurfaced, along with another thought: that muddy wet leaf on the kitchen floor. I'd never satisfactorily explained that to myself, either.

I tried to ignore the prickle of disquiet that was crawling over my skin, closed the cloakroom window, and followed Paul into the kitchen.

'Perhaps we could think about getting a cat ourselves,' Paul said, straightening up from stacking the first load of carrier bags against the leg of the kitchen table. 'Or even a dog, when you're here more. That would take care of Oscar and restore relations with Molly and Jeff. He wouldn't be so keen to invade if there was a dog here. And they do say a dog is the best deterrent to burglars that you can possibly have.'

'I'd like a dog,' I said. We'd had one at home when I was growing up, a lovely soft-mouthed golden retriever who ran great circles in the long waving meadow grass at the back of our house and lay, nose on her paws, at my feet whilst I was doing my homework. With both of us out at work and me away all week it had been out of the question for us to even consider getting a dog, and still was, at the moment, I supposed. But maybe some time in the future...

I had a sudden vision of myself pushing our baby in his buggy down the leafy lanes with a dog trotting alongside. There was a cosy warmth about it that temporarily dispelled the demons.

We'd unpacked the groceries and put them away, and I was chopping herbs for the omelette when we heard a car on the drive. Paul went to the window and looked out.

'It's Josh.'

'Oh no!' I groaned. Were we never going to get any time to ourselves this weekend?

Paul went outside to meet Josh and I went on chopping herbs with as much vigour as my still-weak wrist would allow. It was some time before they came inside, and it occurred to me that perhaps they were discussing something they didn't want to talk about in front of me. Business, perhaps? Or something to do with Ruth's murder? Whichever, I didn't much like it. Paul and I had never had secrets from one another that I was aware of. Now I found myself wondering if there might be something he was keeping from me.

I had the eggs whisked and the salad tossed by the time they came into the kitchen. Josh was looking as handsome as ever – no hotch-potch of weekend gear for him. He'd gone casual, it was true, wearing jeans and a leather bomber jacket instead of his business suit, but he still managed to look as if he'd stepped out of the pages of a Sunday supplement – coordinated, understated, drop-dead-gorgeous.

'Josh dropped by to fill us in on what's happened to Ruth,' Paul said, confirming at least part of my earlier suspicion. 'He thought as we've been away we might not know about it.'

'We could hardly have missed it,' I said tautly. 'The headlines were big enough to see. And we've had the police here asking questions.'

I didn't add that Josh himself had left a message on our answering machine to alert Paul.

'They've been to see me too,' Josh said. 'Mostly they were interested in Jim, I have to say.'

'Poor Jim! Why can't they leave him alone?' But it was a rhetorical question. Though personally I thought Jim was the last person to be guilty of Ruth's murder, I'd come to understand that to the police he was the prime – perhaps the only – suspect.

'I've asked Josh if he'd like to stay and have a spot of lunch with us,' Paul said.

'Oh – right.' I must have sounded less than overjoyed, because Josh said hastily: 'Not if it's any bother, Julia. I know this isn't the best of times for you.'

'No bother,' Paul said firmly. 'It's only omelette, but we're well stocked up with eggs and I'm sure the salad will stretch to three. Can I get you a drink while we're waiting? Beer? Lager?'

'A beer would be nice.'

Paul went off to fetch the cans from the fridge.

'Are you feeling better, Julia?' Josh asked.

'I guess so. I'm going back to work next week.'

'That should take your mind off things a bit. And you've got over your fright of the other night?'

'More or less.' I didn't want to admit I was still a bit spooked by it; still had my doubts as to just what had happened.

'I could kick myself, frightening you like that,' Josh said easily.

'Not your fault.' I put a knob of butter in the omelette pan and turned on the gas, glad of the excuse to keep busy. What on earth was it about Josh that I found so disconcerting?

'Here we are.' Paul was back with the beers. He handed one to Josh, who broke it open and leaned comfortably back against the sink, drinking straight from the can.

'So – did you enjoy your holiday, Julia?'

A natural enough question, but I couldn't help being aware that the subject was being changed to a brighter topic for my benefit.

'It was good, yes,' I said.

'And nice to see your family, I expect.'

'Yes.'

'The most peculiar thing, though,' Paul said, breaking open his own can of beer, 'an old friend of Julia's from her backpacking days happened to be staying at the very same hotel.'

'Good lord! Quite a surprise for you!'

'Yes, particularly since I don't remember her from Adam.' I glanced up from the sizzling butter in the omelette pan to see the men exchanging a look. 'I really don't,' I said, irritated. 'I don't think it has anything to do with my memory lapses.'

'Well, I guess we all meet eminently forgettable people in the course of a lifetime,' Josh said easily, covering the moment's awkwardness.

'Anyway,' Paul said, 'it could turn out to be a blessing in disguise. As you can imagine, we're pretty desperate to fill the vacancy left by Ruth's ... well, by Ruth ... and this girl seems to fit the bill perfectly.'

Something jarred in me, a half-worked-out thought. Helen fitted the bill perfectly. Yes, she did. Almost too perfectly. Was that what was bothering me about her? We needed a housekeeper, and suddenly there was Helen – a Cordon Bleu chef who'd also looked after children for a living, no ties, desperate for a job, and claiming to know me into the bargain. When I had no recollection of her at all.

'Paul virtually offered her the position on the spot,' I said.

Josh laughed. 'You don't waste much time, old son.'

'He'd had rather too much to drink at the time,' I said tartly. 'He's landed us in a situation we're going to have some trouble getting ourselves out of.'

'Oh!' Josh raised a quizzical eyebrow. 'You mean...?'

'There have been a few sticky moments,' Paul said ruefully. 'Julia was none too pleased, as you can tell. But I think she's coming round to the idea. Anyway, this girl – Helen – is coming down tomorrow to talk it over. We'll see how it goes. At least this time I'll be sober,' he added, with a wry glance at me.

The first omelette was done; I slid it on to a plate. It was thick and fluffy and I felt unreasonably pleased with myself. Long ago, at school, I'd been quite good at domestic science, but recently I'd done so little cooking I'd forgotten what fun it could be, and I'd thought I'd lost the knack too. Obviously not! Glowing with satisfaction, I put the plate down on the table.

'One of you make a start on this while I cook the others ... Josh?'

'No – I'll wait for you two. I am the cuckoo in the nest, after all.'

'No, start, please. It'll only go rubbery keeping warm in the oven. And you're not a cuckoo in the nest, anyway. Paul invited you, didn't he?'

'Just as he invited this friend of yours to come and work for you?' He said it lightly, but he was giving me a sympathetic look at the same time. How well Josh understood me! I thought. He always seemed to know exactly what I was thinking.

I'd just cooked the second omelette and put it down in front of Paul when we heard the fax machine in Paul's study begin whirring. Paul went to get up; I forestalled him.

'I'll get it. You have your omelette before it gets cold.'

I pulled the pan off the ring and went through into the study. The message was already half through, and as I leaned over the machine, taking hold of the thin sheet of paper, I felt a twist of anticipation. It was addressed to me – from the Hong Kong authorities! I waited, watching the printout appear on the page and reading it as it materialized.

Re your query regarding Kowloon and Victoria Enterprises. This matter is being dealt with. Will inform you of result of enquiry as soon as possible.

I tore the sheet off and stared down at it, chewing on my thumbnail. Nothing yet, then, but at least I hadn't been fobbed off with some guff about the matter being classified information, as I'd half expected I might be. How long would it be before I heard from them again? That was anyone's guess. Some enquiries of this sort were dealt with in a matter of days, others took weeks – or even months. I put the sheet of paper down on Paul's desk and went back to the kitchen.

'Well?' Paul enquired.

'It's all right – it wasn't for you. It was for me – an answer to an enquiry I made with the Hong Kong authorities.' I glanced at the clock, doing a mental calculation. 'Good heavens, they're working late! It's evening there, isn't it?'

'Hong Kong!' Josh raised an eyebrow in my direction. 'What's your interest in Hong Kong, Julia?'

'Oh, she's been doing a check on Sutherland Dewar for one of her clients,' Paul said. 'They want to team up...' He broke off, glancing at me apologetically. 'Sorry, love, it's confidential, isn't it? But Josh won't say anything, will you, Josh?'

'It is confidential, yes,' I said. 'But actually that wasn't what the fax was about. It was that other thing ... you know? The one I was telling you about.'

'Oh, that,' Paul said shortly. He put down his knife and fork. 'Perfect omelette, Julia. Go on and cook yours, for heaven's sake.

We've finished, and you haven't even started.'

'What other thing?' Josh asked.

I hesitated. Paul had been so dismissive of my suspicions regarding Kowloon and Victoria that I'd decided to say nothing more to him until I had some definite proof that something was amiss. But I hated the feeling that I was going behind his back. And in any case, if Stattisford were dealing with a company that had something to hide, then Josh had as much right to know about it as Paul did. In fact, there was every chance he would take it a good deal more seriously.

'Something a bit odd,' I began, but Paul cut across me.

'Cook your omelette, Julia! We don't want to hear about all your legal stuff, do we, Josh? Drives me barmy. Unless, of course, it's a good courtroom thriller on TV. Were you into *Murder One*? Now there was a programme to get hooked on! I'm not a telly addict by any means, but that was one I set time aside for. With the phone off the hook, to make sure no one interrupted while it was on...'

I glanced at Paul, puzzled. What on earth was he going on about? He had enjoyed *Murder One*, it was true. And I could vouch for the fact that he'd taken the phone off the hook when he was watching it. But it was unlike him to rabbit on at such length. And murder, even as a fictional television serial, wasn't a subject I would have thought even he felt comfortable with, given the present circumstances.

'Yes, it was addictive stuff...' I could tell from Josh's tone that he was almost as surprised as I was by Paul's unexpected departure from the conversation we'd been having. 'What was it you were saying, Julia? About Hong Kong?'

But somehow the moment for wanting to share my suspicions had passed. I'd wait to hear what the Hong Kong authorities had to tell me before saying anything to either of them, I decided. Knowing Josh, he might well go in with all guns blazing if I put him in the picture, and there was no point causing mayhem and possibly bad business relations if it was all a mistake.

'Nothing, really. As Paul said, it's just boring legal stuff.' I slid the omelette pan back on to the heat. 'Do you two want an ice cream or some cheese or something?'

Josh glanced at his watch. 'Actually, I must get going. I've got one or two things to do.'

'You won't even stay for a coffee?'

'Julia, don't hassle the man!' Paul chided.

'Well, fine! You were the one who asked him to lunch!'

'And very nice it was too,' Josh said, smiling at me. 'Just one thing, Paul. Do you think I could borrow the Fischer catalogues?

You've got copies here, haven't you? It will save me going over to the office.'

'Yes, sure. Actually there are some quite interesting new lines in the most recent one...' Paul got up, heading for his study, and Josh followed him. As I waited for my omelette to set I could hear them discussing the relative value of the Fischer components, poring over the catalogue, no doubt, and engrossed in technical detail. And Paul had the nerve to call *law* boring! Oh well, it was a good thing we were all different.

I suspected that now they were on to their favourite subject, whatever the things Josh had been going to rush off to do, they would have to wait!

'Do I understand you're still pursuing this Kowloon and Victoria thing, Julia?' Paul asked when Josh had finally left.

'Well, yes,' I admitted. 'I know you think I was imagining it when I saw their name on the file of companies who have been investigated for corrupt practices, but I know I wasn't. I'm concerned about it, Paul. I don't like to think you might be involved with a dodgy outfit.'

'For heaven's sake!' Paul exclaimed impatiently.

'It's all very well for you to bury your head in the sand,' I persisted. 'That's typical of you. But if there's some irregularity we

213

should know about, I intend to find out what it is.'

'I wish you'd just stick to your own business!' Paul's tone was unusually sharp. It shocked me.

'Excuse me...?'

'I'd have thought you had enough to do looking after your clients, without poking around in my preserve!'

That damned chip on his shoulder again! 'Oh, don't be so petty!' I flared, stung. 'Your preserve – mine – what does it matter? If Kowloon and Victoria are doing something illegal it could have serious repercussions for Stattisford, and in the last resort that means both of us.'

'A few more employees to the square foot than they should have in their factories?' Paul said sarcastically. 'Don't be ridiculous.'

'Even if that is all it is, I want to know about it,' I said, my crusading instincts now aroused. 'I'd hate to think we were profiting from sweatshop labour. But –' I hesitated – 'it might be a good deal more serious than that.'

'And it might be nothing at all. All this fuss...'

'If it's nothing, there's no harm done, is there?' I argued. 'I just don't understand why you are so against me trying to find out the reason your suppliers were investigated. I should have thought you'd want to know the

214

truth yourself, for your own peace of mind. But I intend to get to the bottom of it, even if you don't. And please don't tell me again that it's none of my business.'

Paul glared at me for a moment, face dark, eyes narrowed. Then the anger seemed to escape him like a deflating balloon. He ran a hand through his hair so that it stood untidily on end. 'I'm sorry, Julia. I didn't mean ... it's just that I ... I just don't want you going on with this.'

I frowned. 'What on earth do you mean?'

Paul was looking at me intently. 'Don't you realize you could be stirring up an awful lot of trouble?'

'For who?' I demanded. 'Kowloon and Victoria? Or Stattisford?'

'Sweetheart –' Paul's voice was quiet but deadly serious – 'I know what you're like when you get your teeth into something. You just can't let go. But hasn't it occurred to you that what you're dabbling with here might be dangerous?'

A frisson of fear chilled me suddenly, an echo of all the other fears. Then I shook my head disbelievingly. 'Dangerous? Oh Paul, really!'

'I'm serious, Julia, never more so.' He leaned towards me across the table. 'We are talking the Far East here. Crime on the sort of scale unheard of in this country. Organized crime. The Triads. The authorities have been trying to wipe them out for years, but they just can't do it. They're too big. Hundreds of thousands of members. And too powerful. They are also totally ruthless and very, very dangerous.'

'I know about the Triads, of course,' I said. 'I just don't see—'

'Say the Triads have an interest in Kowloon and Victoria. Do you really think they are going to sit back while you try to scupper them?'

'Paul – I'm in England. The Triads are in Hong Kong.'

'With contacts all over the world. And hangers-on, greedy for a share of the profits. They'll stop at nothing to make sure their little gold mine goes on keeping them in luxury.'

I shook my head in bewilderment. 'I don't believe I'm hearing this! Are you telling me that Stattisford is knowingly dealing with a company run by the Triads?'

'No, of course not. It's all hypothetical. What I am saying is that if you persist in turning over stones willy-nilly, it's just possible that something very nasty might come crawling out.'

I was shocked. 'And you've been thinking this all the time you were pretending to me that you thought I was imagining things? All the time you were trying to convince me that nothing could be amiss?'

'I've been trying to steer you away from getting involved,' Paul said. 'Always supposing there is something to get involved in. It may be nothing, of course, as you say. But then again, it may not. But if there is something, well, I don't want you putting yourself in danger.'

I gave my head a small shake. What Paul was suggesting was far more serious than anything I'd envisaged. But it did nothing to alter the basic principle.

'I see what you're saying, Paul, but I can't agree with you that we should just do nothing. If Kowloon and Victoria are clean and above board, then we have nothing to fear. If not, then surely you want to know about it?'

'Of course I do.' I had never seen Paul look more serious. 'I intend to follow this up, Julia, and find out exactly what is going on. I've already made a start, as it happens. But I don't want you involved. I want you to promise you'll stop asking awkward questions and drawing attention to yourself. I want you to leave it to me.'

'That's all very well, but if you think I could be in danger for simply asking a few questions, where does that leave you?' I asked shortly.

Paul smiled wryly. 'I don't go in with all guns blazing the way you do. I play things a little more subtly. Besides, I can take care

217

of myself.'

I snorted. 'Famous last words! If there is something going on, and these people are as powerful and ruthless as you say they are, I'd like to see you do it! And what about Josh? Does he know there's the possibility of some irregularity?'

'I haven't mentioned it to him yet, no,' Paul said. 'I want to clarify a few things first, find out the lie of the land.'

Just as I'd been doing, I thought. And then remembered the way Paul had talked over me – all that nonsense about *Murder One* – when I'd been about to explain what lay behind my fax from Hong Kong.

'That's why you were trying to shut me up,' I said. 'To stop me telling Josh about my suspicions.'

'More or less, yes. The fewer people who know you've started an investigation into this, the better.'

I stared at him. 'You're not suggesting that *Josh*—?'

'No, of course not,' Paul said. 'But we can't be too careful until we really know what the position is. Look – I think there's a pretty good chance that this is a lot of smoke without fire. But if Kowloon and Victoria is involved in something illegal, which by implication contaminates Stattisford, then I give you my word I'll do something about it. Even if it is only sweatshops or a sideline in counterfeiting. Does that satisfy you?'

'I suppose so...' I was very tired suddenly. Tired of arguing, tired of speculating, tired of shadows and suspicions and a world gone mad. Tired, tired, tired.

But even as I said it, I knew I was not going to let this go so easily.

We dropped the subject then, and the rest of the day was, to all intents and purposes, a perfectly normal Saturday. But I couldn't forget it any more than I could forget about the terrible thing that had happened to Ruth. It was on my mind as we pottered about the house and garden, and when we settled down in the evening to watch television, I couldn't concentrate. Everything had the aura of nightmare about it – the manic enthusiasm of the National Lottery, the film which followed.

'I'd like to watch the football really,' Paul said, and I marvelled that he could summon up the interest to care about something so unimportant when the whole of our lives seemed to be disintegrating around us.

'In that case, I'll go to bed,' I said.

'You don't mind if I don't come up yet?'

'No, of course not.' It was actually quite a relief to be on my own, not to have to keep up the pretence of normality any longer.

I went into the bedroom to pull the curtains. The night was very dark, no moon that I could see, but the stars were bright and sharp against the velvety blackness. I stood for a few minutes staring at them, deep in thought. More than ever I was convinced there was something odd going on which somehow involved Stattisford, and the fact that Paul was worried too made it all the more sinister. He wasn't the sort to get worked up over nothing. But for the life of me I couldn't see how all the things that had happened could be connected. My fall in the car park had been the morning after I'd first spotted Kowloon and Victoria on the list of suspect companies, long before I'd set any investigation in motion, and Ruth's association with Stattisford was minimal. It was two and a half years since she had worked there as an office cleaner, and Jim was just a storekeeper. He had nothing to do with the running of the firm, no direct contact with overseas suppliers. No, it had to be coincidence that all this had happened just now ... didn't it?

Again I remembered the quotation about troubles coming not as single spies but whole battalions. My grandmother used to say something very similar: *It never rains but it pours.* Misfortunes and traumas often come in clusters, I told myself. Sometimes it seems as if the whole planet is under some malign influence. The news is full of disaster and tragedy and everyone around you seems to have something to worry about, something going ghastly wrong in their lives. Just as at other times the world and his wife seems to have a smile on their face. Perhaps it is one of the unwritten laws of nature – or the stars and the planets. Ruth had been a great one for the stars. She'd never failed to read her horoscope. I'd teased her about it. What had it said, I wondered now, on the day of her death? A chill whispered over my skin. I'd always said it was nonsense. Now I wasn't so sure...

The moon had come out, throwing deep shadows across the lawn. I stared at them unseeingly, then stiffened as something moved in the bushes, just on the periphery of my vision. Someone was out there in the garden! I jerked my head round, my nerves taut and twanging – and saw Oscar's furry form slink out of the shrubs and stalk haughtily across the lawn.

The release of tension was so acute I laughed out loud. What an idiot! I was turning into a bag of nerves!

I undressed and got into bed. But the feeling of unease was still there, hanging over me like a malaise, and when at last I fell asleep, my dreams were as confused and disturbing as my waking thoughts had been.

Twenty-Four

Helen Gibbs arrived at about half past two the next afternoon. We went out to greet her.

'What a lovely house! What a lovely garden!' She looked around appreciatively. 'Oh, I know I'm going to love it here!'

Irritated by her presumption, I glanced at Paul, waiting for him to say that as yet nothing had been decided. But he appeared unaware of the implication in her remark.

'It is pleasant, yes,' he said easily, 'but an old house makes a lot of work, of course. There's a range in the kitchen, and open fires in the living room, and...'

'Oh, I don't mind that!' she broke in. 'I love open fires. And I'm not afraid of hard work either, I promise you.'

'We don't have any big stores on our doorstep either,' I pointed out, hoping to curb her enthusiasm a little. 'There's just a little Spar shop in the village. The nearest supermarket is half an hour's drive away.'

But Helen was not to be put off. 'That's no distance at all, is it?' she said blithely. 'That's what's so nice about Wiltshire. You get the best of both worlds.'

We went indoors, and showed her over the house, and to my chagrin she continued to enthuse about everything she saw.

'Which of these rooms would be mine?' she asked when we went upstairs. I hesitated. I didn't actually much like the idea of her having any of them!

'We thought the one at the end of the landing,' Paul said. 'It's the biggest – apart from ours – and there's a connecting door into the little box room next to it. We've been thinking for some time of making it into an en suite – it's ridiculous having only one bathroom in a house this size.'

Again I felt a twinge of resentment. We had talked about getting the work done, it was true, but I'd imagined it as a guest room for friends or my mother when she came to stay, not for a live-in housekeeper who'd been foisted on me.

'Mm perfect! And I'd be able to have my own television and radio, would I?'

'Oh yes, naturally.'

'What are you going to do with all your things?' I asked.

She gave me a look which was almost bewildered. 'My things?'

'Your furniture – all your bits and pieces.'

She smiled slightly. 'Oh, I haven't got much...'

'But surely if you've had a home for ... how

many years? I know how much stuff we've accumulated since we've been married,' I persisted.

Her smile became almost smug. 'I'm not a materialistic person. And I can't stand clutter.'

I wasn't going to let this go. 'But you're bound to have furniture.'

Paul shot me a look. 'I expect she's going to put it in store, Julia. That's what one usually does when between homes. Shall we go back downstairs – have a cup of tea?'

'That would be nice, yes.' Helen laughed, a little self-consciously. 'I must take notice of where everything is, mustn't I?'

Again I felt a flash of irritation – and misgiving. She was getting on my nerves already. How much worse would it be if she was here all the time?

'Look, I have to be straight with you, Helen,' I said when I had filled the kettle and put it on to boil. 'We don't really need, or want, anyone here at weekends. Our last housekeeper came in on Monday to Friday only, and whilst I appreciate that you would have to live in during the week, given your situation, I personally feel we need a certain amount of privacy.'

'Your last housekeeper.' She looked at me gravely. 'Was that by any chance the woman who's been in the news the last few days?'

'I'm afraid so, yes,' I said. 'Look – given all

the circumstances, Helen, I'm sure Paul and I will quite understand if you're no longer interested in the position.'

'Oh, but I *am* still interested – more than interested!' That irritating little smile was back on her face. 'You have no idea what a godsend this is to me, Julia. What happened to that poor woman is perfectly ghastly, but I can't see how it affects me. I mean – it wasn't you or your husband who killed her, was it? At least – I hope not.' She gave a small nervous giggle, and went on: 'As for the weekends – well, if you didn't want me here, then I'm sure I could spend them with my sister. She lives on the outskirts of Swindon and she has masses of room. We never seem to see enough of one another...'

So why don't you go and live with her? I thought crossly. No matter what objection I raised, Helen seemed to be able to counter it. She was like a limpet, latching on and holding tight.

'By the way,' she said now, 'I looked out some of my old photographs of Magnetic Island. I brought a couple down with me if you'd like to see them.'

Without waiting for my reply she fished in her bag, pulled out a paper wallet, and extracted a snapshot. Me – wearing the yellow bikini, sitting in the driving seat of a Moke, with a good-looking chap called – I think – Daniel, beside me.

'Who's that?' Paul asked, pointing to him.

'Oh, good heavens, just one of the crowd...'

Another photograph, another group, me centre-stage again, still wearing the bikini. The flavour of the pictures, as well as their content, was hauntingly familiar. I felt I'd seen them before.

'You aren't in any of them,' I said to Helen.

'Because I was taking them! Actually, I did manage to get in one. I think that's me there – hidden behind that girl's enormous sun hat. What was her name?'

'Can't remember. Sarah, was it?'

'I'm not sure. It seems like it happened in another lifetime now, doesn't it?'

The kettle was boiling. I made the tea, setting out cups, milk and sugar while it brewed.

'So,' Paul was saying, 'if we were to come to an arrangement, when would you be able to start?'

'As soon as you like. There's nothing to stop me from starting right away.'

'Don't you have things to sort out first?' I asked, still stalling. 'Your house, for instance, if it's going to be sold?'

'I should be able to see to that at weekends if you don't want me here then. I might have to ask for a couple of days off if things move faster than I expect, but that wouldn't be such a problem for you as not having anyone here at all, would it?'

'We haven't talked about money,' Paul said.

Quite suddenly I realized I needed to visit the bathroom rather urgently – one of the less pleasant side effects of being pregnant, I'd discovered. 'You'll have to excuse me for a minute,' I said.

As I went upstairs I found myself noticing with love and pride the little things I normally took for granted. The big arrangement of dried flowers and leaves in a pottery vase on the hall table which I'd had the local florist make up specially to complement the subtle shades of the carpet and curtains. The basket of soaps in the bathroom. The bathroom itself, which we'd had completely refitted after we moved in and which I'd chosen myself in a blissful couple of hours, from a carload of samples the man from the bathroom company had lugged in and spread out on the living-room floor. 'Have whatever you fancy,' Paul had said. 'I'll leave it entirely to you. As long as there's a shower and the mirror is high enough for me to shave in, I don't mind what it is. Though I'd rather it wasn't pink,' he'd added as a typically male afterthought. It wasn't pink. It was a lovely soft green with a huge white cast-iron bath, and marred only by the ugly but very necessary electric wall heater.

My home. Mine and Paul's. I couldn't believe how proprietorial I felt about it

suddenly. I didn't want to share it with anyone else, even though most of the time I
wouldn't be here when she was. Ruth had
been different. Ruth had gone off to her own
home at the end of the day. Ruth, let's face
it, had been perfect. But Ruth had gone. We
had to make other arrangements and whatever they were, they were likely to be less
than ideal. We couldn't possibly be so lucky
again.

But if I was feeling so possessive about the
house, how much more so was I going to feel
it about the baby? I'd always blithely
assumed I'd be quite happy to have a nanny
so that I could pursue my career. Now,
suddenly, I was less sure about that either.
Leave my child with someone else in the
most formative years of his life? For the first
time, I found myself wondering whether,
when it came to the point, I'd be able to
bring myself to do it.

When I went back downstairs, Paul and
Helen seemed to be getting on like a house
on fire. I joined in the conversation, but my
feelings of unease remained.

'Well,' Paul said when we had finished our
tea, 'Julia and I will talk it over and be in
touch.'

'Fairly soon?' Helen pressed.

'The minute we've come to a decision.'

'Right. It's just that ... well, if you're not
going to offer me the job, I'm going to have

to make other arrangements.'

'Of course. We understand that,' I said.

She slipped into her jacket. 'I do hope though ... I would so very much like it to be here. If you take me on, I promise you won't regret it.'

'We'll phone you,' Paul said.

'Well,' I said when he came back from seeing her out, 'I honestly don't know what to think, Paul.'

He lifted the teapot, swishing it round. 'Is there another cup in there, do you think? Or is it going to be stewed?'

'I expect it's still all right,' I said, my thoughts still preoccupied by Helen. 'You like her, don't you?'

'I must admit I think she's ideal,' Paul confirmed. 'You don't, though.'

'I'm not convinced...'

'I could tell that. What is it about her that bothers you?'

'I don't know,' I said truthfully. 'I honestly don't know. Perhaps it's not her at all. Perhaps it's me.'

He frowned. 'What do you mean?'

I chewed my lip. 'I don't ... feel myself. I'm getting all sorts of thoughts and feelings I've never had before. Is this what happens when you're pregnant?'

'I wouldn't know. I've never been pregnant.'

'No – you'd make history if you were!' I laughed, but the light relief was only momentary. 'Seriously, though, I really don't know what we should do. I mean – you're right. She *is* about as close to ideal as we're likely to get. And yet ... there's something about her that grates on me. Perhaps it's just that she's so persistent.'

'She is fairly desperate to sort herself out,' Paul suggested. 'It's making her come over as too keen.'

'I suppose so. But there's something odd. What about all her things? Her house. Her furniture. Her life!'

Paul looked perplexed. 'I thought she explained all that.'

'She came up with an explanation, yes. But it's just all too convenient.' I sighed. 'Oh, I don't know.'

'It's that lawyer's mind of yours,' Paul teased. 'You see problems where none exist.'

'Hmm, maybe. But I'm not even sure if I like the idea of a live-in housekeeper. It feels a bit ... well, claustrophobic.'

'I'm sure you'd get used to it,' Paul said. 'And whatever, if we don't make up our minds soon we'll lose her. You heard what she said – she's got to find something fairly urgently. I should imagine that means she'll continue to look elsewhere. Someone like her is going to be snapped up pretty smartly, whether she realizes it or not. She's well qualified, personable, with no ties...' He sipped his tea and pulled a face. 'Ugh! This *is* stewed.'

'I suppose you're right,' I said reluctantly. 'People of her calibre don't grow on trees. Do you think she'd agree to a trial period? I'm a bit loathe to offer her a job just like that, feeling as I do. But I have to admit I'm probably reacting all wrong. If she came for a period of three months, say, on the understanding that if either she or us was dissatisfied with the arrangement it could be terminated, then we wouldn't be losing much, would we? We wouldn't be committing ourselves to something we might regret. If she's a gem, then we could make it permanent. If not, we could get rid of her without fear of her running to an industrial tribunal.'

'I'm not sure she'd agree to an arrangement like that,' Paul said thoughtfully. 'She could sell her house, then find herself out on the street.'

'If she's as good as you say she is, that's not going to happen is it?' I said, determined to stick to my guns. 'Either we'll keep her, or someone else will snap her up. To be honest, Paul, that's as far as I'm prepared to go. A three months' trial period, no promises, no strings. If she's happy, then fine. If not, then I'd like to feel free to look around some more.'

'Even if it means we're without a house-keeper indefinitely?'

'Yep – 'fraid so.' I smiled. 'Who knows? I might decide we don't need a housekeeper. I might just come home and take care of things myself.'

'Promises, promises!'

'Don't laugh – I just might.'

'You, Julia? Pigs might fly!'

I laughed again. Suddenly I felt ridiculously light-hearted. 'Oh look!'

'What?'

'There goes a pig! Over the top of the church tower!'

He pulled me close. In the delicious intimacy of the moment, all our differences were forgotten.

'Shall I phone Helen this evening?' Paul asked much later. 'Put it to her that we're prepared to give it a try?'

And, warm and mellowed by our love making, and assailed by a thumping great dose of conscience for the past which Helen and I had shared, but which I had totally forgotten, I heard myself saying: 'Perhaps I should be the one to do it. After all, she is supposed to be my friend.'

Twenty-Five

I left for London on Monday morning. The sun was bright, though a brisk wind was making the shadows it threw blink and shift, and the daffodils bent low before it, brushing the dew-wet grass.

I'd spoken to Helen the previous evening and she had agreed to our terms. She said she would start on Wednesday or Thursday, and telephone Paul to confirm which it was to be. I did wonder whether I should have taken another week off to see her settled in, but I'd already been away from the office too long. With all my clients waiting on me, expecting me to make their problems a priority, I simply couldn't afford to take any more time off, and I didn't want to. Already, just getting dressed in my business suit and packing my files and briefcase in the car had fired my enthusiasm and made me eager to be back in harness.

I was anxious, too, to be able to get on with my investigations into Kowloon and Victoria without Paul looking over my shoulder all the time. With this in mind, I'd put a fax through to the Hong Kong authorities before I left, asking them to reply to my query at my London office. Since Paul was so opposed to me pursuing the matter, I didn't want their response coming through to the house in my absence.

As I drove through the village, I passed a police car and wondered if it had anything to do with Ruth. I leaned over and switched the car radio on, just catching the local news bulletin.

'Police searching for the killer of Ruth Wood are warning women in the area to exercise extreme caution whilst the murderer is at large. They are also appealing for anyone with any information to come forward. The victim's car, a white Fiesta, had been abandoned in nearby Hawley Woods, and police are anxious to talk to anyone who saw it during the afternoon or evening of the Friday on which she disappeared. They would also like to talk to anyone who was in the area at the time, in particular the driver of a dark BMW saloon which was seen parked on the edge of the woods.'

A nerve jumped in my throat, and suddenly I was thinking – Stattisford again! All the staff cars were dark-grey or midnight-blue BMWs, leased from a dealership in town – Paul's, Josh's, even a couple of pool cars which they had kept when they had traded up to newer models themselves. Of course, I told myself, it probably meant nothing at all. With the thriving dealership so close by, there must be hundreds of BMWs in the area, many of them dark in colour. And there was nothing to suggest that particular car had anything to do with Ruth's death anyway. A car parked on the edge of the woods could have been there for any number of perfectly innocent reasons – ramblers, a courting couple, someone walking a dog, a sales rep parked up to make up his books or kill time for an appointment. I was probably letting my imagination run away with me by attaching any significance to it. But all the same I couldn't help wishing the car they'd mentioned had been red or green or sky-blue-pink, and any make other than a BMW.

I reached over abruptly, switching channels, and some vaguely familiar piece of easy-listening music blared out of the speakers, deafening at the level I kept the radio turned up to because I usually listened to talk shows. I reduced the volume, but didn't change station again. Radio Two wasn't exactly to my taste, but at the moment it was just what I needed.

Everyone at work seemed pleased to see me back, enquiring solicitously after my health, but as always, a busy atmosphere prevailed and soon I was cocooned in my office surrounded by all the familiar trappings and faced with a mountain of paperwork.

I'd had every intention of putting a call through to Tony Bowman as a priority, but with client queries and urgent contracts to be dealt with, I simply could not find the time. However anxious I was to get to the bottom of the Kowloon and Victoria Enterprises business, I couldn't follow it up at the expense of those who not only trusted me to look after their affairs, but also paid me handsomely to do so. My own personal crusade would have to wait.

By five thirty I was feeling very tired – perhaps I wasn't as completely recovered as I'd thought – and I'd worked straight through the day, eating a salad roll from the sandwich man's basket at my desk.

I gathered up a few of the more urgent files, planning to look at them during the evening when I'd had a break and something to eat, and set out for my flat in Canary Wharf.

It was a tremendous relief to let myself in through my front door, dump the files, and kick off my shoes. I'd had the place carpeted throughout in deep natural-coloured wool pile – something I'd never have dared to put in at home, where the leaves get trodden in from the garden and Paul mostly forgets to take off his shoes. I curled my toes, loving the softness, loving the feeling of luxury it gave me. But I was less enthralled by the faint shut-up smell that lingered. I went around collecting dead daffodils from vases and dumping them in the bin, and opening the windows.

As always, the view from my one vast living room was spectacular – the setting sun glinting on the still smooth waters of the Thames and reflecting from the acres of glass in nearby buildings.

I stood for a moment, looking out. London. I loved it. Just as much as I loved Wiltshire, though in a different way. The buzz. The feeling of being at the centre of things, and yet at the same time independent, a free spirit, my own person. Home – in Wiltshire – was the hub of my life, the nest I shared with Paul. Canary Wharf was mine and mine alone. There I was quite a different person, and it was as if I needed those two separate parts of my identity, one complementing the other, coming together to form the whole. But for how much longer could I go on this way? My days of having no one but myself to answer to were numbered – had been, really, ever since I had married Paul. He had been prepared to go along with that other side of me, the side that needed to retain independence. But soon Paul wouldn't be the only consideration. I would be a mother, and my whole life would be altered forever.

I went through to the bedroom and changed out of my business suit. Then I went back to the kitchen, made myself a white wine spritzer that was more water than wine and investigated the contents of the fridge. As I'd expected, the lettuce and tomatoes I'd left there had gone off, and I had to dump them into the bin on top of the dead daffodils, but I'd brought fresh salad from home, and the little freezer compartment was well stocked with packets of ready meals. I chose a salmon and broccoli bake and popped it in the microwave.

I was emptying the bag of mixed lettuce leaves into a bowl when the telephone rang.

'Hi, sweetheart! You're there, then.' Paul. I'd guessed it would be.

'Yes, I've been in half an hour or so.'

'Good! I was afraid you might be tempted to overdo things and stay at the office until God knows what time.'

'No, I'm trying to be sensible.'

'So how was it?' he asked. 'Being back at work, I mean.'

'Tiring,' I admitted. 'I think I must have begun to adapt to being a lady of leisure. But I'm sure I'll soon get back into the swing of things. How about you?'

'Me?' There was something about the way he said it that gave me the distinct impression he was stalling.

'Yes, you. What's been happening at your end?'

'Well, it has been a bit dramatic,' he

admitted hesitantly. 'The police have had Jim Wood in for questioning.'

I went cold. 'You mean ... he's been arrested?'

'No – at least, I don't think so. It's what's known as "helping the police with their enquiries", I believe. But he has been at the police station all day. They came and picked him up quite early this morning, and he wasn't back when I left. Well, at least, his car was still in the yard.'

His car. The pool car he used. A dark-coloured BMW.

'Oh God,' I said.

'I know. I can't believe he had anything to do with it, but we did say, didn't we, that the police were obviously looking in his direction.'

'Yes.' I didn't mention the news item, which had talked about the suspect vehicle. I couldn't bring myself to. But probably Paul had heard it anyway.

'Of course, they won't be able to keep him there much longer,' Paul went on. 'They'll either have to charge him or let him go. But what an ordeal for the poor chap, on top of everything else!'

'You don't think he had anything to do with it then?' I said tentatively.

'No! Not in a million years! He's a decent, hard-working bloke.'

'Aren't they all?' I said. 'Or most of them,

anyway. Murderers, I mean. Aren't a lot of them the sort of person you'd sit next to on a bus without a second thought? They don't have wild staring eyes or manic grins, any more than burglars go round in stripey jumpers carrying bags marked "swag". Most of them seem perfectly normal, or so I understand. And they are all someone's husband or father or son.'

'That's a bit sexist, Julia!'

'Well, I should think most murderers are men, aren't they? And certainly whoever killed poor Ruth. I can't imagine her letting another woman strangle her. I can't imagine her going to Hawley Woods to meet another woman, come to that.'

'And why the hell should she go to Hawley Woods to meet her own husband?' Paul asked.

'I really don't know.' I hesitated. 'Was he at work that Friday afternoon?'

'I suppose so.'

'What do you mean – you suppose so?' I pressed him.

'Well, I didn't actually see him. I was out and about quite a lot that day,' Paul said. 'He could have been out. For any number of reasons. No one would think anything of it.'

'The police must have asked around, surely?'

'As far as I know, no one can say for certain whether or not he went out that afternoon

240

for some reason.' Paul sounded testy. 'Look, I've had all this with the police, Julia. I don't want to go through it again.'

'All right. Fair enough.' I heard the microwave ping. 'My supper's ready. Can I call you back later?'

'If you like. But I'm going out to eat. I've arranged to go into town with Josh, grab a curry. I'll be back by half-ten or so, I should think.'

'The way I feel at the moment, I'll probably be in bed by then,' I said. 'If not, I'll give you a call.'

'An early night would do you good.' Paul's tone was caring again. 'Look after yourself, sweetheart. I'll speak to you tomorrow if not before.'

I put the phone down and realized just how shocked I was by what Paul had told me. Poor Jim – perhaps sitting at this very moment in some bare interview room being questioned relentlessly about the murder of his wife. Had he done it? I couldn't believe it of him, and yet ... Perhaps in some ways it would be a relief if he had. At least it would mean there was no madman on the loose, roaming the lanes around our village. At least it would mean Ruth's death was a domestic matter, nothing to do with Stattisford.

I shivered suddenly. Now that the sun had dropped behind the tall buildings on the opposite side of the river, it was very cold in the flat. I turned up the central heating and collected a sweater from the bedroom. I knew my supper was ready in the micro-wave, but suddenly I wasn't hungry any more. I curled up on the cream leather sofa closest to the radiator, resisting the urge to top up my spritzer with something a good deal stronger, and stared into space.

It was quite a while before I could bring myself to go back into the kitchen and give my salmon and broccoli bake another few minutes' whirl. The only thing driving me was the thought of the pile of files waiting for me when I'd finished eating. In spite of my promise to Paul not to overdo things, in spite of my tiredness, it had all the makings of a long night.

I was in bed at half-past ten but still awake, reading through yet more papers by the light of my bedside lamp and propped up against the pillows. I reached for the phone and dialled our number, longing to hear Paul's voice, but there was no reply. Obviously he was not back yet. Half an hour later I tried again. Still no reply.

'Paul, you are a dirty stop-out,' I said to the endless ringing tone.

With a sigh of resignation I replaced the receiver and turned out the light.

Twenty-Six

Next morning I listened to the radio while getting ready for work, but there was no mention of Ruth or Jim. I wasn't sure if that meant that no charge had been brought, or simply that it wasn't a big enough story to make the national news. There was no point in calling Paul either. He would probably have left for work by now, and even if he hadn't, he would be in as much of a rush as I was. I couldn't risk being late in on a Tuesday – it was practically written in stone that we lawyers had an informal meeting first thing on a Tuesday morning to discuss the cases we were working on and sort out any problems we might have. It was also a time for forward planning. One of these days, I was going to have to mention the fact that I was pregnant. But not yet. I didn't want to go public on that one until I'd had a chance to sort out in my own mind what I intended to do.

The meeting that morning was longer than usual, and by the time I'd dealt with all the points that had arisen from it and dictated some notes to Marian whilst it was all fresh

243

in my mind, it was almost twelve thirty.

Without much hope of success, I picked up the telephone and called Tony Bowman. As I'd expected, he had already left for a lunch appointment, and knowing how Tony worked, I guessed it would be at least three before he was back in his office. No one liked long boozy lunches more than Tony! I left a message with his long-suffering secretary asking him to call me, and went back to my work. But it took every ounce of will power to concentrate. Too many other things were buzzing around the perimeters of my mind, and I was half-listening for the sound of a fax coming through from the office beyond the glass screen, in case the Hong Kong authorities should send me a reply to my enquiry with them.

It was almost half-past four before Tony Bowman rang.

'Julia. You've been trying to get me.'

'I have. You're pretty elusive, Tony.'

'Oh, you know how it is. These clients like to wine and dine one, and a refusal often offends; as the saying goes.'

'Yes, I know how it is,' I said wryly. 'You've never really shaken off the colonial way of life, have you?'

Tony chuckled. 'I've tried very hard not to. Work hard, play hard, that's my motto. Now, what can I do for you?'

'I wanted to pick your brains, actually,' I

said. 'About Hong Kong. When you were there, did you ever come across a company called Kowloon and Victoria Enterprises?'

'Kowloon and Victoria ... Julia, there are a great many companies in Hong Kong, and most of them have names just like that.'

'They make electrical components,' I offered by way of clarification.

'Are they independent, or one of the big Hongs?' Tony asked.

'I really don't know. Independent, I think. You don't know them?'

'Offhand they don't spring to mind, but as I say, Hong Kong is a seething mass of industries and businesses. I doubt even the authorities know them all.'

My heart sank. I'd been pinning my hopes on Tony's inside knowledge. Now I realized I'd been clutching at straws. The number of companies packed into the trade-rich area between China and the sea was, mile for square mile, phenomenal. It really had been a shot in the dark that Tony might know the particular one I was interested in. But he was wrong about one thing. The authorities did know of the existence of Kowloon and Victoria Enterprises. Or had done when that Internet file I'd chanced upon had been compiled.

'Oh well, never mind. It was worth a try.' I tried not to sound too disappointed, and failed miserably.

'Why are you interested in them, anyway?' Tony asked.

'Their name came up in something I'm working on. A suggestion they might not be legal – or at least, that they are contravening the law in some way.'

'You could always check with the authorities,' he suggested.

'I am doing. I thought speaking to you might get me results faster.'

'Yes, they can be a bit slow when it comes to dealing with someone outside their immediate sphere,' Tony agreed. 'And also a bit cagey. Quite honestly, you never know how they will react. It's just the same the way they deal with corruption cases and so on. They like to give the impression of being tough, of cracking down on crime and all its attendant evils. The ICAC, for instance – the Independent Commission Against Corruption – is incredibly active. They were set up in the seventies to try to combat the fact that half the police force – high-ranking officers included – were in the pay of the Triads. They follow up thousands of reports each year and bring prosecutions when they can, but it's like pouring water into a colander, and quite often they go after the small fry and leave the big fish alone. It's a whole different world out there. Values are different from ours. They talk about "reducing corruption to an acceptable level". Can you imagine the outcry there would be in this country at the suggestion that any level of corruption was acceptable?'

'It's a way of life there then.'

'Well yes, it is. Oriental as opposed to occidental. They know they'll never wipe out the Triads. Triads rule – OK? Get rid of a dozen members and a hundred take their place. If they even try to get rid of them. With such rich pickings, plenty of high-ranking officials find it very much to their advantage to turn a blind eye.'

'So you don't think I'll get an answer to my enquiry about Kowloon and Victoria Enterprises?'

'I didn't say that. You might do. It all depends how profitable they are to the person dealing with your query. Always assuming, of course, that there is something dicey about them. But since you're interested in them, I take it there is?'

I bit my lip. 'I don't know, Tony. I hope to God not.'

'You sound very … involved, Julia,' he said perceptively.

'No – no!' I said hastily. 'It will make things difficult for my client, that's all.'

'And you need the information urgently.'

'Well yes, I do really.'

'Tell you what – I'll see what I can do,' Tony said. 'I'll have a word with a few people I know. I can't promise anything, of course, but...'

'Tony, you are an angel!' I said.

'I know. Sprouting wings. Look, Julia, I'll have to love you and leave you. I've got masses of work to get through.'

'Me too. I really am grateful, Tony.'

I put the phone down deep in thought. From what Tony had said, it sounded as if Hong Kong was a hotbed of crime, vice and corruption. There must be legitimate companies operating from there, of course – the one I'd investigated for Poyson Associates, to name but one – and I was hoping desperately that Kowloon and Victoria Enterprises were just as squeaky clean. But somehow I didn't think that they were. All my instincts were telling me otherwise. Kowloon and Victoria had been – were – involved in something nasty, and by implication, Stattisford Electronics were involved too. But until I had something more concrete to go on, there was very little I could do about it.

When Paul phoned me that evening he was able to tell me that Jim Wood had been released.

'He doesn't think they've finished with him, though. They just didn't have enough evidence to charge him, and they had to let him go. My guess is the minute something new emerges, they'll have him in again.'

'Have you seen him?' I asked.

'Yes, believe it or not, he came straight in to work from the police station! Needless to say, we sent him home. He was in no fit state for anything. Unshaven, bleary-eyed, and half-demented. I think he turned up because he just didn't know what else to do.'

'He's probably in a state of shock – going through the motions,' I said.

'Probably. Whatever, he was in no shape to be here. No use to himself or to us. I called round to see him on my way home from work, and do you know what he said? "I felt like telling them I'd done, it, Paul, just so they'd leave me alone." I told him the last thing he must do was to confess to something he hadn't done, and all he could say was: "If I did, perhaps at least they'd let me bury her." '

'Oh God,' I said, feeling sick.

'Anyway, to more cheerful things,' Paul said, changing the subject. 'Helen is coming down later on.'

'Later on?' I repeated, surprised. 'Tonight, you mean?'

'Yes. She phoned me this morning. Said she'd be arriving about eight.'

'I thought she wasn't coming until tomorrow or Thursday,' I said.

'Apparently she's sorted herself out and is eager to start as soon as possible,' Paul informed me. 'I must say I'm glad. I'm getting fed up with fending for myself.'

'You've hardly had to!' I exclaimed. 'I didn't leave until Monday morning, and this is only Tuesday evening. And you ate out last night. You were very late, by the way.'

'What do you mean – late?'

'Well, I phoned at eleven and you weren't back then.'

'I thought you were supposed to be having an early night!' Paul said accusingly.

'I did, but I couldn't sleep. Where were you until that time?'

'Oh, Josh and I were talking. You know how it is,' Paul said vaguely. 'And we stopped off for a drink. Actually I think I heard the phone when I was locking the gate, but I never dreamed it would be you. I must have just missed you – I was in by five past. And I'd accidentally switched off the answerphone. Sorry!'

'It's all right, Paul, you don't have to go on about it,' I said, laughing. 'I'm not checking up on you.' And then I caught myself thinking: Wasn't that exactly what I was doing?

'By the way, Helen will be here at the weekend,' Paul said. 'I know we agreed that in the normal course of events she'd have weekends off, but it seems her sister is away at the moment, and it seemed like a good idea anyway for her to be here for this one, since you're in London now. It will give you the chance to iron out any problems, put her right on anything you're not happy with, and get to know her again.'

'Yes, I suppose so,' I said.

Why did my heart sink every time Helen's name was mentioned? Why the hell was it I couldn't remember what it was I didn't like about her? Why the hell couldn't I remember *her*?

'How's work?' Paul asked, changing the subject again.

'Oh, you know – as always...'

'Taking it easy, I hope.' I didn't answer. 'Julia...' His tone became guarded. 'You have dropped this silly idea of poking about into Kowloon and Victoria, haven't you?'

I hesitated. I couldn't lie to Paul. Not a direct lie. I could omit to tell him something and not feel too bad about it. I could even hedge. But asked straight out, I couldn't bring myself to be less than truthful. 'Not entirely,' I said carefully. 'I spoke to Tony Bowman about it. He's the financial consultant I told you about the other day – remember? He knows a great deal about Hong Kong – he worked there himself, and still has a lot of contacts. I just asked him if he knew if there had ever been any rumours about Kowloon and Victoria.'

'Julia!' Paul exploded. 'I thought we'd agreed you should leave well alone!'

'No,' I said, 'you told me I should. I didn't actually agree to anything.'

'Oh, you are impossible!' There was a brief

pause, then he asked, a little nervously, I thought: 'What did he say?'

'He didn't know,' I said. 'He said he'd never heard of anything.'

'There you are then!' Paul sounded immensely relieved. 'So now you know they're all right, will you forget about it?'

'But I don't know they're all right,' I argued. 'Just that Tony didn't know anything about them offhand. He's promised to get back to me if he finds out anything fishy. If he doesn't, then I suppose I shall have to give them the benefit of the doubt.'

'I should hope so!' Paul exclaimed. 'But look, Julia, if he does come back with anything ... well, suspicious ... you will let me know, won't you? Straight away?'

'Yes, of course...'

'What I'm saying, Julia, is that I don't want *you* pursuing it,' Paul said firmly. 'If there's anything that needs following up, I'll do it myself.'

Frustration nagged at me. 'Oh Paul...'

'Look, sweetheart, it's as I said before. I don't want you getting into something you can't handle.' There was a certain urgency in his tone and once again I had the distinct impression that Paul knew more about all this than he was letting on. I thought suddenly of the envelope with the Hong Kong postmark – the letter which had arrived on the day he'd denied that any post had been delivered. Was it possible that he suspected Stattisford was deeply involved in whatever was amiss at Kowloon and Victoria and was conducting his own enquiries already?

After we'd finished our conversation, whilst I made myself an omelette and salad, I was still thinking about it, and the more I thought, the more worried I grew. I'd assumed that the main problem for Stattisford would simply be by association with any wrongdoing at Kowloon and Victoria, because I'd felt sure nothing seriously criminal would get past Paul and Josh. But if Paul was looking into something, and seriously worried about the consequences of doing so, then it shed a whole new light on the subject. Jim Wood. As he came into my mind I stopped what I was doing and stood with my fingers pressed to my mouth, deep in thought. Clearly the police had Jim down for their prime suspect for Ruth's death, and not just for the obvious reason that most murders are committed within a fairly tight circle – a husband, a lover, a friend, or at the very least, someone known to the victim.

There were other factors involved too. No one had given an alibi concerning his movements on that Friday afternoon. A car just like the one he drove had been seen in Hawley Woods. And I was fairly sure that Ruth had made a phone call to Stattisford just before she disappeared. I'd dismissed him as a suspect because I believed he and Ruth were very happily married, and because he had always seemed a nice, ordinary man. But supposing there was something more sinister behind it all?

Jim had been at Stattisford from the very beginning. He knew the business inside out. Also, as head storeman, he was in a unique and trusted position, and was responsible for checking inbound consignments. Supposing Kowloon and Victoria had set up some kind of import racket through Jim, smuggling God alone knew what? If things arrived at the depot that weren't supposed to, no one else need ever know. But perhaps Ruth had found out about it. Perhaps she had disapproved and threatened to spill the beans. Or perhaps she had demanded a bigger share of the proceeds for herself and her husband. It all seemed terribly far-fetched, but I was very aware now just how little I had known Ruth, and it would explain the feeling I'd had all along that all the terrible things that had happened were connected, and that Stattisford was the common factor.

I still found it hard to believe that Jim had actually killed his own wife. But the kind of organization Paul had described to me was so powerful and its tentacles so far-reaching that it would deal with anyone who crossed it as easily and with as little compunction as swatting a fly.

No wonder Paul was so afraid for me. If Jim or his contacts had been prepared to kill once – his own wife, no less – then they would certainly not draw the line at killing again.

'Oh hell!' I said aloud.

My omelette was totally dried up, sticking to the pan, and I could smell burning butter. I pulled the pan off the heat.

I was feeling totally unreal, as if this whole thing was a bad dream. It was so completely incredible, a sort of wild fiction I'd dreamed up to fit the facts. And yet the aura of sick dread and horror remained.

It might be a nightmare – a flight of horrible fantasy. But it was one I'd strayed into. And somehow, like a blind man in a maze, I was overcome by the suffocating fear that I was never going to find my way out.

Twenty-Seven

It was about ten o'clock the following evening when the telephone rang. I was working on some papers for a client, curled up on the cream leather sofa with legal books spread out, open, all around me.

I shifted the one on the arm of the sofa beside me and reached over for the telephone, wondering vaguely who it could be calling me at this time of night. Paul and I had already had our daily chat. He'd told me Helen had arrived and settled in, and added that so far he was very pleased. She had cooked him a superb meal – 'a bit over the top, but she was probably trying to impress' – and it had been a great treat to come home from work and not find his dirty breakfast things looking at him accusingly from the sink. When she'd cleared up, he said, she had gone to her room to watch television on the portable set he'd installed for her there, and he had high hopes that the arrangement was going to be a success.

Had something gone wrong after all? I wondered, reaching for the receiver. Or was there news about Jim Wood? It must be

256

something fairly out of the ordinary for Paul to ring me again. And I wasn't expecting a call from anyone else.

'Hello?' I said in the rather silly sing-song voice I sometimes use when I think it's someone I know on the other end of the line.

There was a moment's silence. Complete silence.

'Paul? Is that you?' I said, beginning to feel slightly uneasy.

And then a voice spoke. Not Paul's voice. Not anyone I recognized or was likely to. A muffled voice, whispering words that made no sense to me at first.

'You'd be well advised, Mrs Wilson, to mind your own business.'

'Excuse me?' I heard the slight tremble in my own voice.

'You're poking about in things that don't concern you. I think you know what I mean. Unless you want trouble, you'll leave well alone.'

'Who is this?' I was trembling all over now. 'Who are you?'

The person on the other end of the line – a man – didn't answer that. Instead he said: 'I suggest you take a look out of your window, Mrs Wilson. See what's happened to your car. A nasty accident, really. Lucky for you that you weren't in it. But next time you might not be so lucky. Unless you stop asking awkward questions.'

'What...?' I dropped the phone, leaped up, scattering books and papers. My ankle, still a little weak, almost gave way as I put my weight on it suddenly and unthinkingly, but I managed to save myself and scramble over to the window. Then I turned, first hot, then cold, with utter disbelieving horror.

When I'd come home earlier I'd been lucky enough to get a parking space on the cobbles at the wharf's edge, right where I could see it from the window. Now I could scarcely see across the road for dense black smoke. And at the heart of it, where my car should be, a ball of orange flame.

For a moment I was paralysed by shock, then I heard someone gasp, a sharp horrified intake of breath, and knew it was me.

The night was suddenly full of another sound, the wail of sirens, and two fire engines came into view, mottling the weird orange light given out by the street lamps with flashing blue. I could see people milling around in the street; obviously someone had phoned for the fire brigade. From my flat on the third floor, with the curtains drawn, I'd seen and heard nothing.

I turned back into the room. The phone was still off the hook, lying where I'd dropped it. I grabbed it up.

'Who are you? What have you done?' I was almost screaming.

But there was only the dialling tone. Whoever it was who had called me – threatened me – had gone.

I found my shoes, which I'd kicked off earlier, hidden beneath the cascade of books, and stuffed my feet into them. I had difficulty with the safety chain on the door because my fingers were all thumbs. I ran out on to the landing, realized I hadn't locked the door behind me, ran back again. I wouldn't even leave my flat unlocked in normal circumstances, for God's sake! How could I almost forget to do it when there was some madman down there who had set fire to my car?

For someone had. I knew it without a shadow of doubt. Someone had set fire to my car as a warning to me. To lay off. To stop asking questions about Kowloon and Victoria Enterprises. Perhaps about Stattisford too.

A moment's blind panic made me almost run back into the flat and lock myself in. But what was the point of that? Whoever had done this knew exactly where to find me. They knew my car. They knew my telephone number. Presumably they knew which of the identical front doors was mine. If they could burn the car, they could burn the flat. A bundle of petrol-soaked rags through the letter box, or even a Molotov cocktail ... I turned cold again; pushed the thought away.

I had to go down. I'd be safe enough in the street, milling with firefighters and policemen. I couldn't just not go down when my car was going up in flames!

The night air was cold, but even from across the street I could feel the heat radiating from the fire. I felt sick. My poor car! A flash of anger that someone could do this made me forget my fear momentarily.

I found a policeman standing by the kerb. He looked very young, much younger than the policemen back home, and somehow more aggressive.

'Keep back now, please! Right back! There's nothing to see.'

'That's my car!' I said. 'Someone's set it on fire!'

In the weird kaleidoscope of light – orange, scarlet, flashing blue – I saw his expression, pitying but sceptical.

'Yours, is it? Electrical fault, I expect. Happens all the time.'

'No – it was deliberate!'

'Yobs you mean? Well, could be, I suppose. The firemen will be able to tell us where it started. But if it was, they'll be long gone. We'll never catch them now.'

'No – not yobs...' I stopped abruptly. He'd never believe me. It sounded melodramatic, absurd. And even if he did believe me, what would he do about it? What could he do? They certainly wouldn't give me twenty-four-hour police protection. And how could I be sure that whoever had done this wasn't here, in the crowd of onlookers, watching? Would it simply make them more dangerous if they thought I was telling the police about the telephone call? Or would they just laugh up their sleeves because I was obviously so totally helpless?

'Better give me a few details, love,' the policeman said. 'Just for the record. And we'll have to get it taken away, once the fire's out. Would you like me to arrange for a recovery vehicle? Or are you in the AA or the RAC?'

I stared at him for a moment, wondering how on earth he could say something so incredibly stupid. And then, without knowing why, I was laughing. Laughing and crying both together. And I couldn't stop.

By the time it was all over, it was very late – too late, I thought, to ring Paul. I really don't know why I thought that – I was desperate to speak to him, to tell him what had happened, desperate just to hear his voice, but at the same time my muleish independence was throwing up excuses not to.

What was the point of worrying Paul tonight, perhaps waking him, and Helen too? There was nothing he could do. And what was he going to say except 'I told you so'? He'd warned me to leave well alone and I'd ignored him. This was the result. But at least it had confirmed all my suspicions. There was something going on, and someone prepared to go to these lengths to try to stop me finding out what it was. But if they thought – these thugs, whoever they were – that they could frighten me off, then they were very much mistaken.

I looked at the phone, still undecided, almost reached out to pick it up, then finally decided against it. Time enough to tell Paul tomorrow when I'd had time to think.

I didn't sleep much, of course. I lay awake for hours, still seeing the flames leaping into the darkness, hearing the voice of the caller, unrecognizable, muffled, and each time a timber settled or a door slammed somewhere in the building, I tensed into a state of tingling awareness. When I did drift off, it was to vivid but disjointed dreams, all overlaid with the aura of nightmare. And in the end, towards dawn, I slept so heavily that when I did wake I felt thick and nauseous as if I'd been drugged.

I could tell by the broad daylight streaming in through the crack in my bedroom curtains, as well as by the hands of the clock, that it was late – in all the upset the previous night, I'd forgotten to set my alarm. No time to ring Paul now. I went into the living room, drew the curtains, looked down at the black-ened square of road where my car had been, and felt sick all over again. I could scarcely believe it had really happened. But it had. And so had the threatening phone call. This morning, however, I didn't feel overwhelmed by fear and dread. I felt angry and determined. I wasn't going to just sit back and let this go. Now, more than ever, my mind was made up. I was going to get to the bottom of this if it killed me.

I grabbed a cup of coffee, drinking it while I showered and dressed and phoned for a taxi. I'd call Paul later, from the office. Though quite what I was going to say, I hadn't yet decided.

I'd only been in the office a matter of half an hour or so when my phone rang. I picked it up, only half concentrating. It was Tony Bowman.

'Julia. About Kowloon and Victoria Enterprises. I've talked to a friend who's ... what shall we say? ... in the know.'

'And?' I was tensely alert.

'You're not going to like this. It seems Kowloon and Victoria were investigated a few years ago. No charges were ever brought, for whatever reason. Friends in high places, maybe. But the cloud of suspicion remains. My informant is of the opinion the irregularities are still going on.'

'And what are these irregularities, Tony? Did he tell you that?'

'Yes, Julia, he did. He thinks it's drugs. He

reckons that Kowloon and Victoria are a cover for an illicit organization, probably run by a Triad. He thinks they are into drug smuggling. In a very big way.'

Drugs. I think that deep down I'd already realized that must be it. Until Ruth was murdered, I'd been thinking in terms of something relatively minor, like illegal working conditions. But what had happened to Ruth, coupled with the telephone call I'd received last night and the firing of my car, had opened my eyes. There was a great deal at stake here for somebody, profits beyond what I had previously imagined. A goldmine. Even Paul's warnings tied in to that. And only one commodity was really big enough to warrant such measures as murder and arson. That commodity was drugs.

Of course, Hong Kong was an ideal staging post. Hadn't the colony been built on the opium trade? But in spite of everything, it was still a shock to hear Tony actually say it. Kowloon and Victoria were using their export market to smuggle drugs. And as wholesalers for their electrical components, Stattisford were providing the gateway to the UK. Dear God!

I stared at the pile of files and papers on my desk. Work had always been a priority with me. Suddenly it seemed unimportant, petty almost. I flipped through them, trying to decide which called for urgent attention and which could wait. Then I buzzed Richard Havers.

'Richard – can I talk to you?'

'Right now? I'm due in a meeting shortly.'

'I'd appreciate it, Richard, if you could spare me a few minutes. Something has come up – something very important. I'm going to have to take a few days off.'

'But Julia – you've only just come back from sick leave!'

'I know, and I'm sorry. But I'm afraid it's unavoidable.'

'In that case you'd better come through.' He sounded annoyed, as well he might. Only yesterday I would have been concerned about the image I was projecting. Not now. Nothing mattered but sorting out what the hell was going on. My future and Paul's, not to mention the future of our baby, depended on it.

An hour later I was on the motorway, driving a car I'd had delivered by a hire firm. I didn't like it much – after my nippy little hot-hatch it felt sluggish and unstable. But it was wheels. I had to put up with it.

I put my foot down, moved into the fast lane. Whatever it was that had invaded and taken over our lives had to be sorted out, and quickly. Now that my mind was made up I couldn't wait to get on with it.

Twenty-Eight

When I pulled into our drive, a car I recognized as Helen's was parked there, bang in the middle, as if she'd been out this morning and not bothered to put it away when she came back. I was momentarily irritated – my instinctive reaction to Helen, it seemed – but I knew it was irrational, since she wasn't expecting me, and might be intending to go out again for all I knew.

I parked behind the car – an almost brand-new Renault Clio – grabbed my bag and briefcase from the back seat, and went round to the back door. There was no one in the kitchen, but as I dumped my bags I heard the sound of someone moving about in the bedroom above. I went along the hall, kicking off my shoes, and went up the stairs, my bare feet on the deep pile carpet giving no warning of my approach. The door of our bedroom was ajar, and through it I saw Helen with the drawer of the dressing table open, ferreting around inside.

'Helen,' I said.

She jumped out of her skin, not surprisingly, and swung round, a dark-red flush

266

flooding her face and neck.

'Julia! How did you get here?' she asked, and then added hastily, and rather guiltily: 'I'm just putting Paul's clean shirts away.'

'That's not Paul's drawer, it's mine,' I said.

'Oh dear, is it?' She really was dreadfully flustered.

I went into the room. I couldn't actually see any of Paul's clean shirts in my drawer, and I was fairly certain there weren't any. Helen had been poking about and she'd used the excuse of the shirts in panic. Pretty stupid, really, since I was bound to notice it was patently untrue.

'What are you doing home?' Helen asked. A note of accusation had crept into her voice now, as if I had no right to be here. 'I thought you were in London.'

'Well I'm not, am I?' I snapped. I had not the slightest intention of explaining, at least until I'd spoken to Paul.

I'd intended to telephone him, ask him to come home, but it suddenly occurred to me that home was no longer the sanctuary it had once been. Our precious privacy was now lacking. A woman who snooped through my drawers might very well eavesdrop outside doors, or even on telephone extensions. I'd never felt that way with Ruth. Never even thought about it. I felt a pang of longing for the old, safe days before remembering the mysterious telephone call Ruth had made on the day she had died, and realized there had been things I hadn't known about Ruth, too, for all that I had trusted her implicitly.

'I have to go out for a little while,' I said, putting the emphasis on the 'little while'.

'Oh! Where...?'

I didn't answer her. If I had done, if I'd told the truth, I would have said there was only one person I wanted to be with at this moment, and one place where I knew I could find him and talk without fear of anyone overhearing.

I was suddenly more desperate than ever to be with Paul.

At Stattisford I parked the hire car in the yard next to Paul's and headed into the office block. If I could have avoided the reception area, I would have done, but there was only one way in, past the desk where Mary Stalker sat typing up invoices in between answering the telephone and greeting the occasional caller. She looked almost as startled to see me as Helen had done, and almost as guilty, too, due to the fact that she was munching her way through a cream bun, I guessed.

'Julia!' she spluttered, trying to dump the bun and showering her desk with icing sugar in the process.

'Is Paul in?'

'Yes, but he's got someone with him.' She

licked her fingers. 'Police again, I think.'

My heart sank. 'Does that mean there have been developments?'

'I don't know. I haven't heard. Still pursuing their enquiries, I presume. It's awful isn't it?'

'Awful.' But I couldn't feel anything for Ruth at the moment. I'd run the gamut of emotions over what had happened to her; right now it was what had happened to me that was uppermost in my mind.

'Do you want a coffee while you're waiting?' Mary asked.

'No...' I changed my mind. 'Yes, all right then. Perhaps I will.'

She swivelled her chair to reach the filter machine on the shelf behind her, and as if on cue the telephone shrilled.

'I'll get my own coffee,' I said. 'You answer that.'

I squeezed past her desk. Had I begun to put on weight already?

'Good morning – Stattisford. How may I help you?' Mary's voice was robotic, the tone of someone who repeats the same phrase over and over again, day in day out, and suddenly it occurred to me that she must have answered the phone to Ruth if she had indeed called on the day she disappeared. I poured my coffee, squeezed back around the desk, and sat down in the visitor's chair.

'Mary,' I said when she had dealt with the

caller, 'did Ruth Wood ring here on that last Friday?'

Mary looked at me curiously. 'The police asked me that, too.'

'And?'

'I wouldn't know. I wasn't here. I had a dentist's appointment, a wisdom tooth out. That was at midday, and I was too groggy to make it back to work.'

'So who would have answered the phone?'

'Whoever happened to be around. Paul – Josh – even Jim. It's a question of all hands on deck if I'm not here.'

A door opened along the passage. I glanced up hopefully. But it wasn't Paul. It was Josh.

'Julia! I thought I heard your voice, but I thought I must be imagining it. What are you doing here?'

'Come to see Paul. But he's got a policeman with him.'

'Oh, right. The place is crawling with them these days. How are you anyway?'

'Oh, you know...' I hesitated. I really did not want to tell Josh or anyone what had happened last night until I'd had the chance to tell Paul.

I was saved from answering by another door opening, and voices in the corridor. Paul and the detective who had come to see us at home, DS Wright, if I remembered correctly. Paul didn't look surprised to see me as the others had done. He looked pleased, relieved almost, smiling at me before ushering the policeman to the door and going outside with him. Through the glass panel, I could see them talking, but I couldn't make out what they were saying, and frankly I didn't much care. Then the policeman walked away and Paul came back inside.

'Sweetheart.'

'Paul, I expect you're busy, but I have to talk to you,' I said.

'It's OK.' He put an arm round me, kissing me on the forehead. I had the distinct impression he was trying to stop me blurting out the reason I was here. He need not have worried. I had no intention of doing that.

Paul glanced at his watch. 'We'll go for a spot of lunch, shall we?'

'Bit early isn't it?' Josh commented.

Paul ignored him. 'I'll just get my jacket.'

Why hadn't he asked me what I was doing here when I was supposed to be in London? I didn't know and I didn't care. In a few minutes I would have Paul's undivided attention. Nothing else mattered.

Twenty-Nine

'So – is that your hire car?' Paul asked, nodding towards it as we left the office building.

I glanced at him in surprise. 'How did you know I'd come in a hire car?'

'Richard Havers telephoned me. He was worried about you.' His hand tightened protectively around my waist. 'Sweetheart, you should have rung me. Why on earth didn't you?'

'I was going to,' I said. 'But Richard doesn't know the whole story. It's more than just my car catching fire. And ... I just felt that I needed you, Paul. Not on the end of a telephone. Right beside me. And we really do have to talk.'

'OK.' He unlocked his car, hung his jacket on the hook in the back, and slid in. I climbed into the passenger seat beside him. I couldn't believe how shaky I suddenly felt, as if shock had suddenly hit me, sickening, debilitating.

'Where shall we go?' Paul asked. 'Home?'

'No!' I said sharply. '*She's* there – Helen Bloody Gibbs. Anywhere but home, Paul.'

He didn't comment. 'OK. What about the Blue Bowl?'

'If you like.' I'd been to the Blue Bowl with Paul before when I'd met him at his office. It was a pleasant enough pub which was popular with executives and secretaries who worked on the various business parks and industrial estates within striking distance, but I knew the influx wouldn't have begun yet and it would be quiet enough to have a serious conversation.

We drove in near silence. Now that the moment had come I was oddly reluctant to start telling Paul what had happened to me, and what I had found out about Kowloon and Victoria. It just made it all the more horribly real, and I couldn't summon up the energy to deal with it. I just wanted to cocoon myself in warmth and safety, hide my head in the sand like the proverbial ostrich and pretend that would make the world go away. As for Paul, he seemed to realize that what I had to say would require his full attention, and though I guessed he must be bursting with impatience to find out the reason I had come hightailing it home, he contained it, driving with a set expression and studied concentration.

As I'd expected, the Blue Bowl was still virtually empty, but we installed ourselves in a little alcove as far away from the bar as possible so that we could be sure of our

273

privacy when people did start coming in. Paul got in the drinks – a beer for himself and a mineral water for me, and asked if I wanted to order something to eat.

I shook my head. 'I'm not really hungry.'

'You really should have something,' Paul said, looking at me anxiously.

I shook my head again. Food would stick in my throat. 'I really couldn't, Paul. Maybe later.'

'OK, just as long as we beat the rush.' He sat down opposite me. 'Just try and calm down, sweetheart. You're in a right state. I know it's upsetting, having your car torched by vandals, but...'

'I don't think it was vandals,' I interrupted him.

Paul froze in the act of wiping beer foam from his upper lip. Above his hand his eyes had narrowed. 'What do you mean?'

I told him. About the threatening telephone call, and also about what Tony Bowman had told me. I told him everything in one long rush, because when I started I couldn't stop, and Paul listened, his face growing darker by the minute.

'So, you see, there definitely is something going on, and Stattisford is almost certainly involved,' I finished.

'Oh Julia!' Paul looked angry now as well as worried. 'I warned you, didn't I, to leave well alone. Do you see now the sort of people you're up against?'

'Well yes, I do,' I admitted. 'And it's hardly surprising, is it? Drugs, Paul. Hard drugs. That's what's behind all this. Someone is using Stattisford to get them into the country. And do you know what that sort of stuff is worth? Cocaine, for instance? Ounce for ounce it beats gold hands down. The most valuable commodity in the world.'

'I do know that, Julia,' Paul said quietly.

'We have to go to the police.'

'No!' Paul's tone was sharp.

I frowned. 'But Paul, we must! Supposing it was discovered in a consignment headed for us? Or even on the premises? If it's coming in through Stattisford then there must be times when it's actually in your warehouse. Nobody would believe you knew nothing about it, and the consequences don't bear thinking about. And besides that...' I hesitated, unwilling to put my deductions into words, but knowing I must. 'Jim Wood has to be involved. He knows more about those consignments of components than anyone. And now his wife is dead. Murdered. For that reason too we simply must go to the police, and the sooner the better. Before someone else is killed.'

'Julia.' Paul leaned forward, elbows on the table, his expression intense. 'This is my business we're talking about. Our livelihood. You say quite rightly that this could ruin me.

But things could be much worse if we alert the police and they come in heavy-handed.'

'They wouldn't do that, surely?' I protested. 'The drug squad must be used to dealing with this sort of thing and...'

'But if they did ... If they frightened off whoever is responsible. Then I would end up carrying the can. And even if I managed to convince them I had nothing to do with it, the mud would stick. I've got to get to the bottom of it first. Find out exactly what has been going on, and who's behind it.'

I sighed at his seeming intransigence. 'And how do you propose doing that?'

'By going to Hong Kong and following the trail from that end,' Paul said, and his expression told me he was deadly serious.

'You can't do that!' I exclaimed, horrified. 'That could be really dangerous! I've already been threatened, Paul.'

'I know, and if I could get my hands on the bastards, I'd throttle them with my bare hands. But at the moment I'm just not sure who it is we are dealing with. I'm going to Hong Kong, Julia, to make some enquiries. I don't honestly think I have any choice.'

'We should leave it to the police!' I argued. 'I can see you're worried about the consequences of doing that, but whatever, it's got to be better than ending up in Kowloon Harbour in a concrete overcoat. And that's what might happen if you go charging in.

These people will stop at nothing, Paul.'

'I'll be careful,' Paul promised me. 'I won't go charging in, as you put it, just make some enquiries. I'll be all right. It's you I'm worried about. I just wish you'd never got involved. Now you are, and they know you are, I am seriously concerned for your safety, Julia. But at least you're at home now, not in London. And you won't be on your own. Thank goodness for Helen Gibbs is all I can say, no matter what you think of her. At least with someone else in the house you should be safe.'

All my misgivings rose to the surface once again. 'I don't trust her, Paul.'

'I know. So you keep saying. But...'

'I don't like the way she's insinuated herself into our home,' I said, trying to shuffle my impressions of our new housekeeper into some coherent order. 'I feel she's managed to foist herself on us somehow. You don't think she's involved in all this somehow, do you?'

'Helen?' Paul's expression was frankly incredulous. 'What on earth makes you say that?'

'I don't know. Everything really. There's something very shifty about her. This morning when I arrived home unexpectedly I found her poking about in my drawer. She said she was putting your shirts away, but I'm sure that was just the first thing that came into her head. And she looked really guilty.'

'I expect she was just trying to familiarize herself with where things are kept,' Paul said.

'Then why did she look so guilty? Why did she lie?'

Paul smiled slightly. 'You can be quite intimidating when you get the bit between your teeth, Julia.'

'Oh, all right, she was just trying to familiarize herself with things. But I wouldn't have been suspicious in the first place if I wasn't already uncomfortable about her. There's something, I know there is. I just can't put my finger on what it is. But my gut feeling is that it's all too convenient. The way she suddenly appeared on the scene just when we needed a housekeeper. The speed she moved in, though she must have sensed I wasn't keen on the idea. Everything, really. And I still don't remember her. I honestly don't.'

'I thought we'd decided she was just one of the many people you met on that trip,' Paul said reasonably. 'She has photographs of you in Australia, after all. That proves she must have been there.'

'I suppose so,' I agreed reluctantly. 'But I don't like her, Paul, and I don't want her in my house.'

Paul spread his hands helplessly. 'Well, we

278

can't do anything about it at the moment, Ju. We've agreed to a trial period and I don't want to find myself up before an industrial tribunal on top of everything else. Besides –' his eyes met mine – 'just now, as I already said, I feel a lot happier knowing you aren't alone in the house. If I'm going to be away for a few days, I'd rather know that someone was with you, whether you like them or not. She can't possibly have any connection with this other business – it makes no sense at all – and the very fact that she's there with you is bound to be a deterrent to anyone who means you harm.'

I sighed, feeling trapped. Paul seemed to have a total blind spot where Helen was concerned, and I really couldn't understand it. But he was right about one thing. I really didn't like the idea of being alone in the house at the moment, even for a few days. The incident when I'd thought there was an intruder was still uncomfortably fresh in my mind, and after what had happened last night, I did feel dreadfully vulnerable. Helen couldn't have anything to do with all this. She was just a rather obnoxious girl from my past who had got her claws into what she saw as a cushy little job. Perhaps she even fancied Paul! But she certainly wasn't a Triad, and she didn't seem to have enough about her to be involved with any sort of crime beyond poking and prying into things that were none of her business, let alone the kind of big international crime racket I felt sure we were on the point of uncovering.

'When this is all over, we'll think again,' Paul promised. 'If you still don't like her, we'll look for someone else.'

'Mmm, unless I decide to come home for good.' Just at the moment, the thought was a very inviting one. 'I don't see why I shouldn't be able to work as a freelance. Between feeds and nappy changes and visits to the supermarket, of course.'

'You know I'd absolutely approve of that.' Paul's hand covered mine on the bare stained-wood table top, pressing it gently. 'And don't worry, sweetheart. Everything is going to be all right. We'll get through this, and laugh about it one day.'

'I certainly hope so,' I said.

And wished with all my heart that I could believe him.

Thirty

For all my doubts about the validity of the credentials Helen had claimed for herself, it certainly seemed that she had told the truth about her talent for cooking. The meal she had prepared for us that evening was superb. The fillets of sole veronique with sugar snap peas, haricots verts and baby new potatoes not only tasted good but were also presented as beautifully as any top-class restaurant would present them, and I was only sorry I was still too churned up inside to be able to do them justice. Paul, however, ate heartily and I marvelled that, whatever he had on his mind, it didn't seem to affect his appetite.

Helen ate with us, at the dining-room table, which she had set as if for a dinner party. As Paul's eyes met mine over our best Waterford crystal, he seemed to be saying: *See? She's a real find! You are just being paranoid!* And I wanted very much to reply that in my opinion, Helen was trying far too hard.

When we'd finished eating, Paul went upstairs and I followed him. It felt peculiar, somehow, leaving Helen to load the dishwasher and clear the table, though I'd never felt that with Ruth. Perhaps because she'd never eaten with us, I decided.

'You're really going then?' I asked as he retrieved a hold-all from the top of the wardrobe and began stacking shirts, socks and underwear in neat piles. 'Oh Paul, I wish you wouldn't.'

'You know I have to.' He added a sweater to the pile of clothes. 'But I won't be away long, I promise. Just a couple of days.'

I stared at him. 'Just a couple of days? To Hong Kong and back?'

He gave me a look. 'You don't know where I'm going.'

'But you said Hong Kong. That was the whole point. That you were going to start from the other end...'

'Maybe I've changed my mind.' His tone was deliberately non-committal. 'It's just a business trip, OK?'

'But...'

'Julia, will you just stop asking questions! And stop worrying.'

I laughed shortly. 'Oh yes, and how can I do that, I'd like to know? I'm out of my mind with worry!'

Paul dropped a pile of handkerchiefs into the bag and put his arms round me.

'I know it's not easy, but you've got to try and relax a bit, sweetheart. It's bad for you and the baby to be in such a state as this.

Please – for me. Just try to put it all out of your mind and let me do the worrying.'

'Oh Paul, that's easy to say...'

'Trust me.'

'But ... *are* you going to Hong Kong? Or...?'

'I'm going away for a few days and it's better you don't know any more than that,' Paul said. He was looking down at me, his face serious. 'As far as everyone at work is concerned, I'm meeting with a contact to tie up a new contract, and if anyone asks, I want you to back up that story. Be vague. You've never had anything to do with the business or known much about it, so stick to that and no one should think anything of it. I'm sure you can handle it, no problem – just as long as you stay calm. The state you're in is a dead giveaway.'

'Is it any wonder I'm in a state!' I exclaimed.

'There's no need to be,' Paul said, talking slowly and patiently, as if to a child. 'I shall be fine. As for you – well, I expect whoever set fire to your car the other night thinks he's scared you off. And as I said before, you should be safe enough with Helen here. But promise me you'll take care anyway. Stay around the house. Keep the doors locked whenever you can. And –' he grinned impishly – 'no going off with strange men!'

'As if I would!' I laughed nervously.

Paul returned to his packing and I stood watching him. After a minute he glanced at me over his shoulder.

'It was definitely a man, by the way, who drove Ruth's car to Hawley Woods.'

I started. 'How do you know that?'

'The detective sergeant let it slip this morning. It hasn't been made public knowledge, but it seems the seat was in a position too far back for it to have been Ruth driving. She was quite small, wasn't she? And there was no way she could have reached the pedals. It had to be someone a lot taller than her driving – the implication being that it was a man.'

'Jim is quite tall,' I reflected. 'Were they saying that's something else that makes them think it was him?'

'He didn't say that.'

I frowned, a sudden thought occurring to me. 'Why did he tell you at all? If they're not making it public, why did he tell you? He must have had a reason. He doesn't strike me as the sort who'd say something he didn't intend to.'

Paul shrugged his shoulders. 'I don't know. Does it matter? Look, sweetheart, I really need to think about what I have to take. I'm leaving first thing in the morning.'

'What do you call first thing?' I asked.

'I'll be gone by the time you wake up, I expect.'

'Oh Paul,' I said. I felt bereft and anxious, as if the troubles of the world were on my shoulders. And also that I had no control left over anything that mattered in my life.

Of course, I wasn't asleep when Paul left. I'd hardly slept at all, and his alarm put paid to any final hopes of it. Cold grey dawn was creeping in at the windows, the relentless beginning of another day.

I lay listening to Paul moving about, the gurgle of the pipes as he ran his shower. When he came back into the bedroom for his jacket, creeping, so as not to disturb me, I heard myself whisper: 'Hi.'

'I thought you were still asleep.'

'Is it likely?'

He came over to the bed – it dipped as he sat down – and took me in his arms.

'You take care of yourself, yes?'

'You too.'

'I've already told you. Don't worry about me.'

He held me and I clung to him, desperately wishing I could persuade him not to go, yet knowing that nothing I could say would do any good. When his mind was made up, Paul could be every bit as stubborn as I could.

When he had gone, I buried my head in the pillow and wept.

The bad feeling stayed with me all day,

hovering over me like a dense fog, and Helen's presence made me feel yet more tense and stressed. To add to this, I felt nauseous, with a headache threatening. I tried to work but concentration was beyond me. I found myself staring into space, bombarded by chaotic thoughts and emotions.

The post came late, as usual. Wandering into the kitchen with some idea of making a coffee, I found it stacked neatly on the table. Of Helen there was no sign.

I flipped through it, discarding the inevitable junk mail. That left a square white envelope and a small Manila one, both addressed to both Paul and me. I opened the white one first – a wedding invitation from friends we hadn't seen in ages. A church wedding in June – that would be something to look forward to. I'd have to buy something new to wear – I'd certainly be showing by then. Feeling slightly cheered, I tore open the Manila envelope. Inside was a bill from a local builder for some work we'd had done – new guttering and fascia boards on the rear of the house a couple of weeks ago.

The bill was handwritten, and bore the legend in neat capitals: 'Prompt settlement would be appreciated'. Understandable, really. Small businesses suffer dreadfully from late payments, and it always annoys me that big organizations – and some people who aren't short of a penny or two – hang fire for as long as they can in order to grab that extra bit of interest whilst their money is still in the bank.

I'd pay the bill straight away, I decided – write a cheque and put it in an envelope and Helen could post it. Paul usually dealt with that sort of thing, but I had no clear idea of how long he was going to be away.

I got the coffee pot on and went into Paul's study, yanking the relevant file down from the shelf where it lived to look for the cheque book he used for household accounts. There was a sheaf of papers secured loosely by the metal spring and I glanced at them idly, then found myself frowning as I uncovered a building society statement headed up with the name of a society I didn't recognize as one we dealt with.

Curious, I pulled it out from the clip, then gasped as I saw the balance it was credited with. I had no idea we had such a large investment with these people! No idea we had such a large single investment full stop. We had a portfolio of stocks and shares and a certain amount of ready money that we could draw on if we needed to, of course, but this … I was staggered.

The account was in Paul's name, and though to a certain extent we kept our finances separate, I could hardly believe he had never mentioned having such a nest egg tucked away. He dealt with our money matters, of course, but we always discussed how we should best invest any windfalls or surplus cash. Why hadn't he told me about this?

As I stared at it, puzzled and disturbed, I found myself remembering that other occasion a couple of weeks – a lifetime? – ago, when I'd offered to pay a bill for him. He'd been uncharacteristically sharp with me, insisting that he would deal with it. Could it be that he hadn't wanted me to come across this book? And were there others I didn't know about either?

I hesitated, sorely tempted to go through his files to see what I could find. But I couldn't bring myself to do it. It would be almost as bad as Helen snooping through my drawers. When Paul came home I'd ask him about it. In the meantime, well, to be honest, I had enough on my mind already.

I found the cheque book, wrote a cheque to the builder and sealed it into an envelope. But the unease I felt knowing that Paul had secrets from me was still there, another shadow to add to the gathering gloom.

Thirty-One

I'd hoped Paul might telephone me but he didn't, and the uncertainty weighed heavily on me. All very well for him to tell me not to worry – I would have been less than human if I could have managed that. I didn't even know where he was, for heaven's sake. But his original plan had been to go to Hong Kong, and I couldn't see any reason why he should have gone back on that, for all that he had been deliberately vague about it this morning. Was he there yet, I wondered? Would he call me when he arrived?

I thought of getting out the atlas to check flight times, but decided against it. If Helen noticed, it would be a dead giveaway that Paul was out of the country, something he had appeared to want to keep secret from everyone, me included. Then it occurred to me that I could find the information on the Internet. I went back to Paul's study, switched on the computer, and logged on. A few moments later, via my web browser, I was scouring the sites of the major international airports, and soon found what I was looking for.

A Cathay Pacific flight had left Gatwick this morning en route to Kai Tak. And it was due to arrive ... I checked my watch, calculating. He wouldn't have landed yet then. If he was on the flight at all. For a few moments I sat staring at the screen, feeling my anxiety spiralling into something close to panic. Then, not wanting to let my fear crystallize into visions of what might happen when he reached Hong Kong, I deliberately disengaged my thoughts, fiddling restlessly with the mouse, clicking on one link after another. I wasn't consciously looking for anything in particular, but subconsciously I must have been drawn to the key name in the whole dreadful business – Kowloon and Victoria Enterprises. Suddenly it was there on the screen before me in glorious Technicolor. The Hong Kong connection. The people who were using Stattisford to smuggle drugs into the country.

Unable to stop myself, I began delving deeper, and the details unfolded before my eyes. Status – dates of registration – list of directors ... I scrolled down. Chinese names, picturesque, conjuring visions of men in sharp suits and white shirts with oriental features. And then, bringing me up short, making my heart stop beating, a name that leaped out at me from the screen.

Paul's name.

Disbelieving, I stared. I must be mistaken!

But I wasn't.

Kowloon and Victoria Enterprises. Paul Wilson. London.

The confused emotions that had been chasing around inside me all day churned again, muddying my thoughts, dizzying me. I stared at the screen, breath coming so short and fast it made me feel faint. I released the mouse, clenched my hands so that my nails bit into the palms. I could feel a sheen of perspiration breaking out all over me, making my skin cold and clammy.

Paul was a director of Kowloon and Victoria Enterprises. And I hadn't known.

I couldn't understand it – didn't want to understand. But there was no way I could avoid the thoughts that were chasing in. Shaking like a leaf, I switched off the computer, switched it on again, went back online. I was in such a state it took me several goes to find the information again. But when I did, it was unchanged. Clear. Unavoidable. Not simply a figment of my fevered imagination.

Whatever Kowloon and Victoria were involved in, Paul was involved in too. Not passively. Not by default. Not because Stattisford was being used without their knowledge, but directly, by design. Repugnant though the idea was to me – as repugnant as it was unbelievable – there was no getting away from it. Paul was a director of Kowloon and Victoria Enterprises, and must have known all along what was going on. At first he'd tried to smooth things over, make out that I was chasing shadows. And then he'd intimated that he intended looking into it himself. Whilst all the time he must have known that I wasn't chasing shadows at all, that I was on the point of uncovering something he didn't want me to know about because he knew I would never, never, condone such a thing.

Drug smuggling. I'd discovered that Stattisford – and Paul – were involved in drug smuggling, and by doing so I'd thrown a very big spanner in the works. Endangered the whole operation.

Was that why he had gone to Hong Kong? Not to investigate, but to sort things out, or to warn the suppliers that they'd been rumbled? Perhaps he couldn't trust to telephone calls or faxes in case they were intercepted. He couldn't be sure who I had or hadn't told of my suspicions. I'd admitted to speaking to Tony Bowman and that meant that the cat could be out of the bag and the authorities alerted. I could see now why he had refused to go to the police. Why he'd talked of being ruined. Everything was falling into place.

Suddenly, startlingly, the telephone began to ring. I froze. Paul! What if it was Paul?

What was I going to say to him? Nothing, I thought in panic. I must say nothing yet. But could I keep my knowledge from him? Wouldn't it be there in my voice, in every word I spoke? My lip trembled. Only this morning he'd held me and kissed me good-bye and I'd wanted to hang on to him, never let him go. Now, suddenly, I couldn't bring myself even to speak to him.

Somehow I got control of myself. The phone had stopped ringing now, and from the kitchen doorway I saw that Helen had answered it. For the first time I was actually glad she was there, a buffer between me and reality.

'Who is it?' I mouthed, and she waved a hand at me, raised her eyebrows, and said into the receiver: 'I don't think we're interested, thank you, but I'll just check.' She covered the mouthpiece with her hand, turning to me. 'Double-glazing salesman. You don't want anything like that, do you?'

'No – get rid of them.' I could hear the tension in my voice, but Helen didn't give me so much as a second glance. Only when she replaced the receiver did she turn to me, looking at me narrowly.

'Julia – are you all right?'

'Fine. Why?' I snapped in the same tight voice.

'You look really pale.'

'I'm just tired,' I didn't want to talk to her.

'I think I'll go and have a bath.'

'Right.' She smiled, that annoyingly intimate smile. 'That will help, I'm sure. You'll feel better for it.'

'What are you going to do?' I asked.

'Watch TV in my room. Unless you want me to keep you company?' I shook my head and she went on: 'Would you like me to make you a hot drink, then? I think you need something, Julia. You really do look very peaky.'

'No, it's all right, thank you.' I just wanted to be alone, to try to make some sense of my chaotic thoughts, though I was dreading, with an awful sick dread, where those thoughts were going to lead me.

'Well, if you're quite sure...' She was still looking at me intently and there was something in her expression I could not read, though I have to confess I didn't make much effort to do so.

'I'm quite sure,' I said. 'I'll have a hot bath, and afterwards I'll probably go straight to bed.'

I ran my bath and got undressed. Steam filled the tiny room, misting the mirror. I managed to get the top off a bottle of fragrant oil with fingers clumsy with nerves, and sloshed a good measure into the water, which scalded my ankles as I climbed in and paddled around. I got out again hastily, started the cold tap, and stood shivering as so many unwelcome thoughts came flooding into my mind.

Everything was fitting together now that I'd seen Paul's name on the list of directors of Kowloon and Victoria Enterprises, all the puzzling details that I'd been unable to make sense of before. The letter from Hong Kong, for one thing – the letter he'd denied had arrived, though I had seen the envelope in the waste basket in his office. I'd thought it was odd that it should have come here rather than to Stattisford, and even more odd that he had lied about it. Now the explanation seemed all too obvious. Neither Paul nor the person who had sent it had wanted it to fall into the wrong hands.

Then there was his insistence that I should leave well alone and stop trying to find out what Kowloon and Victoria were up to. Of course – he'd realized that if I continued, I'd find out about his connection with them. I remembered his fury the day he'd come home and found Ruth helping me to search for the file – and shivered again. He had been afraid she might find out too. And now Ruth was dead...

No! I blocked the thought almost before it had time to take shape. Ruth's death was coincidence. It had to be. Whatever else Paul had done, he was no murderer. And I couldn't believe he would have been party to harming or threatening me in any way either. But that didn't mean the others involved – and there must be others – would be so scrupulous. And Paul had warned me about them. Thugs who would stop at nothing. Torching my car to warn me off because I was getting too close to the truth. Killing poor Ruth perhaps, though I couldn't for the life of me see why. Unless, of course, it was because she, too, knew more than she should...

I thought again of Jim. As head storeman it seemed unlikely that he was unaware of what was going on. And if he had asked his wife to drive out to Hawley Woods, she would have done so without a second thought. But there was something that didn't quite fit there. If Jim was involved in such a profitable enterprise, then why was his wife working as a glorified domestic help and driving a ten-year-old Ford Fiesta? If he was helping to distribute drugs worth a small fortune, he wouldn't be doing it for just his storeman's wage while Paul took the profits.

I thought again of the savings account I'd stumbled upon this morning, and wondered numbly how many others there were, tucked away in offshore holdings or foreign banks. How could he do it? Dear God, how could he do it? And how could I have known him so little that I had not realized...?

I turned off the cold tap, swished the

water. It was too cold now, and I was cold too, the chill of shock seeming to start in my bones and spread outwards. I reached over the bath, pulling on the cord to switch on the electric heater. It clicked and connected, and then...

It's not easy to describe what happened next. It took me so completely by surprise that for a moment I simply couldn't understand what the rending noise was, why the cord seemed to be coming away in my hand, why I was being showered with crumbs of dry plaster. And then all at once I realized – the heater had parted company with the wall. For a split second it hung out at a crazy angle, then the weight of it proved too much for the remaining screws. There was a last protesting creak, and it came crashing down. It seemed to fall in slow motion and yet very fast, both at the same time. I leaped back instinctively, catching my hip on the towel rail and losing my balance. Almost simultaneously there was an appalling crash and a loud hissing noise as the fire landed in the bath. Water flew everywhere like a tidal wave and I think I saw a flash, but that might just have been me closing my eyes so hard I saw stars. And then the light went out.

'Oh my God! Oh my God!' I was gibbering with shock, my whole body turned to jelly. If I hadn't already been on my bottom on the bathroom floor, my legs would certainly have given way beneath me, and my hip was hurting where I'd bumped into the towel rail. I couldn't see anything, but there was an awful smell that seemed to be choking me. For long moments I stayed exactly where I was, too shaken to move, or even think.

A hammering on the bathroom door. Helen calling my name. 'Julia? Julia – are you all right?'

I tried to answer, failed. My vocal chords seemed to be paralysed like the rest of me. The door opened cautiously and I saw her silhouetted against the light from the landing, head and shoulders poking forward, body hidden, as if she was deformed in some way. She was peering round towards the bath, and all her body language was telegraphing dread. Incongruously I found myself wondering why, if the lights had fused, the landing light was still on, then remembered. We'd had the house rewired in two stages – it was on a different circuit.

'I'm here,' I managed.

She jumped as though she'd been shot. 'Julia?'

'Here. I'm here!' I began to pull myself up, leaning first against the loo, then hanging on to the wash basin. The door opened fully and more light flooded in. suddenly aware of the fact that I was stark-naked, I grabbed a towel from the toppled towel rail, winding it around myself.

Helen was still in the doorway. She seemed to be using the door for support, much as I was using the sink.

'The fire came off the wall,' I said. 'When I pulled the cord to put it on, it all just ... came away!' My voice was weak, shaking.

'My God!' Helen said. 'You could have been killed, Julia!'

I wrapped my arms tightly around my trembling body.

'I know,' I said.

And so I had a second sleepless night. And this time my waking thoughts were worse than nightmares. I didn't want to think them. I fought against them desperately, with my heart shrinking as well as my consciousness. But there was no avoiding them. No way of shutting them out, much as I wanted to. Awful, insidious doubt was nibbling away at the foundations of my world, my whole life.

I'd pulled that 'on' cord so often, almost every day, throughout the winter and the chilly spring, and I'd never noticed even the slightest give in it. Surely, surely if the heater had worked loose of its own accord there would have been? Surely if the wall had been collapsing beneath the securing screws, there would have been little showers of powdery plaster, flurries of dust, at the very least? But I'd noticed nothing. The fire had seemed perfectly secure. Now I could not help but think the unthinkable. The screws had been loosened recently – and deliberately. Loosened by someone who knew I used that fire almost every time I took a bath. And there were only two people who could have done that.

Helen – or Paul.

Shivering still in spite of the two hot-water bottles packed one each side of me, I went over and over it and tried to convince myself it was the lesser of the two evils.

Helen. It had to be Helen. Right from the start there had been something I didn't like about her, and I'd known that her coming into our lives was simply too convenient.

But Helen was no taller than me, and I couldn't have reached the fire without standing on something – the edge of the bath, perhaps? I tried to envisage the angle, how high one would have to reach up in order to loosen the screws. Not that far – but it wasn't the lower ones that had been missing. I'd actually seen them sheer away from the wall. For that to have happened, it must have been the top ones that had been removed, so that the weight of the fire became unevenly distributed. And the top screws, behind the jut of the fire itself, would be very difficult to reach indeed.

And besides ... when would Helen have

had the opportunity to do something like that? Since I'd come home unexpectedly, the only time she'd been alone in the house was when I'd gone to Stattisford to see Paul. But she hadn't known then that Paul intended going away – at least, I presumed she hadn't. For all she'd known, it could have been Paul who would be on the receiving end of a live electric fire in a bath of water. Either she'd done it with that intention – or at least the risk of it happening – or she hadn't done it at all.

Which left Paul.

Everything in me was screaming a protest at the very idea that he could have done such a thing, yet there was no getting away from the awful logic of it. Whether I wanted to believe it or not, the pieces of the jigsaw were coming together all too neatly.

Did I really know Paul at all? Do we ever really know another person? How can we ever be certain of what goes on inside their head? We live with them, love them, and yet see only what they allow us to see – or what we ourselves want to. This time yesterday I would never have entertained for a single second the thoughts that were assailing me now. But already today I'd come so far along the path of admitting there was a side to Paul I knew nothing about that it no longer seemed beyond belief. Doors had opened in my previously closed mind and what was behind them had to be faced. For I was beginning to be able, albeit unwillingly, to explain so much that had previously been inexplicable.

Paul had tried to kill me because I was a threat to his illegal operation. Not just once, but twice. The first time in the multi-storey car park immediately after I first discovered the irregularities with Kowloon and Victoria and told him about it. I'd always known I'd been pushed down the stairs that day. I'd been so certain about the hand that I'd felt in my back before I fell. But Paul had pooh-poohed my assertion, made me believe that I'd imagined it, or that I was confused, because of the concussion I'd suffered. No wonder he'd been so keen to discount my version of how I'd come to fall – if it had been him who had pushed me! Of course such a thing had never entered my head before, but now it seemed all too possible. Paul was the one person who would know that I parked each week without fail on the top deck. He even knew the time, more or less, when I would be returning to my car. And he was the only person who had known at that stage that my suspicions had been aroused concerning Kowloon and Victoria. Motive and opportunity, the police always went on about – in detective stories, anyway. Paul had both.

The same went for Ruth's murder. Paul

had discovered Ruth helping me with my enquiries on his computer. He'd known we were logged on to the Hong Kong site and perhaps thought I'd told her what it was we were looking for. As for the car seen in Hawley Woods, it could just as easily have been Paul's as Jim's. They both had access to dark-coloured BMWs. And when it came to moving Ruth's Fiesta to the spot where it had been found, Paul, like Jim, would have had to move the seat back from Ruth's normal driving position to accommodate his long legs. Could that be the reason the policeman had told him about it? Because he too suspected Paul and was trying to panic him into some admission of guilt or hasty action? I hadn't believed at the time that DS Wright had 'let it slip', as Paul had put it, and I didn't believe it now.

And there was so much else besides, so many details I hadn't even considered as suspicious before. Now they were suggesting themselves to me and fitting together with a sickening inevitability. There were the times when I'd tried to contact him only to be told he wasn't where I expected him to be. No one at work had known where he was when I'd tried to phone him there on the morning of my accident in the multi-storey, and the day I'd learned I was pregnant. On my first night back in London, when he'd supposedly gone out for a quick snack with Josh, I'd been surprised that he was not yet home when I'd phoned quite late. And the night when I'd thought I heard an intruder downstairs and been frightened out of my wits, I'd rung the country club where he was having his Round Table meeting only to be told that he had already left. But there had been an incredibly long time lapse before he arrived home. Where had he been? A possible explanation occurred to me now. Had it been *Paul* I'd heard downstairs? *Paul* who had come home for something and gone out again, inadvertently letting Oscar in in his haste and treading a wet leaf into the kitchen? I couldn't imagine what he could have been doing, but then there was so much I still didn't understand about this whole business.

Then there was the peculiar saga of Helen. All along, Paul had pushed for her to take over Ruth's job and done his best to squash my objections. And all along I'd felt that her turning up when she had was just too convenient. Now, I replayed it in my mind and didn't like one bit the conclusions I was forced to consider. I'd thought Paul had offered her the job in the first place because he was a bit drunk and not thinking rationally. But supposing that wasn't the case at all? Supposing he'd known exactly what he was doing? Offering her the job so that she would be on hand to keep an eye on me, and drinking a little too much because he was nervous as to how the whole thing would go. Offering her the job because that was the way they had planned it between them – that she should be staying in the same hotel as we were and pretend to recognize me.

Incredibly, considering I was actually exploring the possibility that my husband had tried to kill me, the thought that he might be enjoying some kind of liaison with Helen plumbed new depths of despair, another betrayal which hurt on quite another level and so had the power to inflict yet more pain. Paul and Helen. Plotting together. Paul and Helen together under our roof. Making love in our bed for all I knew. The idea made me feel sick all over again.

Oh, why hadn't I trusted my instincts where she was concerned? I'd known there was something wrong – known that I had never met her before in my life. But it had sounded so weak, given that I had been suffering from concussion, lapses of memory and apparent delusions about my accident. And when she'd produced the photographs of me on Magnetic Island it had seemed that I must indeed have simply forgotten her. Now, it occurred to me that they could be my own photographs, the ones I'd kept all these years. Paul could have given them to her. No wonder they had looked vaguely familiar to me!

For a moment I toyed with the idea of going downstairs right now and sifting through my mementos to see if any were missing. But it would take forever and I still couldn't be sure after all this time what should be there and what had been mislaid. And in any case, I really didn't want to leave the safety of my room. Didn't want to meet Helen on the stairs, or see her hateful face peering round the door of Paul's study as I searched through my boxes of photographs and keepsakes, as she had peered round the bathroom door tonight...

Had Paul warned Helen what was going to happen when I yanked on the cord of the electric fire? I wondered. When I had gone to take my bath, did she think it was the last time she would see me alive? Certainly her body language had suggested she was shrinking from what she might see. Oh, dear God, the more I went on with this, the worse it got. I couldn't believe it, and yet at the same time I did – or at least, the badly frightened, confused part of me believed it.

What the hell was I going to do? I honestly didn't know. But I was horribly certain of one thing. The decision I came to must be the right one. My very life depended on it.

Hour after hour I lay awake, hearing the clock downstairs mark their passing with its hollow, echoing chime. At last the sky began to lighten with cold grey dawn, and in the dark womb of despair and fear the familiar items of bedroom furniture began to take shape around me. But they were of no comfort now; like Paul they had become insubstantial and almost threatening artefacts of an anchorage I could no longer depend on, where I no longer felt safe, and nothing was as it seemed.

I got up and got dressed, throwing on the first clothes that came to hand – jeans and a sweater. The house was silent; Helen must still be asleep. Not wanting to face the evidence of what had happened last night, I used the downstairs cloakroom instead of the bathroom, finding a new toothbrush and paste in the cupboard on the landing where we kept fresh supplies. Then, as if needing some kind of armour against what lay ahead, I put on a little make-up.

I went to the foot of the stairs and stood listening. There was still no sound of movement from Helen's room. I grabbed a jacket, my handbag and car keys. I had to get out while I was still in one piece, and I didn't want to face Helen either. Didn't want to talk to her. Didn't want to look at her and wonder if she knew my husband better than I did.

I should go straight to the police, I realized, and tell them what I knew. But I didn't want to do that either. Not yet. I was

307

still clinging desperately to the hope that there was another explanation for all this, that somehow I was wrong in the deductions I had made.

Instead, I had decided to go to the one person I felt I could trust. The one person who would listen to what I had to say and know what to do about it. The person who, above all others, had a right to know what was going on, and who might just be able to come up with an alternative explanation.

I was going to Josh.

Thirty-Two

Early as it still was, there was no reply when I rang Josh's bell. His car wasn't on the drive, and when I peered in through the grime-encrusted windows of the garage, I could see only the BMW motorcycle which was his pride and joy, and various items of garden equipment. He must have already left for work, I guessed. Paul always said Josh liked to make an early start. It enabled him to slope off early too, for a round of golf, a workout at the gym, a ride on his motorbike or even, sometimes, a flight in the single-engine PA28 aircraft which he owned as part of a syndicate with three others, and which was kept in one of the vast hangars at the rear of the local flying club.

I got back into my hire car and headed it towards the industrial estate. I wondered what Helen would think when she woke up and found me gone. But I really didn't care much what Helen thought. Only the unpleasant possibility that she might know where Paul was and be able to contact him when I could not made me put my foot down harder on the accelerator.

As I'd expected, Josh's car was parked in the space reserved for him. Jim Wood's car was also in the yard, outside the rambling shed that housed the stores. He was obviously another early starter – or perhaps he had become one since Ruth's death. I realized just how little I knew about the day-to-day workings of the company that was my husband's life.

I went in through the main entrance. At least Mary was not yet at her desk; a neat pile of invoices lay under a crystal paper-weight, and her computer screen was dark. I walked past it, along the corridor. The door of Josh's office was open; through it I could see him sitting at his desk. He had taken his jacket off and there was something strong and comforting and extremely attractive about the way he had rolled the cuffs of his pristine white shirt back almost to the elbows, revealing bronzed arms. Not that 'attractive' came into it – it was the 'strong and comforting' which appealed to me.

He looked up and saw me, his eyebrows lifting a fraction in surprise. 'Julia! What on earth are you doing here? Is everything all right?'

'No, not really,' I said. 'Not at all, in fact. I'm really worried, Josh.'

'Come and sit down. You look terrible.' He got up and came around the desk, pulling out the visitor's chair and holding it for me.

'Would you like a coffee or something?'

I remembered I hadn't had any breakfast, and realized with a slight shock that at least this morning I didn't feel nauseous. Well, not the pregnancy nausea I'd become used to feeling, anyway. Just sick with worry and fright. Perhaps the other sort was coming to an end, as Bev had predicted it would.

'I could do with a cup, yes,' I said.

'The machine won't be going yet. Mary does that when she gets in. But if I don't fill it too full it shouldn't take long.' He disappeared along the corridor and I sat waiting, hands pressed together in my lap, until he returned a few minutes later.

'Clever things, those. Fresh coffee almost on tap.' He perched on the edge of the desk. 'What's this all about then, Julia?'

I looked down at my hands, wondering where to start.

'Paul's all right, is he?' Josh asked sharply.

'Yes ... well, to be honest, I don't know...'

Josh looked at me narrowly. 'He's away, isn't he?' I nodded wordlessly. 'Haven't you heard from him?' I shook my head.

'Julia,' Josh said gently. 'Whatever it is ... you can talk to me.'

'I know. That's why I'm here. Only ... can I have my coffee first?' My mouth was bone dry, and anyway, once I began I wanted to be able to go through my terrible story, I didn't want any interruptions.

'Yes, sure. Whatever you like. I expect it's ready by now.' He disappeared again briefly, came back with two mugs and set them down on the desk. 'Milk?'

'No thanks. Nor sugar. I'll have it just as it is.'

'OK.' He sat down opposite me, eyeing me gravely and sympathetically. 'So – tell me what the problem is.'

There was no way out now. I took a couple of sips of coffee, so hot it scalded my lips, and began.

'God,' Josh said with feeling when I'd finished.

He got up, crossed to the window, and turned, looking back at me.

'I know,' I said. 'It's a complete nightmare. I just can't believe any of it. But something is going on, Josh. And I thought ... well, that you should know about it.'

He rasped his hand over his chin. Above it his eyes were narrowed, thoughtful. 'As far as I was aware, Paul had gone up north to sort out a new contract. But you think he's gone to Hong Kong.'

Tears were pricking my eyes. I was remembering what Paul had said before he left: 'It's best you don't know where I am...' But best for whom? And in any case, it seemed to me that Paul had forfeited his right to my loyalty. But still it stuck in my throat to tell

312

anyone, even Josh, what Paul had expressly asked me not to.

'I honestly don't know,' I said. 'That's where he said he was going in the first place. To see if he could investigate from that end. But since he is a director of Kowloon and Victoria, that simply doesn't hold water any more. It would have to be that he'd gone to warn them that there was likely to be trouble. And this morning he was very vague indeed. It was as if he was trying to convince me he'd had a change of plan. Why would he do that?'

'That's what I'd like to know.' Josh's face was understandably grim. 'This is something of a bombshell, Julia.'

'I know.' I bit my lip helplessly. 'I'm so sorry, Josh.'

'Not your fault,' he said more gently. 'You've come to me now, that's all that matters. I just can't believe though that all this has been going on under my nose and I never for one moment...' He broke off with a frustrated shake of his head.

'I know. How do you think *I* feel?'

'I can imagine. No – I can't. That's a very patronizing thing to say. I can't imagine at all how dreadful it must be for you. I'm only his partner, for God's sake. You're his wife!'

The tears stung again. At any moment I was going to dissolve and make a complete fool of myself.

'You really think he tried to kill you?' he went on incredulously.

'I don't know what to believe any more,' I said miserably. 'But someone did. It's too much of a coincidence for me to believe otherwise, however I might try to avoid it. And Helen is involved somehow, I'm certain of it. She's there to keep an eye on me – make sure I don't blow the whole thing sky-high. And without a doubt she knows what's going on. Last night, when she came into the bathroom, she thought she was going to find me dead. I know she did. It was written all over her.'

'OK.' Josh's mouth was a tight line. 'So we have to decide what we're going to do. I guess the first thing is for me to do a little investigating of my own.'

'Rather than going straight to the police, you mean?'

'Well yes. I'm going to look a bloody fool, aren't I – my company involved in drug smuggling and me not knowing a thing about it.'

I had a sense of déjà vu and the lump tightened in my throat again. Paul had said much the same thing. But I was glad, all the same, that Josh wasn't going straight to the police. I still hoped, rather vainly, but hoped none the less, that it wouldn't come to that. That there would be some simple explanation I'd somehow missed, that even now it might turn out that Jim Wood or someone like him was behind it all and no more guilt would attach to Paul than to Josh. That he would be guilty of naivety, guilty even of professional negligence, perhaps. But not of drug smuggling. Not of murder and attempted murder.

'The devil of it is, I trusted Paul,' Josh said savagely.

A car was pulling into the car park. Mary – arriving for work without the slightest inkling of what was going on. She'd be at her desk in a few minutes, cheery, curious as to why I was here ... my heart sank. I just didn't know how to cope any more.

'The thing that's worrying me most, Julia,' Josh was saying, 'is your safety. There have already been two attempts on your life, not to mention your car being torched. I think before we do anything else at all – arouse anyone's suspicions that you have got even closer to what's been going on than they think you have – we need to make sure you're somewhere they can't get at you.'

I managed a rather hollow laugh. 'Like where?'

'I know the ideal place. Trust me.' He leaned over, touched my hand, letting his fingers rest on mine. 'Julia, look, we have no idea who else is involved in this. Helen, you think. Paul, almost certainly. Jim Wood, possibly. But it's not just them. There will be

315

others. There have to be. Whoever was responsible for torching your car, for a start. I would guess there must be a ring of some sort – the organizers who deal with the distribution, and the heavies who take care of any problems, the troubleshooters, if you like. There may even be a Mr Big, for want of a better description, who would almost certainly be surrounded by some very dangerous characters indeed. We simply can't take any chances. So far you've been lucky...'

'Lucky!' I echoed wryly.

'I want you out of harm's way before I begin muddying the waters,' Josh went on, ignoring my interruption. 'I have a cottage in North Wales. A place I use as a fishing lodge. It's in pretty wild country, very isolated. No one knows about it. I like my privacy, in case you hadn't noticed. You'd be safe there until all this is over.' He glanced at his watch. 'I could fly you there.'

'But I haven't got anything with me,' I objected. 'I'd have to go home and get a few things.'

'Not a good idea,' Josh said decisively. 'The last person you want to alert is Helen, and you'd certainly do that if you went home to pack a bag. She's obviously in this – up to her neck – and she might have you followed. No, it's best you go just as you are. You can buy anything you need at the little local shop when we get there. Oh, for heaven's sake,

Julia, which is the more important? Having your party frock with you – or being safe?'

'Well ... put like that...'

'Exactly. Come on now, finish your coffee and we'll go.' He got up, moving with purpose now, then glanced back at me. 'And don't say anything to Mary, either. I don't suppose she's involved, but until I get to the bottom of this it's better to trust no one.'

He was hustling me now; uncharacteristically compliant, I let myself be hustled. It was good to let someone else think for me, particularly when that someone was as solidly reassuring as Josh. He propelled me along the corridor, a hand under my elbow.

Mary, in the process of taking off her coat, glanced at us in surprise.

'Morning, Mary. I'm just going out for a bit. Won't be long.' He made it sound as if he was just making the short journey into town.

'Oh, right...' She was still looking at me with a puzzled expression.

'Morning, Mary.' I could hear the tremble in my voice, and hated myself for it. But who wouldn't be cracking up with this nightmare unfolding around them? I reminded myself.

Josh unlocked his car with the remote control, opened the door for me, helped me into the passenger seat.

'Don't worry, sweetie.' He smiled at me briefly, but there was both warmth and comfort in that smile. 'Uncle Josh will look after you.'

I closed my eyes against those still-threatening tears. If I hadn't turned up that file on Kowloon and Victoria, would any of this have happened? Would I still be living a normal life in blissful ignorance? Perhaps. But it was too late now to turn back the clock. I had discovered the file, and in doing so had changed my life forever.

'Let's just go, Josh,' I said.

Thirty-Three

We drove the couple of miles to the local airport where Josh kept his PA28, entering it not by the main entrance, but a service road that led directly to the flying club, and I waited in the car whilst he disappeared into the hangar. A few minutes later the doors opened and Josh and a mechanic pushed the little plane out, parking it on a small expanse of grass between the prefabricated club buildings and the taxiway. I watched, numb now, as Josh prepared for the flight, walking round the plane, checking fuel and oil, running his hand along the ailerons and tail-plane, operating the flaps. He disappeared into the clubhouse, emerged again and handed me a packet of biscuits from the vending machine.

'Thought you could use these if you've had no breakfast.' I was touched by his thoughtfulness, though I thought that any food, especially dry biscuits, would choke me. 'I won't be long. I just have to work out a PLOG.'

I glanced at him, puzzled. 'A PLOG?'

'Pilot's log – a flight plan. Bearings, wind

speed and so on.'

'Oh, right.'

'Try and relax, honey.'

Easier said than done! I couldn't imagine how *he* could be so relaxed, in the light of what I'd just landed on him. But that was Josh all over – the consummate Mr Cool. And it wasn't his whole world collapsing around him. The business might be important to him – it was, of course – but it was just business. The betrayal of a partner, however devastating that might be, could in no way compare to the total betrayal I was experiencing. As for the threat of physical danger, I couldn't imagine that would faze Josh either. Judging by what I knew of him and his lifestyle, he might even enjoy it.

Ten minutes later he was back. 'OK, let's go.'

I followed him over to the PA28 – white, apart from a single blue flash, the paint gleaming in the morning sunshine – and clambered up into the right-hand seat. Josh climbed in beside me and began flicking switches and dials, starting up the engine. The single propeller cranked into life, slowly at first, then faster, so that the blades disappeared into a whirling mist. Josh plugged in his headset and fished a spare one from his briefcase, handing it to me. 'So we can talk to one another without shouting.'

I put it on. It felt heavy and unwieldy and

I couldn't get the little microphone arm to stay at the right angle. Josh fixed it for me, and I realized that at least it gave me the advantage of being in touch with what was going on. Through the earpieces, which felt like enormous tight earmuffs, I could hear his conversation with the control tower, as they gave him updated information about air pressures and wind speeds and instructions for departure. Most of it sounded like double-dutch to me, but I understood 'proceed to holding point C' when Josh released the handbrake and moved off.

He taxied slowly, following the centre line, then parked again at a slight angle to the main runway, where he ran through a sequence of power checks that made the little plane throb and vibrate impatiently. My heart was in my mouth. I'd never thought I minded flying, but this was quite different to being in a passenger jet, with a stewardess moving confidently up and down the aisle and nothing much to see but a comfortingly large expanse of wing beyond a thin double-glazed window – if you were lucky. The smallness of this little aircraft made me feel nervous and vulnerable – there was less room inside than in Paul's BMW! But my nerves were already on edge, I reminded myself, and in any case it would probably get better when we were off the ground.

'Ready for departure,' Josh said, and

321

through my headset I heard the air traffic controller reply.

'Cleared take-off.'

Josh turned on to the runway, held for a moment, building up power, and then we were off, rattling along the narrow grey strip between the expanses of green, faster and faster until the nose lifted, the expanse of green dipped away, and I realized we were airborne.

In spite of all my churning emotions, I felt a moment's supreme exhilaration. There was something about climbing gently, watching the countryside spread out beneath us in a patchwork panorama of fields and woods, that momentarily made me forget everything else. Then Josh was banking to the left and I was hanging on to my seat, feeling fear again – fear that we'd tip over, fear that I'd roll out of my seat, just ... fear.

He turned his head and winked at me. 'It's OK. Relax!'

I half-smiled, wanly. 'This is new to me.'

'We'll do it again sometime – under different circumstances.'

'If you say so.' Suddenly I was very aware of how very close we were, that strong brown arm I'd admired earlier almost brushing mine as he adjusted the trim wheel between our seats. I pulled my own arm in tight to my side and looked out of the window.

'Your house – look.' He nodded to the

right.

'Where?'

'There. See it?'

'Oh – yes.' But I couldn't. Couldn't make any real sense of the familiar countryside beneath me. From this angle it seemed to have flattened out, and nothing was where I thought it should be. Like my life, it was distorted beyond recognition.

I didn't want to see it, anyway. Didn't want to see Helen's car parked in our drive, know that she was there in my home, making free with my things. I felt the violation as keenly as I felt all the other emotions, more keenly, perhaps, because it was more clearly defined.

'How long will it take to get where we're going?' I asked, shouting a little, though it wasn't really necessary.

'About an hour and a half.'

We had climbed now to a height which made it less easy to distinguish features on the ground, though I saw clumps of dark green that were obviously wooded areas, clusters of houses, some with threads of smoke curling from the chimneys, and the gleam of a river threading its way between the patchwork of green and gold. The mountains, when we reached them, caused a certain amount of turbulence and I found myself gripping my seat again as the little plane rose and fell, tossed by the capricious updraughts. Then I realized we were descending, but I could see no sign of an airport, only fields, the occasional isolated hamlet and a lake, silver-blue in the bright sunshine.

'Where are we going to land?' I asked.

'Down there.' His voice, through the headset, sounded amused.

'I can't see an airstrip.' I was experiencing a flutter of panic again.

'Because there isn't one. This is rural Wales, remember.'

'But...'

'Quit worrying! I have the use of a very handy field.'

'A field!' I squeaked.

'My cottage is within easy walking distance. There it is – look.'

I looked. This time, although I'd never seen it before, there was no mistaking it. It was the only building in sight, a speck of grey, surrounded by woodland. Remote. Totally isolated.

'You see – I told you no one would ever know you were here,' Josh said.

We sank lower and lower, flying a neat box around the perimeter of the field and beyond. Then Josh turned a straight path back towards the centre of it and suddenly it seemed to me we were travelling very fast indeed, the ground rushing beneath us at an alarming rate. The wheels skimmed a hedge and then, with a slight jolt, we touched down, bumping over the uneven ground, slowing to a taxiing speed. When we came to a stop, I climbed out of the plane, glad to have my feet on terra firma again.

'Come on then.' Josh put his hand under my elbow, guiding me to a gap in the hedge and out into a lane that was little more than a track. Through the trees I could see the gleam of water – his fishing lake, presumably. Strange he'd never mentioned it. But then, as he had said, Josh was a rather private person behind that suave, easy-going exterior.

The cottage was tiny and very weathered. I couldn't imagine who had once lived in such an isolated spot – a forester, perhaps, or a shepherd, but quite honestly that was the least of my worries. It belonged to Josh now. That was enough for me.

'So where is this village you told me about?' I asked.

He grinned guiltily. 'I misled you about that, I'm afraid. The nearest hamlet is a good ten miles away.'

'But you said...'

'I know. I thought you might baulk at coming if you knew you wouldn't be able to buy a toothbrush. And it seemed more important to get you well away, without anyone knowing where you were going, than to worry about a little thing like that.'

'You really think I'm in that much danger?'

I asked apprehensively.

'Don't you?' His hand tightened under my elbow. 'Think about it, Julia. Two attempts on your life ... Anyway –' his tone lightened – 'you can use my toothbrush if you're desperate. I don't mind.'

I laughed shortly in embarrassment. I really didn't think I knew Josh well enough to share a toothbrush!

'What about food?' I asked.

Josh was unlocking the door. 'No problems there. I keep a good stock of canned fish and soup and there's plenty of dried pasta and so on. I like to know I can just drop in if I choose to without having to worry about shopping in advance.'

Drop in. That almost amused me. I supposed that was what he did, literally, when he had use of the PA28.

Considering how basic the cottage had appeared from outside, the kitchen was a revelation – well equipped with bright modern units and matching sink, a small pine dresser stocked with pottery and gleaming copper pans hanging from a rack that was slung beneath a beam. There was nothing of the air of disuse I'd expected – Josh obviously came here quite often. It was cold though, a hovering chill that was striking after the warm sunshine outside.

'It will soon warm up.' Josh wheeled a portable gas fire into the centre of the tiny room and ignited two panels.

I looked around. 'It's very nice. But what on earth am I supposed to do here?'

It was the first time I'd asked myself that; so far I'd simply allowed myself to be led along, rendered almost mindless by shock, fear and anxiety.

'There are plenty of books in the bedroom,' he offered.

'I couldn't possibly concentrate to read!'

'Some lovely walks...'

'Josh – how long am I going to be here?' I asked anxiously.

'Hopefully not long.'

Hopefully. The aura of nightmare was closing in again; I felt totally trapped.

'What are your plans?' I asked.

'Well, I have to go, obviously. Much as I'd like to stay.' His eyes lingered on my face a little too long. I looked quickly away. 'Look – I've got a couple of calls to make,' he said, getting his mobile phone out of his briefcase. 'You have a look around.'

There wasn't a great deal to look at – a very masculine bedroom with an abstract-patterned duvet in shades of dark red and brown, and plain brown curtains as well as the shelf of paperback books Josh had promised, and a tiny bathroom, also very much a man's room with dark towels that didn't match. I spent a while there, washing my face in water that felt as if it had come straight out of a mountain river, in the hope that it might help me to shake off the suffocating muzziness that came from lack of sleep and from despair, and when I emerged, Josh had finished making his telephone calls and had the kettle boiling on the Calor-gas stove.

'I'm making us coffee – only instant, I'm afraid. And I suggest you have a little slug of something stronger.' He indicated a row of bottles on the dresser.

I thought of the baby. 'No, I shouldn't. You have one if you want though.'

'I mustn't either. Not flying. Eight hours between bottle and throttle is the golden rule, and I have to get back. I have a lot to do.'

'Yes, of course.' But I didn't much like the idea of being left alone here, in this tiny isolated cottage which, since Josh had made his calls on his mobile, obviously didn't even have a telephone for contact with the outside world.

Josh poured water on to coffee granules and opened a carton of long-life milk. I like my coffee black, and he thoughtfully took my cup to the sink, topping it up with cold water from the tap. I sat on one of the counter stools cupping the mug between my hands, which were icy cold, to warm them.

'Come on, Julia, drink it up and you'll feel better,' Josh urged me.

I sipped the coffee. Used as I was to freshly ground filter coffee, it tasted slightly bitter. Perhaps it was a little stale, too, I thought. But I drank some of it anyway, not wanting to hurt Josh's feelings when he was going to so much trouble on my account, and hoping I'd have the chance to throw what was left down the sink when he wasn't looking.

'I still can't believe this is really happening,' I said shakily. 'It's like some kind of nightmare. And to think Paul is mixed up in something like this ... it's just incredible.'

'If it's any comfort, I was just as much taken in as you were,' Josh said. 'The planning must have been meticulous, and he must be quite an actor.'

Tears welled in my eyes. 'The worst thing is that he should have tried to harm me,' I said. 'That's what I really can't get my head round. He's my husband! I'm having his child!' My voice cracked. 'I thought he loved me ... and all the time...'

'He probably never intended that you should get hurt,' Josh said. 'I expect he hoped that if you ever found out, you'd go along with it. And you did say he did his best to stop you pursuing your investigations. He was probably horrified at the thought you were going to find out. He must have known you'd never go along with something like that. And that you would have to be disposed of, one way or another.'

'By electrocuting me in my bath.' I gave a small, bitter, humourless laugh. 'How could he do that to me, Josh?'

Josh sipped his own coffee. 'Profits on the scale that big-time drug dealing can bring must be a very powerful incentive,' he said thoughtfully. 'Greed for that kind of wealth takes men over. It's a kind of madness.'

'I suppose it must be.' But it was no comfort. No comfort at all.

Josh got up, reaching for his jacket and briefcase. 'I have to go, Julia. I'll keep in touch, and be back as soon as I can. In the meantime – take care of yourself.'

Icy fingers closed around my heart. Paul had said much the same thing.

I went with Josh to the door. I didn't want to make a fool of myself by crying, or hanging on to him and begging him to stay. But controlling that impulse was one of the hardest things I've ever had to do.

He squeezed my arm briefly. Then he was gone, disappearing down the track towards the field where he had left the aircraft, and I was alone.

I went back into the cottage. All of a sudden I felt dreadfully tired. The muzziness I'd been experiencing all day was suddenly much worse, my eyes so heavy that I longed to close them, and my limbs felt heavy too. The sleepless nights were catching up with me, I supposed, and though a few hours ago I'd thought I'd never sleep again, now I wanted nothing more than to lie down on Josh's comfortable single bed, pull his duvet over me, and find oblivion. But I felt I couldn't do that until I'd watched Josh take off. When his little aircraft became nothing but a dot on the horizon, it would be the last contact I would have with another human being for I didn't know how long, and somehow I couldn't miss it.

I crossed to the door, opening it and listening for the sound of the plane's engine. It was so quiet here I felt sure I'd hear it the moment he turned the ignition key. But there was no sound but the cooing of wood pigeons in the trees and the rustle of branches as they, and other birds, took flight.

And then a telephone began to ring.

I almost jumped out of my skin. I'd already established there was no land-line telephone here, and in any case it sounded more like a mobile.

Josh's mobile! I hurried back into the kitchen, tracking the sound, and saw it, on the dresser, half hidden by the jar of coffee and carton of milk. He must have put it down there when he'd finished making his calls and forgotten to pick it up again. Without even really thinking, I reached for it and pressed the receive button. And before I could say a word, a woman's voice spoke.

'Josh? It's me.'

I froze, wide-eyed with shock and disbelief. I recognized that voice!

'Helen?' I said.

And her voice, just as shocked, gasped: 'Julia?'

Thirty-Four

I don't remember what I said to her, or what she said to me. Not very much, I think. We were both too taken by surprise. The only thing that stands out in my mind is how I stood there with Josh's mobile pressed against my face, unable to move a muscle. I felt as if a steamroller had run over my chest.

I hadn't begun yet to think or reason and yet I knew the truth. Every instinct was screaming it at me.

Josh.

It wasn't Paul who was using Stattisford to smuggle drugs. It wasn't Paul who had insinuated Helen into my home. Or had me threatened. Or tried to kill me. It was Josh. Josh and Helen working together. Why else would she be calling him on a mobile telephone that even I did not know the number of, when, to my knowledge, they had never even met? That one fact had thrown all the pieces of the jigsaw into the air again, and this time they had come down to form quite a different picture, but one that fitted so perfectly I knew without doubt it couldn't be any other way.

For a moment the relief of it was over-whelming. Just to know that it wasn't Paul behind this nightmare that had taken over my life was a huge surge of joy buoying me up, making me want to laugh and cry both at the same time. And then the next wave hit me, and it was a wave of terror, running a stream of ice down my spine.

If it was Josh – and it had to be – I was in greater danger than ever before.

How could I have been so stupid? Why had I trusted Josh and not Paul? All the time I'd been hoping against hope that there was a flaw in my reasoning about all the things that had happened – and there had been. But why had it never occurred to me to suspect Josh? Josh, who had so many of the good things that money could buy, right up to a share in a private plane? Josh, who was in-volved equally with Paul at Stattisford. Josh, who had flown me here to a deserted cottage in the middle of nowhere, not allowing me to tell anyone where I was going. Josh, who also drove a dark-coloured BMW. He must undoubtedly have killed Ruth, and he would kill again without hesitation. Anyone who threatened his illegal gold mine. Me. And I'd let him lead me like a lamb to the slaughter.

I had to get away from here! But where? How? I had no idea of the lie of the land, no idea in which direction to head for help. He had said the nearest village was ten miles away – but in which direction? And I didn't even know if it was true. He'd told me initially that there was a shop within walking distance, and he'd lied about that. I could be dozens of miles away from the nearest living soul – I certainly couldn't remember having seen any signs of habitation when we'd flown in.

Just to make things worse, the drowsiness had begun dragging at me again. The shock of hearing Helen's voice on Josh's telephone had given me such a surge of adrenalin that it had been banished temporarily. Now it was back, worse than before, muzzing my senses, making my eyes feel heavy and dull, and suddenly I remembered the coffee Josh had made me, saw him handing me the mug with a friendly, sympathetic smile that was almost certainly disguising his real feelings, tasted the faint bitterness that I'd put down to slightly stale instant granules. Had he put something in that coffee? Was that the reason the drowsiness was so much worse? Suddenly I knew without doubt that was it, and thanked my lucky stars I had not drunk very much of it.

But I couldn't understand why he should have done such a thing. He'd gone and left me here, in the certain knowledge that I had no way of contacting anyone...

Or had he gone? I hadn't heard the plane take off!

Panic rushed through me like a forest fire, igniting my flagging senses once more. And I remembered. I wasn't quite as cut off as he'd intended. I had his mobile phone. Stupid, stupid woman, not to think of it before! I could call for help. God alone knew how long it would be before help reached me, and Josh might be intending to return at any minute to see if his drugged coffee had done its work. But at least I had a chance.

I grabbed the mobile, my fingers so shaky and numbed that I wasn't able to depress the button properly that would give me a line. I tried again, jabbing at it furiously.

I didn't hear the door open. The first I knew was that Josh was in the kitchen behind me.

'Who are you ringing, Julia?' he said.

I actually felt the blood drain out of my face, out of my limbs.

'Josh!'

'Who are you ringing?' he asked again, taking the phone out of my useless hands.

'No one. I...'

'I thought we agreed no one should know you were here.'

I stared at him, wide-eyed, and knew my horror must be showing on my face, telling him that I knew.

I thought of running, but Josh was between me and the door. In any case, I wouldn't get far. Josh was strong and athletic whilst I was fuzzy from lack of sleep and whatever it was he'd put in my coffee. And there was no-where I could go. No one to run to.

'Oh Julia,' Josh said, and there was genuine regret in his voice. 'I wish it hadn't come to this.'

'Why?' It came out almost as a sob.

'Because I really like you. But I'm sure you know that.'

I hadn't meant why did he wish it hadn't come to this. I'd meant why was he doing these terrible things. But of course I already knew the answer. He'd told me himself.

Money. More money than he could ever hope to make through legitimate business deals. More money than I'd ever dreamed of. It was a kind of madness, he'd said, and I thought that wasn't far from the truth. A madness that made a nonsense of every standard of human decency, created mon-sters out of twisted logic, and fed on itself. A madness that would stop at nothing, even the murder of someone he 'really liked'.

My fuzzy mind, growing ever fuzzier by the minute, battened on to that. Perhaps it was the reason he'd put something in my coffee. He had hoped that when he came back to do whatever it was he'd planned to do, I'd be asleep. He wouldn't have to look me in the eye when he killed me.

'Josh,' I said urgently. 'I won't say anything.

I promise, I won't say anything.'

'But you would, Julia.' He kicked the door shut behind him. 'I wish I could believe that you wouldn't. But you would.'

'No, I swear...'

'Where is Paul?' he asked.

'I told you ... I really don't know.'

'You said he'd gone to Hong Kong.'

'I thought he might have, but...'

Josh sighed. 'Well, if he has, I'm quite sure he'll be dealt with at that end.'

A flood of fresh horror turned my blood to ice. 'You mean...?'

'I've spoken to them – warned them he might turn up. They are very used to dealing with trouble. Very efficient. So ... that just leaves you.'

The drowsiness was closing in on me now. I was fighting to stay awake. Fighting for my life. I didn't know what good it would do in the end, trapped here with Josh and no one having the slightest idea where I was. I only knew I had to buy as much time as I could.

'Tell me, Josh,' I said. 'Tell me about it.'

He shrugged. 'You already know. Except that you thought it was Paul, not me.'

'Tell me anyway. I only made wild guesses. How does it work?'

'It's very simple, just the way you thought. The drugs come in hidden in consignments from Kowloon and Victoria and I handle distribution at this end. It's been working very smoothly. Customs and Excise aren't unduly bothered about electrical components bound for a legitimate electrical components warehouse unless they get a tip-off. There's never been the slightest shadow of suspicion – at this end, anyway.'

'But someone in Hong Kong must have been suspicious,' I said. 'Kowloon and Victoria were investigated a few years back, weren't they? Why wasn't that passed on to the authorities here?'

Josh smiled, without humour. 'There aren't many officials who can't be bought. The higher their rank, the more they have to be paid, of course. But almost everyone has their price, especially in Hong Kong.'

'So why was it still on the file that I pulled up?' I asked.

He frowned. 'An oversight, presumably – one that was attended to as soon as you drew attention to it. Not that it mattered very much – an investigation doesn't mean anything in itself. Practically everyone in Hong Kong is investigated at one time or another. The only real problem might have arisen if someone had decided to instigate a really thorough check on the investigations which had been shelved. It happens from time to time. A big clean-up operation. Heads sometimes roll then, and as you so rightly say, if something like that was passed on to the British Customs and Excise, it could have made things pretty difficult for us. But my friends in Hong Kong are in very high places, and it's well worth their while to turn a blind eye. Every so often one of the big players retires to a life of luxury in the Philippines, but there's always someone else ready and willing to take over what is a very nice little sideline. No, it works very well. And would have continued to do so if you hadn't started poking your nose in.' He gave me a narrow, questioning look. 'Aren't you getting sleepy?'

So I'd been right. He had put something in my coffee, and had expected to find me in a drugged stupor when he came back.

'I am sleepy, yes,' I said, thinking that I mustn't let Josh know I knew what he had done, or how little of that coffee I had drunk. He must have given me a truly knock-out dose; even as it was, I had to fight the drowsiness with every fibre of my being. 'I suppose I didn't have much sleep last night,' I said, and I didn't need to be a great actress to slur my words. 'I really do want to hear the details of what's been going on, though. I think you owe me that much.'

Josh smiled, and I found myself wondering how I could ever have thought it was a nice smile. Now I could see it was smug and self-satisfied. Josh was obviously enjoying boasting of his own cleverness. And whilst he was talking, I was still alive.

'What about Ruth?' I said. 'Why did she have to die?'

'Ruth? Ah, Ruth. Poor, foolish, greedy Ruth. I'm afraid that was your fault too.'

'Mine!' I exclaimed. 'But why?'

'You asked her to help you with searching the computer files, didn't you? And she saw what you saw.'

'But that wouldn't have meant anything to Ruth,' I objected. 'And she didn't really see anything, anyway.'

'Enough to ring bells, apparently. Ruth used to clean the offices at Stattisford Electronics, if you remember. And when she was there all by herself in the early mornings or the evenings or whenever it was she used to work, she'd done some snooping around. She'd obviously seen something that aroused her suspicions and never forgotten it. I think it's possible Jim might have mentioned something to her too, that he had his doubts about the consignments I personally took care of. Whatever, when you asked her to help you with your computer, she realized what it was you were looking for. She put two and two together – and made four.'

'How do you know that?' I asked – although I think I already knew the answer.

'She rang me,' Josh said. 'She asked me to meet her that Friday afternoon.'

So – I'd been right. It had been the telephone call Ruth had made to Stattisford that

341

had sealed her fate. But it had not been Jim or Paul she had phoned, but Josh.

'Ruth had the temerity to think she could blackmail me,' Josh went on. 'She actually asked me for money in return for her keeping quiet about what she knew.'

'Ruth – tried to blackmail you?' I exclaimed. 'I can't believe it! Blackmail – Ruth?'

He shrugged. 'Oh, I don't think she had it in mind to live the high life at my expense. Apparently she and Jim were desperate to start a family. She wanted enough to pay for private fertility treatment. At least, that's what she told me.'

'Oh God!' I said. Poor Ruth! Not greedy at all. Just desperate for the child she had been unable to conceive naturally.

'I'd have given her the money if I'd thought it would stop there,' Josh said, magnanimous suddenly. 'But it wouldn't have, I'm afraid. Once you start paying extortion money there's never an end to it. In any case, I couldn't risk her messing things up. I had to do something to make sure she didn't start shooting her mouth off in the wrong places. And of course, as it turned out, her death was very convenient really, because...' He broke off, looking at me meaningfully.

'Because it left us looking for a housekeeper,' I finished for him.

'Exactly.'

'And who the hell is Helen Gibbs?' I asked, angry suddenly.

And Josh said something which surprised me more than anything that had gone before.

'She's my wife,' he said.

Thirty-Five

I could feel the rim of the stool at the back of my knees, and suddenly, more than anything, I wanted to sit down. But I didn't dare. I was too afraid that if I did I would no longer be able to fight the drowsiness that was threatening to overwhelm me. Josh seemed to notice that I was struggling.

'Why don't we go into the bedroom?' he suggested. 'You could lie down and you'd be much more comfortable.'

I ignored him, picking up on the amazing thing he had said a few seconds before. 'Your wife! I didn't know you were married!'

'Why should you?' He shrugged. 'We haven't shared a home or a life for a long time. We married very young and it didn't last. But the split was quite amicable. We remained friends, though we went our separate ways. And of course I still provide her with a good standard of living, so it was in Helen's interests, naturally, to do whatever was necessary to safeguard the status quo.'

'So when you needed someone to keep an eye on me you got Helen to step in,' I said.

'You knew we were going to Cornwall on holiday, and arranged for her to be at the same hotel. And to pretend to recognize me.'

'Right.'

'And you were able to fill her in about my Australian sojourn because you've heard me talking about it.'

'Right again.'

'Clever, Josh,' I conceded. 'You must have known I'd met so many people during that time I'd never be completely sure she wasn't one of them, let alone convince Paul of it. But the photographs ... how did she come by the photographs of me on Magnetic Island?'

But even as I asked, I knew. That night when I'd been taking a bath and heard someone downstairs. It must have been Josh, looking for them. It was a hell of a chance to have taken, but presumably if I'd caught him in Paul's study he would have pretended he needed business papers urgently and had been unable to make me hear. The thought of him poking about down there whilst I was in the bath, looking through my personal possessions, was sickening.

'I must say you looked very attractive in that bikini,' he said now, with a leer. 'I could wish that you weren't feeling so drowsy and I wasn't in such a hurry. But I really have to get that plane back before they put out a search and rescue for me. I can't afford any more hitches, and that really would draw attention to me. I'm afraid we're going to have to draw this to a conclusion.' A small, unpleasant smile twisted the corners of his mouth. 'I really am very sorry about this, Julia, but...'

He moved towards me. I sidestepped, banging hard against the dresser. Panic was rising in me now in a flood tide that threatened to overwhelm me, but I knew that somehow I must stay calm. What good it would do me in the end I didn't know, but I didn't dare let myself think about that. Every minute I kept Josh talking was a minute more of life. And every minute was suddenly very precious. More precious than I'd ever realized until now.

'Did you say that to Ruth?' I asked wildly.

He checked. 'What?'

'Did you tell her you were sorry about what you had to do when you murdered her?'

A look of incredulity crossed his face, and suddenly I was angry again. He had killed Ruth without a second thought, without a single moment of regret, as he might swipe a fly that was annoying him.

'You won't get away with it,' I said.

He laughed shortly. 'Oh, I think I probably will. The police are convinced it was Jim who killed Ruth. They had to let him go because they didn't have enough evidence to hold him, but they are still looking in his direction. And they can be remarkably blinkered.'

The arrogance of the man! He truly believed he was clever enough not to get caught, and the worst of it was, he was probably right.

'What about me?' I demanded. 'You brought me here, to your cottage, in your plane. How are you going to explain that away?'

Again he smiled, that unpleasant, self-satisfied smile. 'No one knows you were with me when I flew out today. I didn't log any passengers with Air Traffic Control, and I didn't see anyone watching, did you? You were in the car, well out of sight, until I was ready to taxi. Mary knows you left the office with me, of course, but I shall say I dropped you off somewhere and no one will have any reason to doubt me. You won't be found here, Julia. You probably won't be found anywhere.'

I felt my knees go weak, saw the black edges of despair closing in, and this time was powerless to fight them. Josh was going to kill me. For all I knew, Paul was already dead, disposed of by the ruthless men at the Hong Kong end of the operation, and now Josh was going to kill me. I couldn't believe he would get away with it forever, however confident he might be that he would. But in the end there would simply be too many things pointing to him and to Stattisford, and a thorough investigation would uncover the truth. But there was no way I could persuade him of that. He was too vain, too arrogant, to believe it. And in any case, it would not save me – or my baby.

'How can you take an innocent life?' I sobbed. He looked at me, puzzled momentarily, and I went on: 'It's not just me, is it? It's my baby too!'

'I know, and I said I'm sorry, but you really have only yourself to blame,' he said, sounding vaguely irritated. 'You should have kept your nose out of things that didn't concern you. But you couldn't, could you? So I'm afraid you leave me no choice.' He paused for a moment, then went on: 'I think we should go for a little walk, Julia. I really think, since you're still awake, that might be best. And it really is very nice down by the lake. You'll like it.'

I thought of Ruth in the water-filled quarry at Hawley Woods and shrank away, but he caught hold of my arm anyway, pulling me towards him. All my instincts were to struggle, but I knew it would be useless. Josh was so much stronger than I was. And at least out in the open, if I was showing no signs of offering resistance, he might let his guard down and I might get an opportunity to get away. It was a slender hope, but it was the only one I had.

He propelled me across the kitchen and

out of the door. After the dimness of the kitchen, the bright sunshine almost blinded me – or perhaps it was the panic making everything look black. My legs were like jelly now as well as heavy and a little numb; they almost gave way beneath me.

Dear God, I prayed silently. *Don't let me die!*

Josh had a silk scarf in the pocket of his jacket. He pulled it out with one hand, still holding me fast with the other. Again my legs buckled, and this time I fell, feeling the ground graze my knees before Josh jerked me up, holding me like a limp marionette. I sobbed in terror and despair. I was going to faint or pass out at any moment. Whichever, it would make it easy for Josh. I must hold on! But I couldn't fight any more. The world was going away from me, the trees, the sun, all blurred, all edged with black. My senses swam and there was a buzzing in my ears like a swarm of insects, louder than the cooing of the wood pigeons and the creak of the trees as the light breeze stirred in the branches. The overture to total silence.

And suddenly there was another sound, quite out of place amidst the heartbeat of the countryside. Faint as yet, wavering with the bends of the lanes, yet somehow piercing, shattering the stillness. The most welcome sound I have ever heard in my life, though I could scarcely believe I was really hearing it, that it was not just an aural mirage in the desert of my terror.

A two-tone siren.

I wasn't imagining it – Josh had heard it too. He let go of my arm and I crumpled in a heap on the track into the carpet of last year's dead leaves. Still afraid to believe it was real, I raised my head a fraction. And saw a police car, blue light flashing like a beacon of hope, turn into the lane.

I remember very little of what happened next. Perhaps relief finally did what terror and Josh's attempt to drug me had failed to do. I remember shouts and running footsteps, someone crashing through the trees – Josh, presumably, trying to make a run for it, and a policeman going after him. But in the end, of course, there was nowhere for him to go, any more than there would have been for me. I learned later that he got as far as his plane, but in his haste to escape, he failed to gain enough speed before attempting take-off. He clipped one of the hedges bordering the field he used as a landing strip and crashed. He was pulled from the wreckage virtually unhurt, but his beloved PA28 was damaged beyond repair.

At the time, however, I had no way of knowing that. I remember being helped into the back of the police car, the smell of the sun-warmed leather, the crackle of the radio, the way the still-flashing beacon was making weird blue patterns in the trees. And I remember gasping: 'Paul! Oh, please God, Paul!' because I was safe now and only one other thing in the whole world mattered – that Paul should be safe too. Really, that is the extent of it. The rest is lost in that blessedly thick haze which envelops us when physically, mentally and emotionally we can take no more.

They took me, I understand, back to the nearest police station, some twelve miles from Josh's hideaway, and then to a cottage hospital. A policewoman stayed with me while a doctor examined me, and still all I could say was: 'Paul! Oh, Paul!'

'It's all right,' the policewoman said soothingly. 'He'll be here soon.'

'No!' I was becoming agitated again. 'You don't understand! He's in Hong Kong!'

'No, he isn't! Not if you mean your husband, anyway.' She reached over and squeezed my hand. I think she must have thought I was hallucinating. 'He knows you're here, and he's on his way. Just relax and try to rest, OK?'

And he was. I couldn't believe it. I opened my eyes and there he was. And all he could say was: 'Julia! Thank God!'

'Oh Paul!' I was holding on to his hand as if it was a lifeline; as if I'd never let it go. 'Are you all right?'

'Of course I am! You're the one who's had the worst of this. My God, Julia, I'd never have left you for a moment if I'd realized...' He broke off. I could see beads of sweat standing out on his forehead.

'But you went to Hong Kong! And he said ... Josh said...' It was all I could do to utter Josh's name, and to put into words what he had said was going to happen to Paul was quite beyond me.

'What does Josh know?' Paul forced a smile. The strain was written all over his face, but like me he was so relieved that this was all over that he could almost joke about it.

'Look, we'll talk about it later, sweetheart.' He reached over and brushed a strand of hair from my face. 'Just at the moment the most important thing is for you to get some rest.'

Incredibly, I did. Paul was safe and I was safe. Really, nothing else mattered.

Thirty-Six

'What I don't understand,' I said, 'is how the police knew what was going on. I mean – that cottage – it's so isolated. How did they know Josh was there? How did they know I was there?'

Paul was sitting beside the bed, holding my hand on top of the covers. They were keeping me in for observation, they'd said. I presumed that meant they wanted to keep an eye on me because of the baby. But I could feel it moving inside me, the faintest, laziest of flutters that might be the kicking of a tiny foot or the punching of a little fist, and I was confident that no harm had come to it. With luck, they'd let me go home in the morning with a clean bill of health.

'It was a process of deduction, really,' Paul said. 'The only place where we could think that he might have taken you.'

'But ... how did you know he'd taken me anywhere?'

'Perhaps it would be easiest if I explained from the beginning,' Paul said. 'I never did go to Hong Kong. There was no need for me to. It suddenly occurred to me that going back to source was the wrong way to check things out – and probably highly dangerous, as you so rightly said. It came to me that what I needed to do was confirm who was taking the drugs from us once they'd got into the country via our warehouse. I followed up on what I thought was the likeliest lead – one of Josh's accounts who collect, rather than having us deliver to them, and I struck gold. Or rather, cocaine. I went straight to the authorities with what I'd learned – I figured I would get a fairer hearing from them than from the local police, who might very well suspect that I was involved too and waste valuable time trying to prove it.

'This morning I tried to ring to let you know what was happening – that I was all right, and an investigation was being set up. But you weren't at home. Helen Gibbs answered the phone and made some excuse that you'd gone into town to get your hair done. But I know you always go to the same hairdresser in London, so that didn't sound right. I was worried sick then, and I began to wonder about Helen. It had never occurred to me that she might be involved until then, but suddenly I was thinking about all the doubts you'd had about her, and realized I might have been played for a fool. If Helen was involved, there was an enemy right inside the camp. I contacted the police, told them of my fears for your safety, then belted straight home.

'It didn't take long to find your hire car – at Stattisford. Mary said you had left with Josh, and naturally, knowing now that Josh was behind the whole operation, I was frantic with worry. I don't know what made me think of the airport, really. It was just an inspired guess. But sure enough, we found Josh's car there. The people at the flying club confirmed he'd taken off in his PA28. The trouble was they didn't know where he'd gone. He'd told them he was just going for a couple of hours' jolly, and didn't intend to land away, but by then they were beginning to get concerned about him. He hadn't reported landing anywhere, and of course the PA28 only carries enough fuel for four hours' flying. They were about to put a search and rescue into operation. And then I remembered the cottage in North Wales.'

'He said something about being worried that they might start a search for him if he didn't soon get back,' I said. 'But I still don't understand ... Josh said no one knew about the cottage.'

'Well, he was wrong there,' Paul said grimly. 'I knew. I'd seen paperwork about it in the past, though I'd never mentioned it to him. I thought he was entitled to his privacy if that was the way he wanted it. But the cottage was the obvious place he'd take you – isolated, and, as far as he knew, his secret.

The police at home contacted the North Wales police, and...'

'And the cavalry arrived in the nick of time,' I said dryly.

Paul shuddered and held my hand more tightly. 'I can't bear to think of how close I came to losing you.' He was silent for a moment. 'What puzzles me, though, is why you went off with Josh. I thought we'd agreed you were going to lie low until you heard from me.'

I looked away, towards the window, where a tendril of the creeper that covered the old stone walls of the cottage hospital was flapping gently in the light spring breeze.

I didn't want to tell Paul what I'd suspected. I really didn't think that any relationship, even ours, could survive the terrible things I'd believed him capable of, however temporarily. It was beyond me now how I could ever have entertained such an appalling suspicion, however bad things had looked. All he had ever done was try to protect me, and I'd interpreted it as something quite different. Perhaps I had been suffering from my own dose of madness, hardly surprising, really, considering all that had happened in these last weeks.

'I was very frightened,' I said weakly. 'And I just never for one moment thought that Josh...' I hesitated. Paul had to be told sometime that his name was registered as a director of Kowloon and Victoria – presumably instigated by Josh as a cover for himself if things went wrong – but I didn't feel this was quite the right moment. 'In any case, I *wasn't* safe at home,' I went on. 'That damned Helen was there. She tried to kill me, you know. Electrocute me in my bath.'

'She *what?*' Paul was staggered and horrified, almost beyond words.

'I know, it's awful, isn't it?' I said. 'She loosened the screws on the fire – or at least, someone did. Perhaps that was Josh too. I think a woman would have had great trouble reaching them. Perhaps he did it while you and I were at the Blue Bowl. If he went to the house whilst we were out of the way, Helen could have let him in. Anyway, whoever did it, she knew about it, I'm sure.' I hesitated again. 'Did you know she is Josh's wife?'

'I know now.' He shook his head from side to side, looking completely crushed. 'Sweetheart, I am so sorry I fell for her line. She took me in completely. But you disliked her right from the start, didn't you? I should have listened to you – trusted your judgement. I was so concerned about you and the baby, I was only too ready to latch on to her as a solution to all our problems. Big, big mistake.'

'We all make mistakes,' I said with feeling.

'Well, that was a really bad one. To be so

gullible ... but then, I suppose you could say I've been pretty gullible all along the line. Josh has played me for a complete fool, too. If you hadn't come across Kowloon and Victoria on that website and mentioned it to me, I'd still be in blissful ignorance and Josh would still be carrying on with his drug dealing right under my nose. What a fool I've been!'

'No, Paul, not a fool. Just you being you. You like to think the best of people and you take them at face value. It's why you'll...' I broke off. *Why you'll never make a business-man*, I had been going to say. But that would only undermine his confidence further. He had a big enough chip on his shoulder without me adding to it.

'What's going to happen to Helen and Josh?' I asked instead.

'I should think we can safely assume they'll both go to jail for a very long time,' Paul said grimly. 'Personally, I hope they lock them up and throw away the key.'

'And what about the business?'

He sighed. 'I'm just going to have to try to pick up the pieces. Hopefully no blame will attach itself to me. I was the one who went to the authorities, after all, and besides, Josh's connections with Kowloon and Victoria predate my joining the company. According to what you pulled up on the website, it was in 1985 when they were investigated for irregularities. I imagine that put paid to their illegal trade for a bit. They had to lie low – and so did Stattisford, which would explain why things were so rocky for them when I first joined Josh. The mainstay of the turnover had gone down the pan. Not knowing anything about that, I rolled up my sleeves and built up the legitimate side of the business – the best possible cover, if only I'd realized it, for Josh to begin shipping in a few kilos of drugs here and there. I always realized he was a charismatic go-getter. But he was very clever about hiding the fact that he was also a crook on an international scale.'

'Who had you registered as a director of Kowloon and Victoria.' There, I'd said it now.

'So they tell me.' Paul sounded tired, suddenly, totally defeated, and once again I realized what a blow to his ego this must be. He really was just too nice, too honest, and he didn't realize that not everybody was as well-meaning as he liked to think them. Josh – Helen – he'd been taken in by both of them because it simply had not occurred to him that they could be anything other than they seemed.

Suddenly, although I was the one in the hospital bed, I felt as if I was the strong one, and all my instincts were to protect Paul from hurt.

'I don't know how our customers are going

to react to all this, of course,' he was saying now, his tone anxious. 'I can only hope that they've been sufficiently satisfied with the service we've provided to want to carry on dealing with us.'

'With *you*,' I said.

'The idiot who didn't have a clue what was going on.'

'Anyone could be taken in by Josh,' I said fiercely. 'I certainly was.'

'Mm.' Paul pulled a face, then went on: 'Well, if the business does take a dive, at least I've got a bit of a nest egg set aside. I'd intended it for when the baby comes along. To give him a good start, education and so on. Especially if we were managing on one salary. But if the worst comes to the worst it might help us to get started again.'

The money. The money he had been saving without my knowledge and which had aroused my suspicion in the first place. He'd meant it for our child. And he hadn't told me about it, presumably, because he thought I'd kick off at the suggestion that I would be giving up work. I felt thoroughly ashamed.

'You will miss Josh,' I said.

'Like a hole in the head!'

'But he was good at certain things, you must agree. And I don't just mean the illegal ones. He was very good at talking to people, for one thing. Oiling the wheels, persuading new customers to come on board, setting up a stick of dynamite here and there...'

'That's one way of putting it,' Paul said dryly.

'No, seriously. Josh did his bit for the legit stuff too. You really will need to think about replacing him if the business is ever to get back on its feet.'

'I'll manage.' Paul's face was tight. 'I don't much fancy the idea of a partner at the moment, thank you very much.'

'Not even if that partner were your wife?' I said.

His eyes narrowed. 'You?'

'I'm your wife, aren't I? Or is there something else I don't know about?' I asked mischievously.

It had come to me in a moment of inspiration, one of those sudden ideas that gives you shivers down your spine because it feels instinctively so right you can't imagine why you hadn't thought of it before.

It wasn't what I'd trained for, but I'd had plenty of experience on the legal side of the business world, and I enjoyed meeting people. I also had a suspicious lawyer's mind, and enough self-confidence for both of us. Most importantly, if I joined Stattisford, I would be here, working with Paul. There would be no conflict of interests, no more lengthy separations, and I wouldn't have to worry about leaving our child in the care of someone else. I'd have to find domestic help at some point, of course, someone to do the chores and perhaps look after the baby for at least part of the time, but not just yet. A baby could come to the office with me in the early days – or at least, that was how I was seeing it at the moment – and I wouldn't be missing out on those first precious months. But neither would I be confined within a role that I was afraid would soon suffocate me if I had no opportunity to be myself and use my talents.

'Are you quite sure about this?' Paul pressed me, obviously pleased, but still a little apprehensive that I had made this decision on the spur of the moment when my defences were low.

'It's in our interests to keep the business in the family and really make it work, isn't it?' I said, and added, with a smile: 'Do you really think that after Helen I am going to want to trust anyone else with the people who matter most to me in the whole world?'

EPILOGUE

So that's about it really, and now you know as much as I do about the sequence of events that almost cost me my life and certainly changed everything from my career to the way I look at things.

It's a year now since that day when I logged on to the Internet and came up with the information that set everything else in motion, and I sometimes wonder what would have happened if I hadn't. I can't help feeling it would only have been a matter of time before Kowloon and Victoria were investigated again, or the authorities made the connection as I had done. Some vigilant customs man or drug squad officer would have come upon it and traced the stuff to Stattisford, and perhaps Paul would have found it difficult to prove he wasn't implicated. As it was, it was generally accepted he'd been naive, but innocent of complicity.

The case against Josh and Helen came up just before Christmas. It was long and complicated, but Josh is now beginning a lengthy sentence, though Helen, who pleaded that she was completely under his influence, got off much more lightly. They never did prove that she loosened the screws in my bathroom fire, any more than they were able to prove that my fall in the high-rise car park was anything other than an accident. But I'm quite sure Josh was responsible for that too. Hadn't I told him that morning exactly where I was parked – and hadn't I been certain from the very beginning that I'd been pushed? Paul remembers mentioning to him something of what I'd said, because at that stage he had absolutely no idea Josh was involved, and Josh must have decided on the spur of the moment to do something about it. Just what he intended to achieve by pushing me down the stairs I can't imagine – unless it was to buy himself a little time by injuring me so that I couldn't go to the office and continue my investigations. But he must have known that in the long term it wouldn't stop me, and everything that followed had an awful inevitability about it.

For a while I had trouble sleeping because I dreaded the nightmares that wouldn't stop coming almost every time I closed my eyes. But I'm over that stage now and I don't even think too much about what happened. I've got plenty to keep my mind occupied, after all, what with learning the ins and outs of running a business (for which we can have our board meetings in bed if we like!) and caring for Jessica.

She's a beautiful baby, the most beautiful ever – but then, I would say that, wouldn't I? I'm her mother! She has my colouring and Paul's eyes, but otherwise I don't think she's much like either of us. She's very much her own person, and incredibly bright. She'll be walking soon, I'm sure, she very nearly did the other day, and when she does I hope I'll be there to see those first steps. Though I do implicitly trust Marianne, our highly qualified nanny, I've made very sure she doesn't get full responsibility and all the fun!

Jim Wood has left the area. The last I heard he was working in Birmingham. I can't say I blame him, though of course it meant Paul had to find a new store man as well as a partner. I hope that one day Jim will be able to pick up the pieces of his life and find someone as nice as Ruth.

I began writing all this down when I was wide awake in the middle of the night after feeding Jessica, but of course that doesn't happen any more now that she's sleeping through, so I've been doing it in odd moments. The other day Paul came in and found me at it, and when he read the first page he actually laughed.

'What do you mean – you'll never trust normality again?'

I smiled. He was looking rumpled and tired after a long day at the office, and Jessica was tucked into the crook of his arm, sleeping soundly and in blissful ignorance of the patch of dribble she'd deposited on the shoulder of his shirt.

'Is this normality? I asked.

'Probably.' He looked a little rueful, but very content.

'In that case, I expect I'll learn. Just give me time,' I said.